# Not Dead Yet

By T. Reeves

Thank you for continuing to believe in me. Thank you to my loving husband for still appreciating my crazy dreams no matter how unhinged the story sounds without the details. Thank you everyone who have helped these characters develop beyond the pages and answered the questions that aren't internet friendly. Thank you to my family for letting me be the crazy one. Finally thank you to the readers, I hope you enjoy the next step in this adventure like I did.

To my Baby Beau, you weren't here long, but your life changed all of ours for the better. We will see you again one day.

May 14 – Oct 12 2024

# Caution to the Reader

Dear Reader,

    The journey continues. Again, this book contains many of the same dark thematic elements including lots of language, kidnapping, murder, excessive gore, torture, religious extremism, abuse, drug use, sexual scenes, and mention of past rape and child abuse. Once again please consider these before reading.

-Thank you

T.

# Chapter 1

"Hey, did those uniforms get washed?" Catarina asked. Thomas, the owner of the gym poked his head out of the laundry room.

"They are here on the floor, so I'm going to take that as a no." Thomas's voice was clipped.

"I'll get them." Catarina put away the papers for the class that had just left. The temperature was stifling but she felt like she got a good workout. The gym was split into two sections: Commercial Gym, and Control MMA. The commercial gym was just that, but the MMA portion had classes on Brazilian Jiu-Jitsu, Judo, Weaponry, and Maui-Thai. Catarina went to at least one every day except Sunday. She got a special discount for working part time.

"I'm going to throttle Jeff." Thomas grumbled. He walked to the closet to start sanitizing the mats.

Jeff was Thomas's entitled shit of a nephew. He was on his last warning from his parents before they shipped him off to the military. So far on his juvenile record was taking his parents car for a joyride, 'forgetting' to pay for a bag full of clothing at the mall, and beating a kid at school so bad he was in the hospital for a week.

Thomas agreed to let jeff work at the gym to pay off the medical bills.

"Thomas?" Catarina called while throwing the uniforms into the wash.

"Ya?" he poked his head out of the room.

"Make sure to put detergent on the shopping list!"

"Oh, yeah." He gave her a thumbs up. "You coming to the party? Seven people have asked today."

"I don't know." She walked into the main room and watched the old man sanitize the mats. His grey hair slightly moving when the oscillating fan passed him. "It's been a long time since I've been able to go to a party." They both waved at the last of the students to leave, allowing them to talk openly.

"You know what Director Johnston said." Thomas called over his shoulder.

Thomas had retired four years earlier. He had been one of the best government agents of his generation. As he got older his body slowed down and he became a trainer. He took an early retirement when investigating a terrorist cell and a car bomb blew up too close. He had operated a safe house that was compromised due to a loose lipped green agent. Catarina was now running the new safehouse.

"I can't believe I got shanghaied into this." Catarina used the heels of her hands to try to rub away the headache that was starting behind her eyes.

"Would you rather be doing anything else?" Thomas sounded like he was laughing at her.

"Ugh." She walked to the cubbies and plopped onto the ground. She rifled through her things to get her shoes and socks. "No. I know I need to go, but the dogs."

"The dogs will be fine for a few hours." Thomas gave her a well-meaning look.

Officially, she had been hired as a dog trainer with a house and grant from the government. She trained puppies and dogs in basic obedience before they went off to their specialties. They did everything from bomb sniffing to service dogs. It was just a coincidence that she was certified, and her classes paid for by the same government. Immediately after she was cleared by the psychiatrist, she moved into the new house, but she continued to see him on a regular basis as part of her contract. She routinely took in troubled dogs to rehabilitate and get them ready for their forever homes.

"I know." Catarina pulled herself to her feet. "It's just a big step."

"It is kid, but it's worth it." Thomas kept cleaning. "How's that Mastiff Clyde adjusting?"

"You know for a dog that was supposed to be a bite risk and reactive, I think they sent me the wrong one." She laughed and shook her head. "You know, if I go to the party, I'm leaving if I can't hack it."

"I expect nothing less." Thomas laughed with a smile of success.

"See you tomorrow?" Catarina made her way to the door.

"If you don't have to bail me out for killing Jeff." Thomas gave her a wave.

"Deal!" Catarina loaded her things into a matte black Land Rover. It was a good car to take the dogs out and she got a great deal when she paid in cash up front. She stopped and picked up dog treats and sushi on her way home. The twenty-minute drive gave her plenty of time to decompress.

The lights that surrounded the estate lit up when she came up the drive. There were about two dozen cameras all over the property. At first when she signed her contract with the FBI and Homeland to take over the safehouse, it freaked her out. After some negotiations, she was assured that unless something happened, no one would watch her. She pressed a button on her watch that connected to the speakers in the house.

"Watch, watch, watch." She unlocked the door and hauled the groceries inside. All the dogs were perched on their designated elevated dog beds. Rocco, a two-year-old Doberman and Gunner, a one-year-old Boston Terrier, were perched together like they were when they were rescued. Buster, a four-year-old Brindle Bull Mastiff gave her a dismissive grunt. Ralf and Frankie, Neapolitan Mastiff littermates stopped growling after she kicked the door closed. Clyde was two and a half facing the garage door, again.

"You two are assholes." She laughed at Ralph and Frankie when she slipped in the water that trailed from the water bowl to where they sat. Locking the door, she set the home alarm. "Chill out!" Catarina walked to the kitchen. The dogs jumped off the beds and settled around the house. It was an open concept, with an L shaped island dividing the rooms.

After they had all eaten, and she had showered, she plopped on the couch surrounded by the monsters. She had to watch the popcorn bowl like a hawk. They were all learning how to wait and ignore food. Once their training was complete, they would either be claimed by various government trainers for specialty jobs or become companion dogs. Buster was hers though. It wasn't that he had failed his training, but after the events that brought her here, he was trained as a service dog for PTSD.

Almost eleven months ago, she had been the victim of a robbery gone wrong. She woke up in the hospital but ran into the perpetrators a few towns over. They followed her home and abducted her. She fought them the whole trip, several states away, to a remote cabin in the mountains. She was drugged and brainwashed into assisting with a larger robbery with the promise of her release. While she was there, she found out that two of the captors were undercover FBI Agents who were investigating an international serial killer with over six- hundred lives under his belt. He died in a hail of bullets, after stabbing one of the brothers in the group and killing the other.

Tyrese, the psychiatrist, spent three months convincing her that Buster might be beneficial. The nightmares, flashbacks, and panic attacks were rare after she gave in, and buster realized he was hers, they helped each other heal. When they started to creep up, Buster alerted her and when normal exercises didn't work, he did deep pressure therapy. These last few months, she was nearly event free. He stayed home when she went to the gym though, Thomas knew the drill and could help should she need it.

At around ten, she let the dogs out for thirty minutes. She had about fourty-eight acres, with ten-foot fence lines. But there was a shorter fence that covered about four acres, marking where the dogs could roam and play. She filled the filtered water trough and laughed when Rocco started a rampage of all the dogs chasing a few squirrels that taunted them from the trees.

The trees rustled in the wind. Its soft touch on her skin reminded her of him. Roland. One of the agents who had been part of the abduction. During their time together, something happened between them. They gave and drew comfort from each other, and she had developed real feelings for him. There were things that he did that made her think he might have loved her too. They never outright said anything but there was a vague discussion about it in the cabin. Then after…

Through all the meetings, the therapy, the trial, and seeing each other in passing, he never once looked at her, other than a dismissive glance. That first time she wasn't sure, but after it happened again and again, she curled into a ball in her apartment and cried. She was estranged from her family because of a former relationship, so she had no one. She was very aware of the fact that the feelings they shared in the cabin were probably just a product of the extreme situation. That didn't make it hurt any less.

Buster came sprinting across the yard like a bat out of hell. He slid to a stop in front of her and wacked her less than gently with a giant paw.

"Alright, alright, I'm going." She grumbled while scratching his head. She sat down in the grass and he climbed onto her.

She thought about the last time she saw Roland. She had just accepted the offer of the classes to be a certified dog trainer and take over the upkeep of the safehouse. She was nervous but excited. When the elevator opened to the main floor, he was standing there in a crisp suit and tie. She sucked in a breath but when their eyes met, he turned on his heels, walked to the stairs, and disappeared. She didn't cry though she wanted to. The pain made her want to drive into oncoming traffic, but she held her head up and walked out of the building.

Buster growled and stood. She sat up quickly and looked in every direction. All the dogs stared into the woods where the fence line came closest to the house. She stood and pulled her specialty flashlight that could give someone flash blindness if she wasn't careful. A giant black shadow moved across the fence line and the dogs took off.

"Down!" She screeched and all the dogs, but Clyde dropped where they were. "CLYDE DOWN!" Clyde slid to a stop and looked back at her. The black bear growled. Clyde took another step. "Home! Home! Home!" She pitched her voice in a harsh order. All the dogs, including the dipshit Clyde, ran back to the house and sat down by the back door. The bear let out a grunt on his side of the fence and padded away.

"Inside." She ordered while opening the door. The dogs waited until she was in then followed. "You asshole!" She said after the door closed. "You could've been killed!!" Clyde looked away in shame when she wagged her finger at him. That's when her phone rang. She checked the time; it was ten thirty.

"Hello?" She entered the code on the security system to lock their land down.

"Catarina," Director Johnston's voice was clipped and urgent. "Are you home?"

"Yes, Director, and about to head to bed. Why?" She walked to the office by the front of the house and pulled a book off the wall. It opened a door to a security room that doubled as an armory.

"There was an alert along the fence closest to the house."

"Yeah, there was a black bear." She pointed to the dog beds. "Watch, watch, watch." The dogs went to their beds and mean-mugged the door. "It's gone now. You never call for something as small as an alert."

"You're perceptive." He said dryly then with a sigh, he continued. "Listen carefully Cat." She closed herself in the security room and found the live feed where the bear had been. "Tobias Morgan was sentenced today."

"I know." She watched the bear wander into the dark.

"While he was being transported to Cumberland Correctional Facility in Maryland, the bus was hit, and he escaped along with four other prisoners." She dropped the phone. It bounced of the counter, hit the chair, then clattered across the floor. She scrambled to get ahold of it. When she finally got it back to her ear, she heard Director Johnston calling for her. "Hello? Catarina? Are you ok?"

"I'm fine." Her voice sounded breathy and hollow. "The phone slipped."

"Catarina, your formal title is Consultant, but you are in the family. We have agents in route for security until he is caught. When they get there, you will establish their cover story until he is in custody. The introduction code is Sparrow, and the response is Cardinal." He sighed and his voice seemed more human than she had heard it in a long time. "Cat. There is a nation-wide manhunt for him. We will catch him."

"I know." She was shaking.

"Three distant relatives of his have also gone off the radar. Watch you back, use the training you've received, and remember the whole country is searching for them."

"Thank you, Director." She said quietly. "Would it be considered overkill to lockdown the house before turning in at night?" The lockdown system secured all the windows and doors with steel covers. A three-dimensional image was painted on, so the house looked just like any other from the outside.

"I was going to recommend doing that for the time being." Director Johnston sighed. "I am also implementing check-in's three times a day. I will call you with any other updates. Goodnight Catarina, and Godspeed." He hung up with a sharp click.

Catarina turned on the motion sensors for the property. The analysts at headquarters would be watching for any suspicious activity. Leaving the armory, she locked it, and went to the security panel by the stairs. Typing a ten-digit code, the house whirred. Steel plates sliding into place. An all-clear tone rang out, leaving her to sigh with relief.

That night the nightmares came back.


The next morning her alarm rang way too early. Her feet were soaked when she stretched.

"Ugh! Frankie!" She glared at the slobber king himself. She climbed over the mess of dog bodies that were sprawled across the two kings that made up the master bed. Wrapping a silk kimono style robe around herself, she turned on all the security equipment. The screens that covered and entire wall in her bedroom lit up and showed the property in brilliant color.

Reports speckled the screen, along with an all clear by the night team that watched the footage. She finally took a breath and relaxed as much as she could. Pulling out her phone, she sent the first check in for the day and walked to the wall. Entering a code, her bedroom door unlocked with a thud of heavy metal. After she stepped to the side, all the dogs sprung out of bed and torpedoed down the stairs.

She let them outside and went about their morning routine, with some training. Around eight Catarina let the dogs lounge while she got some of the rooms ready. Since she wasn't sure how many people would be coming, she made up all the rooms. There were four other bedrooms besides hers. Two of them had kings and the other two shared six queens. There had been several sets of agents that had used the house in transition to their next assignments, or to keep witnesses safe until trials. She liked the routine.

Recently, there was a high valued witness that had to stay in the bunker because of the threat on his life. He was going to testify for a mafia case. There were even a few people who came around that she had suspected were searching for him. When she gave them the tour for her dog training classes, they looked disappointed, and she never heard from them again.

Taking the dogs outside, they ran and played while she worked one on one with each of them. Catarina's training with Buster was more extensive, and she wanted it all fresh in his brain before the barbecue today.

When they were done, she showered and got ready after sending the second check in. For her outfit, she settled on a familiar favorite, high waisted jean shorts and a black crop top under a sheer black shirt with brightly embroidered flowers. Catarina could never say it out loud, but the flowers reminded her of the garden at Pete and Annibelle's. She tied her hair into a messy bun and put on a little light makeup. She had colored her hair a medium brown and put some layers into it after she moved here. The red hair she was given was too much for her to mentally handle.

Buster pushed the door open, his service dog vest hanging from his mouth. He walked in and sat down. Catarina took the vest and scratched his head. He held still when she slipped it on and buckled it.

Letting the dogs out one more time and getting Buster's lead, she took some of her anxiety medication. She always had some just in case, but it had been a while since she needed it. Under the circumstances she didn't judge herself too harshly, she hadn't even gone to the last cookout.

Thirty minutes later she and Buster were walking into the park. Every month or so Thomas put on a big get-together so people could get to know others at the gym and families could mingle. It was largely responsible for getting new people to the gym besides the atmosphere. More people in and around Springfield had made it a point to go and it blew up into a monthly event that was fully funded by donations.

"Hey Cat!" A few people waved as she and Buster walked in with a dish for the potluck table. Buster was the image of disregard for the food, the noise, and the people. His focus was on her. Thomas was talking to a lady she recognized from a local bakery. The smile he was giving her was something she would tease him about later.

"Hey Thomas." Catarina waved when she set the pie on the table. "This is getting to be a huge event!

"Cat!" Thomas nearly cheered. "This is Donna! From the bakery down the street!" Catarina shook her hand. "Donna, this is Catarina, and Buster." Donna jumped a little when she saw Buster.

"Oh, shit!" Donna laughed. "I didn't even see him!" She smiled and admired him. "Service dog?"

"Yeah." Catarina gave a slight shrug of the shoulder. "He helps keep all the demons in their cages." Catarina laughed awkwardly. Donna gave her a kind smile.

"Thomas tells me you train dogs?" She took a drink from her cup and gave Thomas a flirtatious smirk.

"I do." Catarina smiled. "I enjoy these big guys." She scratched Buster's head. "Well I'm going to look around and see how much Thomas has outdone himself this month!"

She gave them a wave and dove into the crowd. It was a warm day and Cat found a nice spot under some trees where they could sit, and she could eat. Some of her friends from the gym came and sat down with her. They joked and laughed. A few kids came up and asked if they could pet Buster. She politely declined and decided it was time to see if she could sneak out without too much backlash. She was focusing on finding people to say goodbye to, so she didn't hear him until he was right behind her.

"Hello, Angel." He said. Catarina whirled on her heels to face her abusive ex-boyfriend. Trent had dark circles under his eyes and looked like he hadn't showered in a while. Staring wide-eyed at him she hardly recognized the person he had been. Where he used to be strong and lean, he had become soft and round. She never thought she would see him again.

"Trent." She said with as little emphasis as possible.

"That's it?" Trent sneered. "After everything I've done for you. I got a slap on the wrist for that little stunt outside your apartment. Then almost a month later, after your disappeared, my buddy Axle, who worked at dispatch called. He told me he had overheard some of the officers talking about a warrant for my arrest on some bogus charges."

"Those charges are very real." Catarina said. Buster growled beside her.

"Control that mutt or I'll put a bullet in it." He lifted the front of his shirt. A revolver stuck out of the front of his pants. Her heart hit her stomach. She gave Buster a hand signal quieting him, but not one to be friendly. "What did you tell them?"

"I told them everything you did to me. Everything." She whispered. Trent gave a dark chuckle and looked around less than casually. Catarina looked past him at Thomas. The man didn't know what was wrong but could tell something was off. She tried to convey her distress with a quick look.

"You're a lying bitch." Trent growled. She was sure that if they were alone, he would've already started beating her. "Get rid of that thing if you don't want me to start shooting into the crowd."

"Buster, find friends. Friends. Friends." Catarina ordered and dropped the lead. Buster picked up the handle and trotted off to find Thomas. "What happens now?" She stifled a squeak when he grabbed her arm and yanked her to his side. Every action he took was meant to display dominance and power.

"We're going to go spend some quality time together." The ominous statement chilled her to the bone. He wrapped an arm around her shoulder in an attempt to look casual. His other arm held fast to her bicep. He started walking them towards the edge of the park. Catarina stole a quick glance at Thomas who was on the phone with Buster glued to his side, waiting for an order.

"Trent, let me go. We can talk about this." She kept her voice low and calm. He snorted and squeezed her arm tighter.

"You are even dumber than I thought if you think you're getting out of the beating that's coming." He smiled like they were having a relaxed conversation, but it didn't reach his eyes. They were at the edge of the party. She knew if he got her alone, she would be dead. They walked through the old post and rail fence that surrounded the park. There was no one in the parking lot that she could see. Taking a steady breath, she attacked.

Reaching across herself, she grabbed the hand that held her bicep. She pulled her other arm between their bodies, out of his grip, and grabbed the back of his jeans. Catarina stuck her leg behind his and pulled him backwards. Trent sat down hard on his ass, hard enough to crack his teeth together. While she rolled, climbing on top of him, she brought her knee to his groin with a ferocity she hadn't felt in a long time. His mouth opened in a silent scream.

She brought her elbow across his face three times before his eyes glazed over. Reaching down, she pulled the revolver out of his waistband. Aiming it at him, she started to climb to her feet. With practiced form, she tightened her grip on the trigger, and the cylinder rotated. Looking through it, she realized the gun was empty. Focus returned to his eyes, and he lunged at her from the ground. His foot caught her leg, and she stumbled forward.

In a sickening, wet gush, the barrel of the revolver embedded itself in his eye. Catarina stared in horror as the screaming started. Trent ripped the gun from his eye socket and threw it into the grass. She dry heaved, her eyes watering, and climbed back to her feet. His one good eye swiveled to her. Holding his hand over what was left of the other one, his scream transformed to rage, and he pulled his feet under him. Blood oozed between his fingers, and he started to charge at her.

Almost as an afterthought, she heard a growl. when Buster clamped his massive jaws around his ancle. People stood around watching the horrific scene play out, no one wanting to come close with the gun involved. Catarina grabbed the gun and tossed it underneath a nearby car.

Buster yanked the leg back, sending Trent toppling forward, barely missing Catarina. He began to roll to his side to fight Buster, but Catarina slammed her elbow down on the side of his face over and over again until he went limp. Using the cross-body strap on her purse, she pulled his hands behind him and tied them together.

"Buster, release!" She commanded. Buster dropped his leg and sat at attention. "Buster, watch, watch, watch." Buster laid down, and scrutinized Trent. Thomas came running up, with a first aid kit. He had the gun and set the case next to it before helping Trent, who was slowly coming to.

"Zach! Call the police and ambulance." He ordered. A man she recognized from one of her classes pull a phone out. "Tell them the gun is empty and we have the attacker restrained." He looked down at Buster whose muzzle was dripping red, then at Trent's bloody leg. "Also, let them know that the dog is trained and calm."

Catarina watched everything happening around her in a fog. She had climbed off Trent and crawled away in the grass. Thomas ordered buster to go back to her and he immediately began deep pressure therapy, along with other techniques, keeping her mentally present and in the moment. At some point Trent got his breath back and started screaming and yelling. One of the nurses that came to judo, stepped forward with a medical bag and was applying first aid to Trent's ruined eye. After a few minutes she felt ok to get up. The kids had been moved to the playground and everyone else stood quietly while they waited for the police.

"I take it, this is Trent." Thomas asked with asperity. He waved two of the MMA fighters from the gym to take over supervising the struggling man on the ground.

"You guessed right." She nodded. Buster was locked to her side, casual, but keeping himself between Catarina and Trent the way he was supposed to. "Asshole tried it with an empty gun."

"You did good kid." Thomas clapped her on the back. "I called The Director. He's going to make sure he disappears into the system. You know, after he recovers." Six police cars came speeding into the parking lot. They all ran up with guns at a low ready. When they saw that the threat had been handled, they put them away.

Taking statements was a quick process since several people had been filming various events at the time. They got most of it on camera, including a stunning performance by Buster. Animal control pulled up, but a call came in and they didn't try to take him. Instead, they gave him a once over and a few comments on his relaxed temperament.

The ambulance took Trent away followed by a pair of officers. They were all asked to stay until the interviews were over. Several friends from the gym came up and asked how she was doing. When she explained that it was nothing more exciting than a crazy ex-boyfriend, they gave the universal nod that essentially said 'oh, ok.'. Before she really had time to relax, a mountain of a man came running through the crowd. People scurried out of the way in fear of being crushed.

The breath she had been holding came out in a strangled whimper. Thomas turned on his heels to see who it was. When she took several steps back, Buster stood his ground in front of her, and several friends stepped up defensively. The man stopped running and looked like he was fighting to keep his composure. Scars webbed out of the right side of his face, disappearing into his beard and continued down his neck into the collar of his shirt. Roland looked the same as the last time she saw him. Jacob and a tall slender woman with a dark bob came jogging up behind him.

"Sparrow." Jacob gave her the code.

"Cardinal." She damned-near spit out the response, and you could cut the tension with a freaking spoon.

"Cat." Roland's voice was all choked up. He coughed and tried again. "Catarina." She felt like an elephant was sitting on her chest. She remembered how big he was, but standing here in front of her, he seemed nearly colossal, like Popeye on spinach. "It's been a while." Those words knocked all the fear from her and replaced it with rage, pain, and the need to inflict hurt.

"It's been a while?" She repeated back to him. "It's been a while?" her voice rose to a combative volume.

"Catarina," Jacob stepped forward. "I think we all need to talk."

"Two months of the cold shoulder, and then thrown away," She was trying not to shout, "and the best you can come up with is 'it's been a while'?" Thomas touched her arm, trying to keep the situation calm, but the crowd was starting to gather again. The officers that remained started to step forward, but Jacob was having a whispered conversation with one. That officer gave an order for the others to stand down.

"I was going to bring a razor scooter, but we didn't have the time to stop and get one." Roland gave her a weak smile. She choked on a laugh while tears fell down her face. All the emotion of the day was spilling over.

"You fucking asshole!" Catarina was laughing and crying all at once. Buster growled defensively in front of her. "Almost a year later, and now you show up? No call, no letter, nothing?"

"You don't know the whole story!" Roland's voice almost cracked. Catarina studied his face. Buster was still growling at the giant in front of him.

"I think we need to go get settled, then talk." Jacob put a placating hand up. Everyone was watching now. Catarina's face was flushed with a mixture of anger and embarrassment. He was right. Nothing good would come out of hashing this all out here.

"Fine. Let's get out of here." She consented. Thomas grabbed her hand before she could take a step.

"Will you be ok?" he whispered.

"I don't know." Catarina didn't look at him when she walked away.

# Chapter 2

The crowd around them were mumbling questions. Roland had resisted the urge to run up and wrap her in his arms. Now he was glad he did. They missed whatever happened at the park that got the police involved, but Jacob had gotten the police chief on the phone and gave him the cliff notes version of what was going on. Jacob returned the favor and explained what they were doing there.

The massive brindle dog in the vest beside Catarina eyed him like he was on the menu. Clearly, he was still in protective mode. She gave him a subtle hand signal that kept him quiet and subdued when they pushed past them. Catarina avoided any contact with him, and Roland's heart throbbed. He had imagined this day over and over again, but it was never like this. The sunset, sure, but not the hostility.

"You're not riding with me!" Catarina snapped when he reached for the handle on the passenger side.

"But I…" Roland was genuinely hurt by the comment until the dog gave him a low growl. He was hoping to spend the ride explaining, but by the look on the dog in the passenger seat, he decided his life wasn't worth the risk.

They piled into the black Ford Expedition that was armed to the teeth. Along with their suitcases. The entire back of the vehicle was loaded with everything from handguns to short range missiles.

Agent Katie Madison sat in the back. She was Jacob's long-term girlfriend, and the agency's forensic analyst. They had crossed paths a few times before but once their last mission had ended, Jacob finally asked her out. They had been attached at the hip ever since. She was on a different team, so everything was ok with The Director.

"So, this is from your last mission?" Katie asked. "Director Johnston was pretty vague about everything." She had been ordered to come along to collect evidence if it came to that.

"Yeah," Jacob smiled at her in the rear-view mirror. He gave her a detailed version of the events up until they had left her with the ambulance.

"Then what happened to have her acting like that? Sounds like she loved Roland." Katie asked. Roland didn't miss how she said 'loved', in past not the present tense.

"We were given orders of no contact. If she contacted us we were to report to The Director immediately." Roland nearly growled. Then after a harsh look from Jacob, he cleared his throat and continued. "If we contacted her at all before Tobias was permanently locked in prison, we would serve jail time for tampering with a witness." Roland bit back the pain those words brought.

"Wait, what?" Katie pulled herself forward, leaning between the front seats.

"She was a witness for everything that happened in the end, so if we talked to her the defense could push that she was coerced in her testimony." Jacob explained.

"So, she was just left to deal on her own?" She sounded baffled. Even though he didn't think it was possible, the pain in his chest magnified.

"Roland was going to go find her after Tobias was locked up, but now…" He trailed off.

"That was only a day or two away!" Katie gasped. "Now she probably thinks you're obligated to be here."

"What would you fucking know about it?" Roland snarled. Jacob punched him hard in the shoulder, and Katie sat back.

"Get your shit together!" Jacob seethed. If anyone else had said the same thing Roland would've started a fight, but it was Jacob, and he got a lot of leeway. "If you go in guns blazing, she will kick back just as hard, you know that!" Roland readjusted in his seat knowing he was acting childish. "We don't know how long we will be there. It could be a few days it could be months! You have time. Use it to wipe the slate." They drove the next few miles in silence.

"Sorry guys." Roland mumbled. Katie reached forward and gave his shoulder a friendly squeeze.

"We've got your back." Her soft voice was soothing. "I will do everything I can to help." Roland gave her hand an appreciative squeeze before she retreated. They followed her car out of town, past an expensive looking neighborhood, and into a long driveway with a sign that read: All Size Paws, Dog Training.

"When The Director said he found her a good job as a consultant this is better than what I thought." Jacob commented.

They followed the car through two automatic gates and up to what looked like a pristine version of an old ranch house. It was white with an attached three car garage and a wraparound porch. She pulled into the far garage door that opened, and they crept into the one next to it.

Roland watched her speak to her watch before she got out of the car. She sniffed and wiped her eyes before opening the door, followed by the brindle monster. The doors rolled closed, and she used a key to unlock a set of French doors that lead into the house.

"Family, family, family." She called into the house. Turning back to them she said: "I hope you're all ok with dogs! I have six right now. Watch out for the little one, he will pee on you if he doesn't like you. I'm taking them all out. Bedrooms are upstairs, take a U-turn at the top and there are the four doors at the end on the left. Take your pick."

She walked away without another word. They listened to her direct the dogs outside. Jacob and Katie shared a look they thought he didn't see, and he pretended he missed it too. They dragged their bags inside.

To the right was a giant marble kitchen that was boxed in by a high L-style counter. On the left was one of the biggest sectionals he had ever seen in front of two TV's mounted on each wall by the corner. Directly in front of them, the staircase disappeared into the ceiling. He could make out an office past the stairs and the front doors. They marveled at the house, the fifteen-foot ceiling made it look bigger than it had from the outside, and outside it looked huge.

The upstairs was just as extravagant, so they did their best to prevent the suitcases touching and scuffing the steps. They followed the instructions and found two rooms with king beds, a second with two queens, and the last one had four. Roland took one of the Kings closing himself in while Jacob and Katie scurried into the other, barely hiding their smiles.

Roland opened the blinds to look out at the trees over the roof of the garage. If he stood close to the wall, he could see some of the dogs playing in the back yard. Catarina was picking up after them at the edge of his sightline. He laid his suitcase on the chase at the end of the bed and opened it. His pile of unsent letters sat on top. Hand-written letters couldn't be hacked or traced to a home console. Tyrese, his psychiatrist, had recommended it to cope with the separation and process his feelings.

His phone beeped and Roland checked the notification. It was The Director. He walked out of the room, nearly colliding with Jacob and Katie, who were straightening their clothes. No one said anything as they made their way downstairs. A door opened and the dogs flooded the house, running to meet their new guests.

"You guys get the message from The Director?" Catarina waved her phone in the air. "GUNNER!" She yelled at a small black and white dog that had its leg lifted beside Jacob. The dog jumped and ran to sit next to a massive Doberman like a puppy.

"Yeah." Katie held out a hand. "Hi, I'm Agent Katie Madison."

"Catarina Stone." She gave Katie a good shake before walking around to grab a remote. "You know Dumb and Dumber." Catarina said, waving a dismissive hand at Roland and Jacob, who kept silent at the jab. Turning on the TV The Director's face stared back at them.

"Hello, everyone." His voice reminded Roland of Ron Perlman, a deep full tone that never left room for doubt. Director Johnston was a short bald man with seventies glasses and a presence that dominated the room. "You are all together because Tobias Morgan escaped on his way to Cumberland Correctional Facility, and your lives are in danger. Catarina, he blames you for the death of his brother, however delusional that opinion is. You will not leave the house without one of the others with you. Is that clear?"

"Yes, Director." She nodded. Her brindle monster was leaning against her legs, without the vest.

"Agent Katie Madison is our top forensic specialist, but she has high marks in combat training, marksmanship, and undercover operations." The Director gave her a respectful nod. "We hope this is an unnecessary precaution and that Tobias will be caught ASAP.

But until then, you are all to agree on a cover story and help maintain Catarina's routine."

"Yes, Director." The three field agents agreed.

"Catarina," The Director softened his voice to a tone Roland had never heard. "You were literally dragged kicking and screaming into this." Roland watched a faint smile soften her face. "There are a few details that you were deliberately kept in the dark on. I am the person who is responsible for that decision. Any animosity you have about that falls on me, and me alone." The tension in the room was high enough that several of the dogs started whining.

"Hush." Catarina commanded. When she sat down, the black Neapolitan Mastiff climbed onto the couch beside her. She scratched his head lovingly and sighed. With a nod she looked back at The Director for the rest. "Ok, let's hear it."

"Cat." His voice was almost fatherly.

It made Roland uneasy to see the hard man giving an entirely uncharacteristic side of himself to someone who was newly part of 'the family'. He tried his best not to be resentful while listening.

"Due to the extreme nature of the prosecution of Daniel Smith, Samuel Morgan, and Tobias Morgan, the media surrounding this case, and the global scale of it all, extreme orders were given. Agent Andrew Jacob Evans and Agent Ambrose Roland Hoeft were ordered to have no contact with you. If they broke those orders, they would spend the next eighty years in prison for tampering with a witness."

"Tampering with a witness?" Her color was bad when she choked out the words. Roland walked to the fridge and found a can of pop on the shelf. Cracking it open, he brought it back to her, ignoring the low vocalization of the cream-colored mastiff that sounded like a 'no'. She took it without looking at him and sipped the fizzy drink. It seemed to help ground her.

"We caught word that the defense attorneys were going to try to pin the blame on you or try to frame you as an unreliable witness because of the drugs that were in your system. Although those plans were improbable at best, they were putting the highest bet on framing any contact between you and the agents as coaching and coercing you as a witness. They were ordered specifically by me to ignore you completely. They had no say in any of it. I apologize for any turmoil this has caused you."

Catarina stared in shock at the screen. Roland kept looking back and forth between her and the screen until she nodded and excused herself, setting the drink on an end table. All the dogs jumped up from where they were sitting and followed her up the stairs.

"Agents." The Director wasted no time. "The property is to be locked down every night before lights out. You are to update me on the day-to-day goings on, and I will update you immediately with any new information on the whereabouts of Tobias and the three family members that have gone off the grid. This is an official assignment so within reason," He leaned heavily on that last part and smirked, "Your company cards are approved for use."

"Director," Jacob stepped forward, "Are we approved to use deadly force if we are not able to successfully contain Tobias and potentially his family members that are involved."

"I didn't send you in there for a suicide mission, Agent Evans." The Director smirked. "Protect yourselves and Catarina, but if it comes down to it, don't take any shit." With that the screen went black.

"Alright." Katie said. "You two grab the accessories, and I'm going to go check on Catarina." One of Katie's biggest strengths was how she always knew what to say. Jacob gave her a quick side hug and a kiss on the cheek before he and Roland walked back into the garage.

The 'accessories' were all the firepower they brought in case shit hit the fan. They managed to get it all into the dining room, past the far side of the stairs. The table was a sturdy white stained cedar slab on cast iron legs that were attached to a steal plate on the underside. If needed, it could be flipped on its side and used to stop bullets. He was impressed.

"Been a hell of a day." Jacob broke the silence while they lined up inventory.

"She's right here within arm's reach, and she hates me." Roland mumbled. He wanted to punch something.

"She didn't know the whole story." Jacob started sorting ammunition cans. "Give her time. She will come around. Katie is smoothing shit over now."

"Was it all in my head?" Roland plopped into one of the high back chairs, his head throbbing.

"Fuck no." Jacob snickered. "You two idiots almost blew our cover a few times even before she knew who you were." Roland ran his hands through his hair in frustration. "Why are you basing your future off what happened then? Do you want my opinion?"

"Why the hell would I want that?" Roland knew he was being confrontational, but he couldn't seem to stop himself.

"Because one of us is currently in a *successful* relationship." Jacob said coolly.

"You dick." Roland laughed. It was like a pressure valve releasing some tension.

"Start over." Jacob said, ignoring his comment with a smile.

"What?" Roland looked at him like he officially lost his mind.

"Where's that other box of three-fifty ammo?" Jacob distractedly looked around. "Ah, found it. Yes. Go up, introduce yourself again as the real you, and ask to start over." Jacob quietly counted the items on the table again.

"You think that will work?" Roland asked dubiously.

"One thing I'm sure of." Jacob smiled. "Honesty goes a long way. Give her time, and when it's right, give her your letters." Roland was pacing, but the shock of that statement buckled his knees and had him on his ass before he could think. Jacob pretended not to notice his fall. "Yes, I know about the letters."

"How the hell..." Roland pulled himself back onto the chair.

"You're family." Jacob smiled, like that said it all. Roland gave him a well-meaning punch on the arm before standing again and exploring the rest of the house.

Under the staircase, a second flight lead down to a finished basement. Raised dog beds like the ones he saw upstairs lined the wall at the bottom of the stairs. To the left was a giant room with an insane amount of food storage with a furnace room buried in the back of it. Behind the stairs along the back wall was an industrial washer and dryer set. Next to that was a huge closet with linens and Dog training gear. On the other side was a strange bathroom with two dog washing stations. A narrow ramp against the far wall in the basement lead up to a door that went outside.

Back on the main floor he saw Katie lounging on the sectional. It was nearly six o'clock. She had the news on to the local station. He made sure to do a thorough look around to make sure Catarina wasn't close before parking it next to Katie on the sectional.

"How's she doing?" He kept his voice low.

"She's ok." Katie tucked her hair behind her ear. "She's relieved that it wasn't your choice to stay away, but that's almost a year of building resentment. She knows it's not your fault even though it was a high stakes situation. You two only really spent a little over two weeks together." Katie crossed her arms and leaned back. "And in that time, only four days of it were spent knowing the real you as much as she could."

"God…" Roland whispered. "She must hate me. She has every right to, but…." He held his hands out in front of him, waiting for the words to appear.

"True." Katie leaned forward. "But you two have a second chance. Right now, she's wondering if those feelings were something her brain concocted to deal with the trauma. Show her that they weren't and that you feel the same way."

"What if she doesn't like the real me?" Roland had to blink back tears that stung like acid. He had never allowed himself to be this vulnerable with anyone, including Tyrese. The only reason he could be with Katie, is because she was Jacob's other half, and helped him deal with much more than just the last mission. Roland trusted her like he trusted Jacob.

"Why don't you let her decide?" Katie gave him a pat on the shoulder. "She might surprise you."

"She's right." Jacob walked into the room.

"I normally am." Katie got up and wrapped her arms around Jacob's neck giving him a kiss that made Roland scrunch his nose. They knew he teased them to hide his own pain.

"You two make my skin crawl." He mocked while getting up to check the fridge. There was a sound like a dozen stuffed turkey's thumping down the stairs before about eight hundred pounds worth of dogs flooded into the room. Roland had barely grabbed the handle of the fridge before three of them came sliding to a stop at his feet.

"Rocco, Gunner, Clyde. Piss off!" Catarina rounded the banister by the stairs and walked into the room, her extravagant floral robe fluttering. The three dogs immediately turned on their heels, but one of them stopped and looked back. "Clyde!" The dog skittered away to attack a ball on the ground.

"We can make a grocery run tonight if you want?" Katie separated from Jacob and walked into the kitchen.

"I've got us covered for tonight if you don't have any dietary restrictions." Catarina was still tense in a t-shirt and pants pajama set. The peach tone brought out the flush in her skin. Katie shrugged and shook her head. "First things first." Catarina took a steadying breath, and the brindle got up, walking over to her. "I'm ok." She mumbled to him, then continued. "I need to apologize for my attitude towards you all. This last year has been a living hell. It's going to take some time to adjust to the new information, so if my emotions get away from me, I'm sorry." Jacob took a step forward.

"I know I speak for both of us when I say we wanted to tell you more than anything." He walked up and held out a hand. "Truce?" Roland watched Catarina's eyes flood with tears. She was trying to hold them in, but when they ran down her face, his own blinded his vision.

"Truce." Roland heard her say before he blinked his own away. Katie had walked up to them and held her arms out. Catarina accepted the hug, and Roland had to fight back a bit of jealousy. He wanted to do that since he saw her disheveled in the park.

"What can we help with?" Jacob paved the way out of the intense conversation. Catarina and Katie separated.

"How does everyone feel about spinach stuffed chicken over rice?" Catarina asked.

"If I get a pan to myself, I'm good!" Jacob nearly danced in place and the girls smiled.

"If you would get the two packs of thighs and the cream cheese out of the fridge? They can thaw in the sink, just fill it with hot water." She waved to the general area where the items were.

"Roland, would you help me with the dogs?" He nearly jumped out of his skin when she said his name.

"Yeah." He nodded and quickly following her to the back door.

"Oh," she stopped and addressed the room. "Just so you all know, these guys are Rocco and Gunner, they were rescued together and will stay together. Ralf and Frankie are littermates. Clyde is our newest addition who is still learning the rules. And finally, Buster, but he is mine." She pointed to each of them as she said their names then walked briskly out the door.

Roland did his best not to sprint after her. Walking through the French doors, he stepped onto a porch that was lit up with hundreds of vintage lights that hung lazily around beams that towered as high as the ceilings inside. The vast yard had lamp posts scattered to illuminate everything. Catarina had walked into the yard pulling several bags apart to clean up after the giant animals. The dogs ran and played like they didn't have a care in the world. He followed her down the steps.

"I can take a few of those." He reached out a hand to her.

"I've got it, I just wanted to talk." She didn't look at him. He could see the tension in her shoulders.

"I know, but I can still help." Roland grabbed a few of the bags that stuck out farthest from her hand. She watched warily. "I understand if you don't want anything to do with me. I couldn't even blame you. The way the last year has gone you probably hate me."

"I never said that." Catarina's voice was barely a whisper. That phrase rang in his ears and had his heart instantly racing. She had said the same thing to him when they first met back at the bank, and the memory flashed in his mind. He had to resist the urge to reach out to her.

"You need to know." He turned to watch the dogs too. If he kept looking at her, he might not be able to stop himself from wrapping her in his arms. If it happened too soon, she would probably try to shoot him, or sic eight hundred pounds of dog on him, then hate him forever. "I never stopped thinking about you, not for one minute. I hated Director Johnston for his orders. I understand why he gave them, but every day I couldn't see you killed a piece of me." He stole a glance at her and caught the edge of a tear that fell unchecked.

"Did I imagine it? Was any of it real?" Her voice was horse. The two Neapolitan Mastiffs, Ralf and Frankie, along with Buster came jogging up but she flicked a hand, shooing them away. "Or was it just the situation, adrenaline, and emotion?" That question felt like a dagger.

"The first time I saw you, you were in a pair of heels that damn near had me on my knees. Then I found out you were a spitfire that made me feel alive again, even if you did beat me with a fire extinguisher." He smiled when she choked out a laugh at the memory. "I love the way your face is an open book, and your eyebrow can tell someone to 'fuck-off' before your mouth does. I missed your sass and the way you keep me on my toes. But most of all." Roland turned to look at her, waiting until she looked at him too. She was crying softly. "I miss the way I felt more like myself with you than I have in years. You're the first person that has ever created a safe enough space for me to be one hundred percent real. When we were separated, I felt like you took half me with you and I've never felt a pain like that in my life." She looked at the scars marring his face and body. "Never." He affirmed.

They sat there like that for a long time. The dogs had wound themselves up into a comedy act of racing laps around the yard. A long time had passed before Catarina sniffed and wiped her eyes. Roland could see the uncertainty on her face.

"My feelings were just as strong." She whispered. "Because of everything, I can't promise anything." She shook her head slightly.

"My name is Ambrose Roland Hoeft." Roland's heart was thundering in his ears as he held out a hand. "I've gone by Roland for a number of years, and I haven't lived a normal life in a long-ass-time. I've got some baggage and a job that I can't talk about to most people. But if you are open to it, I would like to start over and see where this goes. If you're not, I would really love to be able to call you a friend." She stared back and forth from his face to his hand. Roland was pretty sure he was going to have a stroke if she took much longer.

"I'm willing to give it a try." She shook his hand. Roland couldn't help the smile that took over. They dropped hands and he let out a tense breath. "You ok?" She laughed at him.

"I wasn't sure I would ever get a second chance." Roland was trying to keep the wave of emotion out of his voice with a smile.

"There is one thing though." Catarina looked uncertain.

"Anything." He said, and if he said it a little too quickly, then to hell with it. She gave him a ghost of a smile before taking a breath of her own and pushing through.

"I spent the last year with a lot of anger that I should've delt with in the moment," Catarina wrapped her arms around herself. "I might need some grace if we touch on something sensitive."

"I'll probably need some grace to adjust to the real world too." Roland watched her smile return slowly. "All we can do is try." They both jumped when the dogs came racing between them at pretty much the speed of light. They laughed when Ralf went to turn and slid a good five yards in the grass.

"Maybe we can start this out with a hug?" Catarina's voice was so soft that if not for an implant that gave him hearing on the right side, he would have missed it.

"I would like that." Roland opened his arms and let Catarina make the first step forward.

Her body was more solid than he remembered He had dreamed of this moment every day since the last time he saw her, but no dream he had ever felt this good. The soft scent of strawberries and champagne filled the air around him. She still only came up to his shoulder, so with her arms wrapped over his, he lifted her into the air and spun her in a circle before placing her gently on her feet. He wanted to cheer, run, and take a victory lap, but he didn't want to lose this moment.

"Alright, lets clean up so we can get dinner going." Catarina pulled away with a smile. "I don't want to walk in on Jacob and Katie doing the horizontal tango on my kitchen counter because we took too long."

"I think they have more restraint than you think!" Roland couldn't help but look back to the kitchen window. Jacob and Katie were lip locked and giggling to themselves. "Then again, maybe not." Roland watched the mock horror cross Catarina's face.

They walked around the yard together picking up after the dogs. Roland knew he shouldn't put all his eggs in one basket, but having her here, he couldn't help looking at the future with euphoria.

"Buster!" Catarina called. Roland watched the enormous dog trot up. "Go say hi." She told the dog. Roland crouched when the dog smelled her and started walking up to him. He held his hand out for inspection. "Family, family, family." She affirmed.

"Hi, big guy." Roland gave him a tentative smile when Buster licked his hand and continued forward. Roland gave him a good rubdown while the dog's massive tail made a breeze of its own.

"Buster is mine," She explained, "My psychiatrist thought he would be a good idea. Turns out he was right." Roland climbed to his feet, and they walked back towards the house. "Frankie and Ralf were dumped at a shelter but just needed some training.

They're three and hopefully will become security dogs once they graduate their next stage of training."

"Will you do that?" Roland took the bags and threw them in a designated trash bin.

"No, but I'll house them" Catarina washed her hands in a small outdoor sink nearby. Roland did the same. "Then Clyde is going to start as a therapy dog, and Rocco and Gunner are going together hopefully to be cadaver dogs. If not, they will make a great addition to someone's family.

"So you do the basic training and housing, and they get extra training from specialists?" Roland couldn't keep the admiration out of his voice.

"Yeah." Cat blushed and looked back at the window. "Ok, let's get back inside before I have to have the house sanitized." Roland realized that Jacob and Katie were no longer visible which was dangerous. Funny, but dangerous.

# Chapter 3

Her heart was racing, and Catarina had to focus on taking deep breaths to try to calm it. The pessimist in her was trying to tell her that this was all too good to be true. She was trying to tell that voice to put a lid on it and let her enjoy the moment. He smelled just like she remembered back in the cabin. She let out a whistle calling all the dogs back to the house. Roland stepped back and let her go up the deck stairs first.

"Back up!" She commanded. All the dogs made way for her to open the door. She pretended to focus on them while she went over and over again in her head his speech. She let the dogs run by her and closed the two of them out on the porch. She looked at Roland and smiled. "I know that part about you being ok with just being friends was bullshit. It was written all over your face."

"If it meant you didn't hate me, and I didn't have to say goodbye forever, then I could live with that." Roland searched her face in a very intimate way that made her flush. She tried to hide a smile and they went inside.

"Everyone decent?" She called a little louder than necessary.

"It's a good thing you sent the dogs in first as a warning!" Jacob taunted in a way that gave her a bit of nostalgia. "You might have tried to bleach your eyes after seeing my white ass!" Catarina laughed when Katie gawked at him.

"In case you've forgotten," Catarina smirked, "I've seen that exact pasty white ass before and survived." Roland let out a bellowing laugh that shocked even the dogs. Jacob flushed and Katie's head snapped to him.

"The towels!" Jacob said, digging the heels of his hands into his eyes while trying, very badly, to explain to Katie. "No one replaced the towels in the cabin, so I walked back to my room with my clothes covering myself!"

"After yelling at us!" Catarina mocked. "Don't worry Katie, there are things that I haven't seen."

"I guess," Katie bounced back, "you will have to tell me more details when you were all stuck in the mountains together. I only went over the incriminating information involving Daniel."

"Hey," Catarina walked into the kitchen and pulled a rice maker from a cupboard to distract herself, "Where exactly where we? It seemed like we were on a different planet." Katie drained the sink and Roland started searching the cupboards. "Rice is by the stove on the bottom."

"We were actually about two and a half hours outside of Jackson, Wyoming." Jacob was giving Rocco a good scratch between the ears.

"And just so everyone is aware, this whole house has camera's everywhere." Catarina started measuring out rice and water. She covertly slipped a glance at Jacob and Katie who both gave each other shocked expressions and she had to hide a giggle. She gave everyone instructions to get dinner done quicker. She grabbed a tablecloth and headed to the table. "Hey guys, where are you wanting your fire power?"

"We were going to ask you that." Roland walked into the room.

"How easily accessible do you need it to be?" Catarina wasn't surprised at the excessive display of force.

"As long as we can get to it fairly easily, then we would probably keep a few things with us and store the rest." Roland had walked up behind her and put a hand on her shoulder.

"Define easily." She joked. Reaching up, she squeezed his hand and laid her head on it before starting towards the kitchen. "Come on."

She instructed them to steer clear of one side of the island before pushing a button under the counter. All the blinds around the house closed at once. Then she pushed another button, and the top of the island moved back. A panel on the side slid open to reveal a staircase down to a bunker. She flipped on the light switch smiling at the shocked faces in the room.

"Boys!" Catarina called to the dogs. "Watch, watch, watch!" All the dogs scurried over to their designated raised beds and kept their eyes on the doors. "I will  show you how to get in and out from each entrance."

"I like your safehouse better!" Roland was grinning ear to ear.

They followed her down through the bunker. She showed them the other secret door. And how to access it from the outside and the hidden latch next to the water heater. Then how to get into the main area of the basement from outside. They walked back up to the kitchen and the guys started moving the guns.

"So how long have you two been….?" Catarina asked Katie but left it open for her to label the relationship.

"Dating?" Katie smiled. "Officially about eight months, but we've worked on a few different teams together for years." She laughed and filled the chicken while Catarina seasoned the rice.

"I'm glad you two found each other!" Catarina confided when the guys disappeared down the stairs again. "I mean I didn't exactly know them well, but he looks so happy!" Katie smiled.

"He's such a smartass." She finished the tray and handed it to Catarina who sprinkled cheese over the top. The guys walked past them to take a few things up to the bedrooms. When they were gone, Katie lowered her voice. "How are you doing with everything?"

"I'm ok. I guess I'm still a little shellshocked." She put the chicken in the oven, and they washed their hands. "It's been a shitshow kind of day. I mean with my ex showing up, then you guys, and Director Johnston's information, I would love a drink." Katie chuckled and they got going setting the table.

"Can I say something between us?" Katie looked uneasy, and that didn't help.

"Go for it." She leaned on one of the high back chairs.

"I've known Roland for a long time. Until he met you, he was a hollow man going through the motions. When you were all in the cabin, something in him became whole again. Getting those orders nearly killed him. He spent every spare minute for almost eight months at the gym trying to fight the pain. He kept some of your pictures and had a calendar on his wall counting down the days until he could come find you again." Katie explained softly. "I know this last year has been just as horrible for you, but I hope you guys can be happy. We can't imagine two people who deserve it more."

Catarina was doing her best not to cry but it wasn't going well. Katie walked around and gave her another hug. She had about half a foot on her, and Catarina started laughing.

"I'm the shortest person in the stupid house!"

"Well at least you're not the strangest!" Katie led the way back to the kitchen. "Jacob holds that title."

"I do not!" he laughed.

"Hey, are you all done in the bunker?" Catarina asked when the guys lingered.

"Yeah," Roland looked around to affirm with the others, "Looks like it." Catarina pushed a few buttons on the counter that made a quiet hydraulic hiss that moved the Granite counter back to where it had been, concealing the secret entrance. About fifteen seconds after, the blinds on the windows rose.

"Boys, Chill out!" She called. All the dogs scattered to different parts of the adjoining rooms. "Anyone want a drink?" Catarina asked.

"Sure, what do you have?" Jacob was petting Rocco who seemed to have taken a shine to him.

"Just about everything actually." She led them all to her office on the other side of the house. When they all had their drinks, they plopped on the couch to wait for the food to finish. "Well, I guess we had better have a cover story then."

"You two are cousins." Roland blurted out making Catarina smile.

"That's what I was thinking!" Jacob raised his glass in agreement.

"I'm down." Katie agreed. "Estranged but recently opened communication."

"My crazy aunt divorced your dad because she was sleeping with his boss years ago?" Catarina suggested.

"Jacob is my boyfriend, and Roland is an army buddy that you met the last time you visited and hit it off?" Katie snuggled into Jacob's side.

"We had stopped talking because one of my female coworkers told you that her and I were sleeping together. Then she told me that you met someone else, so we had no reason to talk."

Roland held his hand out for Catarina. After a second's hesitation she took it. The rough edges of his hands sparked a memory of the two of them dancing in a small living room.

"And I found out and played matchmaker." Katie giggled. Catarina was doing her best to focus on the rest of the conversation, but his hand was so familiar and warm wrapped around hers. The whiskey was warming her gut, leaving her relaxed and jittery all at the same time. They hashed out a few more details before the timer went off and dinner was done.

They got all the dogs fed and sat down in the dining room. The conversation was a little guarded, but they were slowly making progress. After dinner Catarina showed them the Panic Room. It was a camera room and gun safe that was hidden behind a bookshelf in her office, comfortably fitting the four of them. Catarina sent the evening check-in to The Director and they all sat down for a movie. The dogs found spots to sit, and Buster chewed on a bone near the end table.

Catarina intentionally sat next to Roland, who had his feet up on the ottoman. She sat where she could tuck her feet under herself, but still left space between them. Gunner got up and made himself at home beside Katie. A few minutes into the movie, Roland reached out a hand and put it over hers. It was tentative at first, but when she didn't pull away, Roland ran his thumb back and forth along the edge of her pinky. The room felt like it was a thousand degrees too warm. She tried to focus on the historical drama and the main character that was going through his own internal peril, but the space next to her was damned near buzzing.

"Hey," Jacob asked, not bothering to whisper, "Where's the bathroom? And is there more than one?"

"Yeah, there's one next to the office, or two upstairs, first two doors on the left." She smiled at them. Jacob and Katie walked up the stairs hand in hand.

When they disappeared upstairs, Roland brought her hand to him for a small kiss. It was soft and tender, a reassurance, rather than an urging. He placed that hand in his other one, wrapping an arm around her tentatively. Neither of them was paying attention to the movie now. She could feel him watching her. Her breath was shallow and tense. She craved his touch, but mentally she was spiraling and didn't know how to voice it.

"Is this, ok?" Roland whispered. Catarina looked at him. Concern was written all over his face. She nodded once sharply. He gave her a sad smile. "It's ok to say no. You're not going to offend me."

"I want this." She whispered firmly.

She made to scoot closer to him when he moved towards the corner of the sectional. Catarina froze, wondering what she did wrong until he reached around and lifted her to sit next to him. Then he leaned forward and pulled her feet up onto the ottoman next to his. He draped an arm over her shoulder, then she leaned back against him and waited. He took her right hand in his and let his thumb trail along the edges again. The seconds seemed to pass slowly. With every breath, they both relaxed a little more, until they finally stopped mimicking bookends.

"That was slightly less awkward than it could've been." Roland snickered.

"I can go sit on the floor if this is too much for you." Catarina tried to keep the laugh out of her voice but let out a little squeak when he wrapped both arms around her and gave her a small squeeze. That seemed to do the trick, taking the edge off. She relaxed into him, the warmth of his body against hers pulled at a memory of the two of them wrapped in each other's arms giving and taking comfort. "I don't want to rush things." She mumbled, but she knew he could hear her.

"My plan was to walk you to your door like a gentleman." Roland leaned down and whispered in her ear. "We never got a fair chance at this. I lost you for almost a year and it nearly killed me. I want to spend the rest of my life getting to know you one second at a time. You know, until you get sick of me." They chuckled and Catarina rested her head against his shoulder, overwhelmed with emotion.

Jacob and Katie came down the stairs a few minutes later. They didn't say anything, but they both sported mischievous smiles. Roland leaned his head against hers and sighed. Catarina could feel the tension in his body melting away, and hers did the same. There was so much she wanted to say and so many questions ran through her mind, but she wanted to savor this moment.

"You two are assholes." Catarina snorted when the movie had ended. Jacob and Katie were smiling triumphantly back at them.

"If that's the worst thing you have to say about us," Katie cackled, "I can live with that!"

The others started in on the dishes while Catarina took the dogs out for a final time. She took the flashlight with her but didn't see the bear again. They were less common around this area, so she wasn't surprised that it moved on. The door clicked but she didn't bother turning around.

"Hey," Jacob walked out to where she was cleaning up after the dogs, "We figured this qualified as 'leaving the house'. You look good, Short-Stack." Jacob gave her a side hug before digging his hands in his pockets.

"You look happy." Catarina smiled. "I don't think I've ever seen you smile this much, it's a little unnerving."

"Yeah," Jacob smiled to himself, "She's pretty great, isn't she?"

"She seems nice." Catarina walked over and threw the bag away. "She loves you. The sparkle in her eye, and the way you're the first person she looks to when she laughs."

"I'm trying to find the right time to ask." Jacob gave her a conspiratorial smile. Catarina flicked an eyebrow at him and smiled. He had a small box in his hand and opened it. A huge oval diamond in an intricate setting sparkled in the light.

"That's stunning! If I can help with anything, I'm all ears." She jumped and yelled out, "Out of the bushes! Ralf, Clyde, OUT!" Turning back to Jacob who was pocketing the box, she laughed "Once a skunk managed to make its way onto the property and we all slept outside until I finally found a recipe that killed the smell." Jacob nodded.

"You know he was going to come looking for you right?" Jacob turned and watched her, but she couldn't look back at him. "Not tomorrow, but the day after was the start of his time off where he was going to come find you. He was going to explain everything and try to win you back. I know that this is all a lot, and you need time to sort this all out, but I needed you to know it wasn't just a 'someday' thing. It was on the calendar and The Director was going to give us your location in two days."

"It's a lot." Catarina tried to keep her voice even. "Thanks for telling me." She gave him a pat on the back. "If its ok with you guys, I do still have a lot of emotions to work through. I never stopped loving him. Even though we barely knew each other, and I mourned the person I did know under the circumstances, I never stopped." She sighed, trying to relieve the pain in her chest. "Is it naive? Absolutely. But I'm beyond grateful to have a second chance to get to know him for who he really is." She gave him a sly grin. "You know, not under duress and all that."

"That sounds like a great start." Jacob smiled with her. "And I'm glad you were able to beat the shit out of Trent." Jacob gave her a playful shove.

"Do I have you to thank for his warrant?"

"Well, the house had surveillance in every room, and the cameras were super high resolution. That was the evidence they needed after contacting his former girlfriends, he never had a chance." Jacob stole a glance back at the house.

"So, I guess she knows too?" Catarina had to fight off the agitation. When Jacob nodded, she sighed. She knew she was more upset about it than she needed to be, so she tried to let it go. "I guess everyone in this house has seen me naked?" She smirked. "The fact that no one has been blinded by bleach or thrown themselves off the nearest cliff says a lot." That shocked a laugh out of Jacob. "Come on, Gimpy, I need to get these loons in bed."

They got the dogs corralled in the house. Catarina showed everyone the protocol for locking it down at night. They all gawked when the steel plates rolled shut over the windows and doors. Katie and Jacob excused themselves to shower, although no one was under any illusion that they were going to be using separate bathrooms. She giggled to herself at the giddy couple.

Catarina wandered into the kitchen, searching the cupboards for a sweet snack. Roland wasn't far behind. She grabbed the peanut butter with two spoons and sat on the island. Handing one to Roland, she smirked.

"I don't suppose you figured out how to eat without getting half of it in your beard?" She smiled at him.

"You think it's cute." He said right before he took a spoonful and tapped her nose with the end, leaving a small remnant behind. She blinked in shock before they both burst out laughing. Roland's laugh slowly ebbed, but she kept going, the laugh pulled at something else, building up speed. Before she knew it, she was sobbing in his arms.

He stroked her hair and whispered calming words in her ear. She couldn't understand a damned thing he was saying, but his touch on her back and the reverberation of his voice in his chest slowly brought her back from her episode. She held tight to him, suddenly feeling ashamed.

"I'm sorry!" She sniffed while wiping away the tears. "I don't know what happened. I had my shit together!"

"Hey," Roland's strong hands cradled her face making her look at him, "sometimes the things that make you laugh can pull out emotions that were buried way down deep." He wiped away her tears and pulled her against him in a hug that melted away the last of the tension she was holding.

"How are you so goddamned calm?" Catarina choked out.

"Because after a year, I finally have you in my arms again." Roland kissed the top of her head. "I don't care if you randomly burst into tears as long as I can be here to hold you and make it better. I mean I will do everything I can to make you smile again, but as long as you are here, I couldn't be happier."

And just like that she was crying again. He patted her back and brushed her hair off her face with a soft smile before pulling her against him. The scent of him wrapped around her, reigniting memories she wasn't ready to deal with. She thought her last memory of him was just that, the last. But now he was holding her, telling her it was all going to be ok, and not shying away from her emotions. She sat up strait when they heard footsteps on the stairs. Jacob walked slowly into the kitchen with his hands up placatingly.

"It's just me." He came and gave her a supportive pat on the shoulder. "Just wanting to know what the schedule is so we can get up and help. We can go get groceries sometime tomorrow if that works."

"I take the boys for their morning walk at seven." Catarina sniffed. "But it's just inside the property, so you guys can sleep in if you want."

"I'll go with her." Roland said quietly. Jacob nodded and went back upstairs. Roland gave her a long hug. With every second that ticked by, she felt another piece of herself relax until she felt warm and safe for the first time in a long time. "Come on, Half-Pint. If you don't get to bed soon, then I'll be the one to blame."

"Promise me you'll still be here when I wake up?" Catarina searched his eyes, not caring that her makeup was probably smeared. She just spent the last fifteen minutes holding onto him like a lifeline.

"I promise that I wouldn't miss seeing you in the morning with bed head, for anything." Roland smiled down at her.

He lifted her off the counter and put the spoons in the sink. They walked hand in hand up the stairs. The dogs all thundered to her room and waited by the door. Catarina's heart was thumping when she opened it, and the dogs sprinted to her bed. She kept steeling glances at him. He was bigger than she remembered and in the time they had been apart, he had toned out immensely. When he held her, his body was unyielding and hard. Roland smiled at her damned near reading her thoughts.

"I've regretted not kissing you every second since that day." Roland took a step forward but stopped when a warning growl came from Buster. Catarina gave him a small hand signal that had him climbing back onto the bed and laying down. Roland's enormous hand pressed into the small of her back, pulling her into him. "You have no idea how much I want to." His voice was low and sultry, leaving her weak in the knees. Catarina's heart was beating so loud he could probably hear the damned thing. His other hand caressed her face in gentle strokes. "But you've had one hell of a day, so I'll leave you with this." Roland leaned down and pressed his lips to her cheek before pulling back and smiling. "I love the woman I got to know, the spitfire, the sassy warrior, and the kind heart. I look forward to getting to know the healing heart, the dog trainer, and I hope, someone who's just as much of a sarcastic asshole as I am."

"If you think that I've lost my edge you've got another thing coming." She smiled at him. "You better get to bed before I'm the one doing the kidnapping this time."

That got a snicker out of him. They hugged for a long time and when he finally walked down the hall to his room, she watched the door close behind him. Closing her own, she managed to climb into bed before the sobs racked her body. The stress was bound to come out sooner or later, so she let it run through her, and when it was over, she slept better than she had in over a year.

When her alarm went off, she nearly leapt out of bed. The dogs all ran to the door, pacing impatiently while she pulled on her shorts and shirt. Yanking a brush through her hair and applying a generous amount of deodorant she sprinted down the stairs. Roland was sitting in a tank top that hung loose over shorts and running shoes.

"You ready to go Hulk?" Catarina teased. Roland's smile damned near took her breath away. He stood and stretched. She had to stop herself from gawking at his physique. "Katie wasn't kidding when she said you lived in the gym after."

"I mean I had to find some way to keep your attention just in case you thought my personality, was shit." He waggled his eyebrows, shocking a laugh out of her. Smiling, Roland added a bit more solemnly. "It helped with the pain of losing you."

"Well," She walked up and held out a hand, "I get it." Roland took it and stood. "Before we go, will you grab the dog bags out of the drawer?" She used the fingerprint scanner to open a secret gun safe hidden in the bottom of the kitchen cupboards. While she was getting it attached to her belt along with an extra magazine, she felt his eyes exploring her.

"I don't know if I should be insulted or flattered that you think you need something that big to fight me off." Roland had his arms folded over his chest almost defensively. It was meant as a joke, but Catarina heard all the undertones that he wasn't saying.

"Hey, "She walked up and took his hand, "You said it yourself, you've not lived a normal life in a long time, so I see how this looks. I know that I'm safe with you." She gave him a well-meaning look when he eyed her dubiously. She let go of his hand to close the safe. "There's been a black bear that's showed up a few times round the edge of the property. I'd rather have it and not need it, than need it and not have it." They walked outside and the dogs practically stampeaded down the walkway. "Besides, I just got you back, and I don't want to risk losing you in an actual bear fight."

They started off walking along the fence following the dogs and cleaning up after them. She could see the tension in Roland's shoulders. Catarina was very aware that he needed as much room to adjust as she did. She didn't want to bombard him while they were still figuring each other out, so she stayed quiet and relaxed.

"I'm sorry." Roland sighed after they had been walking a while. The house had disappeared behind the trees. "It's been years since I've done the whole normal thing." Catarina gave him a slight bump with her shoulder.

"Well, you know I've never dated normal, so this will be new for both of us."

"Is that what we are doing?" Roland asked quietly. She could see him fighting to keep the smile off his face. "Dating?" He kept his eyes straight ahead, but they were damned near sparkling in excitement, and she had to stifle a giggle.

"I mean, if you don't want to, I understand...." Her words were cut off sharply when he pulled her against him, his hands narrowly avoiding the firearm on her hip. One of his hands was wrapped around the back of her neck, while the other pressed her against him with a need that took her breath away. She steadied herself, liking the way his assertiveness put her at ease. It was a feeling she hadn't experienced before.

"Like I said back at the cabin, nothing would happen because you were under duress." His lips hovered dangerously close to hers. "Now you're not and I'm asking: do you want this? Can I kiss you?" He didn't move a muscle, but she could feel the tension buzzing through him.

Every breath pressed her tighter against him. She stared deep into his eyes at the brown that surrounded the pupil, cutting off in a sharp cliff where the blue wound around it like the ocean around an island. His thumb trailed a line of fire along her jaw. The touch was tender and earnest, trying to convey what he couldn't put into words. Catarina slowly nodded and tried to say 'yes' but no sound came out. Roland leaned down slowly, his lips pressing softly into hers. Her breath caught, all the noise in her mind going silent, as she melted into the taste of him.

Pulling away, he looked at her, almost making sure that she was still ok. Catarina didn't want it to be over, she watched relief flood his face when he saw the passion in her eyes. His lips came crashing down on hers as she felt him finally let go. The kiss was electric, burning its way through her body and lighting up every nerve ending. She held him tighter when he deepened the kiss, pulling a gasp from her. Her hands were everywhere, on his body, in his hair, and wrapping themselves around his massive shoulders. They stumbled backwards until she was pressed against the fence.

Several sharp barks shocked them out of the moment. They pulled away gasping and both drawing firearms. It took longer than it should have to realize that the dogs weren't alerting to anything, but instead were unnerved enough by the two of them to start barking. Re-holstering their weapons, they damned nearly collapsed in a fit of laughter.

"You were so upset about me having a gun, but you had one too!" Catarina laughed. Roland pointedly reached down and grabbed her hand when they started walking again.

"I thought you were bringing it because you were afraid of me." He admitted.

"I've already seen you with a boner back at the cabin." Catarina teased, then cleared her throat before continuing. "I think worrying about your self-control after everything would be ridiculous. Besides I watched you face off against a serial killer like a brute and tread around me like I was fragile or something. That tells me that you've either got the best character and integrity I've ever seen, or I'm not your type, and Katie's got one hell of a battle to prep for."

"I'm not saying that Jacob's not a catch...." Roland smiled "But it's hard to see myself in good light after the last several years undercover."

"Then let me help with that, and you can return the favor!" She laughed and held her arms open to him. Roland smiled and pulled her around for another hug. Looking up at the man who had her terrified when they first met, Catarina smiled at the person standing with her now. It was mindboggling to think of everything that led up to this.

Roland leaned down to give her another kiss, this one soft and sweet. They both savored the moment, enjoying the serine comfort of each other after coming so far and enduring so much.

# Chapter 4

Roland didn't want to let her go. The way her skin glowed in the morning had him convinced he had died, and this was his journey to Valhalla. She was still the witty girl he remembered from the cabin. The pain that racked his body mentally and physically for the last year was gone.

Bodies sprinting through the trees broke the moment. Roland turned and pushed her behind a tree before lunging behind the trunk of another. They both had their guns drawn waiting for the intruders.

"Boys, down, down, down!" He heard Catarina's order and immediately heard the runner's footsteps slow to a walk. He noticed each of the dogs taking cover against a tree and low to the ground. He would have to remember to compliment her on her training.

"Sparrow!" Jacob's voice came through the trees and Roland took a calming breath.

"Cardinal!" He responded. "All clear here!" Roland nodded at Catarina, and they lowered their guns.

"All clear! Approaching now!" Jacob and Katie came into view, both had their weapons drawn but at a low ready. Everyone came out from cover.

"We heard the dogs barking." Katie explained, worry in her voice. Catarina slapped her free hand over her mouth and went red when Roland smirked at her before running a hand through his hair. They all put their guns away leaving Katie and Jacob looking confused as all hell.

"Turns out the dogs are protective." Roland smiled proudly. It took a solid three count before it clicked and the others chuckled to themselves.

"You lucky bastard!" Jacob punched him in the shoulder. "You could've been shot! You couldn't have waited until you were back at the house?"

"The soundproofing is awesome, no one would've heard anything." Katie smirked.

"It's not as great as you think!" Roland looked pointedly at her. Katie looked horrified and flushed.

"I'm going to go drown myself in the pond, thank you." Catarina groaned, but she was smiling when she said it. "Boys, Chill out!" All the dogs jumped to their feet and continued sniffing around. Jacob took a few steps back when Gunner tried to pee on his shoes again.

"Seriously what is with this dog?" Jacob grumbled. "Come on Katie, let's get you back to the house."

"Yeah, I was getting my new pump when we heard the barking." She shrugged.

"Pump?" Catarina asked now that she pulled herself together.

"Yeah, I'm a type one diabetic." Katie shrugged.

"Don't worry," Jacob grinned deviously, "I make sure she's always got plenty of reason to keep her sugars up."

"Ugh!" Catarina groaned. "Get back to the house before I kneecap you!" Roland laughed when she shoved Jacob before they walked away.

Roland took in the property while they walked. There was a huge fence that lined the land making him feel better about security. He was able to spot several obvious cameras in the trees but knew for a fact that there were many more hidden. They made it to a clearing where a small pond sat. Catarina called the dogs back when they tried going for a swim. He couldn't imagine having to wash all of them, one after another.

"You know," Catarina's voice was hesitant. "We pretty much had a whirlwind two weeks together, but I didn't really know you." They were walking close enough that Roland was practically able to feel the nervous energy buzzing off her. "Can you tell me about you?"

"Uh, yeah." Roland racked his brain for a good place to start. "My grandparents are Russian, Catalan, and Samoan. I grew up in a place called Granollers on the outskirts of Barcelona. I was born in the US, but we moved to Spain when I was a baby to take care of my grandparents before they died, and we moved back five years later. My parents live in Arizona, and they know I work for the government but nothing specific."

"Do you visit them often?" She threw a stick that Clyde had brought up, the others racing past to try and get it first.

"I have gone about every other month since the trial," He tripped over a loose stone and laughed to himself, "I haven't been the best company to anyone though." Roland was watching Ralf and Frankie chasing a squirrel up a tree before giving a sharp warning bark. A soft hand took his and he looked down at Catarina with a halfhearted smile.

"If you don't want the company, then I'm happy to stay and reminisce in the silence with you." She squeezed his hand gently, leaving him feeling like he was flying.

They made it back to the house after they finished walking the property line. The smell of eggs, sausage and bacon came pouring from an open window. The dogs all sat and waited while they threw away the bags, they had brought with them. When they walked inside, Jacob was finishing loading the dishwasher from last night and Katie was setting the table. After the dogs had been fed and they were all sat down Catarina gave them a rundown of everyday life.

"Ralf and Frankie will be picked up in an hour for their training, they go Monday through Friday. Clyde is going in for evaluation on his behavior so they can decide if he's ok to be a therapy dog. Then Rocco and Gunner will be picked up at one for their training, their schedule is the same as Ralf and Frankie."

"We can go grab groceries sometime today if that works?" Jacob asked.

"Sure." Catarina nodded." I have Jiu Jitsu tonight if you all want to come. There's a gym next door if that's more your style." She noticed Katie look a little uncomfortable. Roland thought it was sweet that she was thinking about everyone, and it warmed his heart a bit.

"Katie and I can hit the gym." Jacob left the door open for Roland.

"It's been a while since I've gone," He shrugged, "but if they won't mind having a boulder rolling around the floor, then I would love to come." That got a smile from Catarina, and he put it in the win column.

"There's always room for one more." Roland watched the way her eyes flicked towards him.

They cleaned up and the girls got together to meal prep while Roland and Jacob did a check in with The Director. There was no update on Tobias' location, but his accounts had been cleared out and the house he had lived in before had gone up for sale. That was bad. Tyrese said that he was sure that whatever Tobias was planning, he wasn't expecting to live through it.

Tyrese had done the psychological profile on the brothers and testified at Tobias' trial. One of the most damning points of evidence for his jail sentence was how fixated he was on Catarina and blamed her for Sam's death, even though Daniel was the one to fire the gun. Sam had jumped to try to stop it, and the bullet tore his throat out. Even though he had just been stabbed, it took eight agents and an excessive use of sedatives to get him to the hospital. They gave him a maximum sentence along with mandatory counseling in hopes of tempering his anger. The reports they received said that he never said anything during those sessions.

They went through the day, helping Catarina with the usual training for the dogs. Finishing lunch, they did their second check in, and continued until all the dogs were returned. They had two hours to kill before the gym, so Jacob and Katie went for groceries, conspicuously leaving Catarina and him alone. Again. Roland was going to have to have a talk with him if this was going to be a regular thing. They were supposed to all be there to protect her.

"Anything I can help with?" Catarina was going through bills in her office when he walked in. She looked up at him and smiled.

"What's your favorite color?" She set her pen down. It caught him off guard and he took a second to answer.

"Green, like the pine trees." He smirked. "Why?"

"Well, if we are dating, "She smiled and walked around the antique desk, "I figured I should know."

"What's yours?" Roland brushed a few strands back from her face needing the reassurance that she was real, and he wasn't just dreaming.

"Blue." Her voice was soft. "I don't want to move to fast." She spoke hesitantly.

"Savoring the minutes with you doesn't have to mean rushing to anything." Roland held his hand out to her. When she took it he gave her a warm smile. "We had our first official double date last night, our first kiss today, and if you let me, I would love to make you dinner sometime." The blush that colored her face had his spirit soaring. "But if it's ok with you, I really need a shower."

"A shower?" Catarina's sheepish grin made him smile.

"If we are doing Jiu Jitsu, I figured no one would want to roll with someone who hasn't showered in a few days." Roland scratched the back of his neck. "And do you have nail clippers? I forgot a few things when I was packing."

In the bathroom upstairs, Roland set his clothes on the counter while Catarina dug through a few drawers to find the clippers. He turned on the shower and peeled off his shirt when he realized she was staring at him. Roland had never been ashamed of his body, maybe a little self-conscious about the scars, but when he caught her watching him, he felt like he needed to cover up. She slowly walked up to him and set her fingers on the lines that marred his arm. Her eyes wandered over the rest of him, following the scars.

"What really happened?" Her fingers gently traced them leaving his skin tingling where she touched.

"We were in a convoy that ran over an IED." He sighed, remembering that horrible day. "Jacob had a giant piece of shrapnel stuck in his leg. I was bandaging it and trying to secure the metal so the doctors could remove it when another one went off. The second one had metal shards and shit in it. I mostly caught ricochets off the side of the Humvee and that saved my life. Didn't make it hurt any less though. We hunkered down and waited for an evac. They threw a few grenades trying to finish the job and I covered Jacob, trying to keep him alive. Part of my clothes caught on fire, and it compromised the vest. We got it put out before another IED went off. We heard the chopper coming in and that's the only reason I was able to push through the pain. I had to get him out. After they took out the small team, I carried Jacob out to the chopper. We were the only ones...."

Steam had filled the bathroom fogging the mirror, and Roland could feel her hands on him, but he couldn't bring himself to look at her. She walked slowly around him, kissing the deepest scars and ending in front of him. Humiliation filled him. Shame at the way he looked, shame at not being better, and shame that she saw him being this pathetic.

"Ambrose Roland Hoeft." His heart jumped hearing his full name. He had forgotten that she knew it. "I'm proud of you for protecting Jacob and making it out alive. Your scars are a badge of honor that show how much you've overcome. I love that you were able to tell me. You are so strong and brave, physically and emotionally, and I'm, proud to call you mine."

Roland wrapped his arms around her ignoring the emotions that built up inside himself. He never thought he needed any validation, or anyone to say anything like that, but the tears he blinked back told a different story. She ran her fingers up and down his back, letting him have his moment of vulnerability. When he was done, she stood as high as she could on her toes, giving him a quick kiss.

"Wash up." She whispered. "I'm going to do your hair for class."

"You think so huh?" Roland smirked at her. "You might have to fight me for it."

"Don't threaten me with a good time." She sassed back, closing the door behind her.

Roland had never had anyone speak to him the way she had when he was feeling low. His parents loved each other but love and admiration wasn't something they discussed in front of the kids. She wasn't speaking to him, the agent, or him, the boyfriend. She spoke to him like she was speaking to his soul, and it excited him.

He jogged down the stairs several minutes later. He had dried his hair as much as possible with the towels. Catarina was parked on the couch watching a historic tv series. He had heard of it before but never watched it. When he got closer, he realized that she was fully intending to do his hair. He plopped down in front of her, but when she went to move her legs, he put them over his shoulder.

"Is this the part where we fight over who does your hair?" She laughed.

"You mean the part where you lose badly, and I let you do my hair anyways?" He tickled her feet.

"Your funeral." Catarina laughed before jerking behind him.

He was going to ask what she meant by that when one of her legs wrapped around his neck, and sinched down. Roland lifted his hips and pushed backwards sending the both of them and part of the sectional off kilter. With her legs still around his neck, Roland hit the front of the couch that was standing straight up in the air, and he went flying back over the sofa. The dogs looked lazily over at the two of them. No help. The bastards.

Roland felt around and tried to dislodge her foot when he started to see spots around the edge of his vision. Surrendering, he tapped her leg. Immediately she released him with a giggle. They were both laughing when he rolled over and crawled up her body. They were still halfway on the back of the sectional that was now on the ground, pillows flung everywhere. Roland intertwined his hands on her stomach, resting his head on them.

"I like this view of you." He smiled at her blush.

"I thought we were taking it slow." She giggled, making his hair bounce when her belly moved.

"I'm just admiring the architecture." Roland smiled. Untangling his arms, he moved higher and rested an elbow on either side of her head. She had wrapped her arms around his waist. He took that as a positive sign, and the smile glowing on her face wasn't giving any arguments. He brushed his knuckles along her cheek, still at a loss for words that she was here in his arms.

Roland leaned down and kissed her. She met his lips with equal fervor. Her hands made their way under the sides of his shirt and held onto him. Roland cradled her face in his hands, his brain buzzing with the possibilities, the future, the passion....

"Oh God!" The exclamation did not come from them. They both looked up to see two horrified sets of eyes gaping down at them. Katie and Jacob both had their arms full of groceries standing in the doors leading to the garage that apparently neither one of them heard.

"Well, hi guys." Catarina said less casually than she meant to. "Um, this isn't what it looks like?" They all cackled while Roland and Catarina got up and fixed the furniture.

"I can't wait to hear this." Jacob set his groceries on the island.

"We were testing the malleability of the furniture." Roland walked into the garage to help with the rest of the groceries. "You know, in case of an intruder."

"Oh, really?" Katie taunted. "Because it looked like you two were about to have sex on the overturned furniture in the living room!" They were all loading groceries into the house now.

"Exactly!" Catarina's smirked but her blush had him turning away to hide a laugh. "Did you guys get the cookies?"

"Yeah, and the whipped cream," Jacob started loading the fridge, "but after what we just walked in on, I don't really want to give it to you!"

"Piss off, after what I heard through the walls last night." Roland wacked him on the side with the back of his hand. Jacob turned and they threw a few fake punches while bobbing and weaving the way they did when they were kids while laughing.

"If you two aren't going to help, then get out of the kitchen." Katie playfully pushed the two of them out.

Roland set to work finding and reorganizing the brush, comb and hair ties that went flying when they tipped the couch. They turned on a football game and plopped down. After a few minutes, the girls joined them. Catarina pushed him to the ground and sat behind him again. It didn't' take long before she had his hair tied into what vaguely resembled a Viking braid. She excused herself to get her own hair done and Katie disappeared to go with her.

"How's it going?" Jacob asked damned near as soon as they heard the bathroom door close upstairs.

"I'm going to need a neon sign to tell me to take it slow." Roland rubbed his face in his hands. It was taking everything he had to keep it simple, but he was failing.

"Is that what she wants?" Jacob asked, leaning forward to scratch Rocco between the ears. Gunner jumped up to get a scratch of his own in a momentary truce.

"Yeah." Roland tried not to grumble. He didn't have an issue taking it slow, but he wanted her forever, not just for right now and he needed her to know that. "If she wants me, I would love a life with her, but it's way too soon to ask that."

"That's what I felt with Katie." Jacob smirked. "It will happen when it's supposed to." They settled in for the game.

The girls came down in their gym gear a little while later. Roland laughed at Catarina's wild pants. Katie was in loose sweats and a t shirt. The down time before the gym was nice but it made it that much harder to get up and go. Roland changed into a long pair of spandex pants under loose shorts that had a slit up the side to maintain flexibility, and a short sleeve rash guard. Once all the dogs had been out and were now lounging in the house, they set off.

The gym was in a massive building that had been remodeled. When they walked in the older man from yesterday was at the front desk. Catarina pulled him aside and they talked for a minute. The three of them were standing around awkwardly while others shambled in, going through the doors on the left that lead into a full MMA gym. They were catching looks from people he assumed were at the park yesterday. God, was that only yesterday? Catarina walked back and made an introduction.

"Thomas, this is my cousin Katie, and her boyfriend, Jacob.' Thomas reached out and shook their hands. "And this is my boyfriend, Roland." She smiled shyly at him. Thomas didn't offer his hand.

"And all that yesterday?" Thomas asked with a hint of fatherly protection in his voice. Roland couldn't keep an appreciative smirk off his face.

"My ex-coworker told her that we were in a relationship and that I was leading her on, and then she told me that Cat had met someone else. We spent a year with nothing before Katie found out and exposed Laura." Roland gave Katie an appreciative smile.

"Laura?" Thomas asked.

"The co-worker." Catarina's nose twitched angrily. Thomas gave her a nod and held his hand out to Roland who shook it.

"Ready to get your ass kicked?" Thomas asked with a smirk.

"After what I've already gotten from Cat, not really, but I'm game." Roland got a laugh from the short grey-haired man.

Jacob and Katie waved, walking into the gym portion of the building. Following Catarina inside the MMA doors, Roland watched everyone freeze. He had to resist the urge to run his hands over his hair. He didn't realize he stopped walking until Catarina took his hand and dragged him over to several sets of cubbies against a wall. She got her things out of her bag and pushed them into the back of one, having him set his bag in front of hers.

"If you don't relax, people are going to think that you're trying to decide which one of them you're going to select to grind their bones to make your bread." Catarina said low enough that only he could hear. It surprised a snort out of him, and he couldn't help but smile at her.

He was very aware that up until he smiled, that everyone was still watching him warily. He used to be described as intimidating, but damn this was a tough crowd. They went and sat in a corner on the mat to stretch. A few brave souls gave Catarina a nod, but no one wanted to talk. Roland felt guilty. She had started a new life, made new friends, and he came in like a tornado messing everything up.

"Alright everyone!" Thomas was standing in the center of the mat, "before we start class, most, if not all of you were at the cookout yesterday and know what happened. You have also noticed we have a new member joining us today." He waved a hand towards Roland. "I think it would be best if Catarina filled in the holes in the story after we heard some wild ass theories being thrown around."

"Sounds good." Catarina grunted as she got to her feet. "Alright, so the cliff notes version for those who need a map to figure out how to wipe their own backsides is," that got a chuckle from the class, "My abusive ex, that's been stalking me for years found me again, he brought an empty gun to try to kidnap me, and thanks to my sessions with you wackos, I handled the situation, and he is now going to prison." Everyone smiled at the jab. Roland could see the comradery they all shared.

"What about King-Kong here?" A twenty something beach boy looking guy nodded at Roland.

"Feeling subsequent, Conner?" Catarina prodded with a smile. Everyone chuckled when he flipped her off in good humor. "This is Roland. I met him when I reconnected with my cousin Katie over a year ago. We hit it off. A coworker of his lied and said that she and him had been dating for a year or so."

"Then she told me," Roland jumped in, not standing but pitching his voice so everyone could hear, "that Cat had met someone else and got engaged and didn't want any contact with me." Catarina reached out a hand and he took it.

"My cousin found out and set the record straight after getting the coworker to confess to everything." Catarina snickered. "Yesterday was the first time we had seen each other after being told that I was being played. We are all good now and he's going to be visiting for a bit." They dropped their hands.

"So, you guys bumped uglies all night then? I'm surprised you two have the energy to be here." The crude comment came from a brown-haired kid with a fat lip. Several people made faces that basically said he was about to get his ass kicked.

"Jeff, ten laps." Thomas barked out. The kid rolled his eyes and got up to run.

"We got everything sorted out, and I'm sorry for making a scene." Catarina continued. "I promise, he's really cool."

"Promise?" An older man in the group said with a smile. "He looks like he eats missiles for breakfast."

"With a side of grenades when I'm really hungry." Roland said with a smile, he watched everyone visibly relax.

"If you're nice, he might give you a demo later." Thomas stood back up. "Alright everyone warmup!"

It had been years since he had done a class, but the movements came back quickly. He did practice with a firefighter. He had Roland beat by a long shot for flexibility, but Roland had more hand-to-hand combat experience. The guy's name was Jamal, and they talked while they did drills. Jamal had a wife and two kids with one on the way. When he talked about his wife, he damned near had stars in his eyes. Roland hoped he could have the same look one day.

He would steal glances at Catarina who would catch his eye every now and again. The guy she did drills with gave her shit the same way siblings do, so Roland didn't worry. He was aware of the fact that the women in the class were getting distracted easily. The whispered conversations weren't as private as they thought. His implant picked up comments that he was sure would start a fight if Catarina heard them. She never gave him the impression she would be one to let comments like that slide. It gave his ego a boost though.

At the end of class, they had three-minute rounds where they switched partners for each round. The kid named Conner came up first with a cocky smile and gave it a good effort. Roland let him come close a few times before switching it up. By the end of it the kid was panting. Next was the guy that made the missiles comment. They were pretty evenly matched with an equal number of submissions and ended with both of them grinning.

Jeff was just what he expected. He tried a few dirty moves and tried to muscle the rest. Thomas was only a few steps away, ready to jump in if either one of them lost their cool. Jeff started to get angry when his tactics weren't getting anywhere. He threw one hell of an elbow that Roland dodged. Thomas grabbed Jeff by the hair and told him to hit the showers. A few people stopped to watch. Roland looked over at Catarina, worried he was about to get booted when Thomas sat beside him.

"I'm sorry," Roland started but Thomas waved with a smile.

"No sweat. He's a hothead and this is his last chance." Thomas explained before lowering his voice so only Roland could possibly hear. "Don't hurt her, she's been through so much."

"I promise." Roland nodded. "And I know, she told me everything."

"At the cabin." It was a statement. Thomas smiled at his shocked face. "The Director called. But I knew him as Houdini back in the day."

After class they met up with the others. They left all the windows down on the way home when Jacob griped and moaned about the smell. Katie found out they had a pool, she thought she might go back to swim a few laps later in the week. Jacob was impressed at the diversity in lifting equipment. There was one part of the gym that was specifically designed for powerlifting. They decided on something easy for tonight and picked up an absurd amount of Chinese food. Roland couldn't stop smiling.

Catarina let the dogs out while the rest of them jumped into the showers. Roland took extra time to scrub down and get all the stink off him. There was a knock on the bathroom door when he was slipping into his shorts. He was surprised to see Catarina standing there.

"Hey." She said with a shrug. "I'm sorry about the comments Jeff made. He's a dick."

"Yeah, I could tell." Roland shrugged. "It happens when people are still trying to figure out who they are in life." She looked like she wanted to say more, so he opened the door with an invitation. She walked in and leaned against the sink. He closed the door and sat on the steps that led up to the tub.

"I know this is a massive change in the last day, but what's your opinion about you and me?" She didn't mince her words.

"Um," Roland was having trouble sorting his thoughts with this being sprung on him, "I knew since that morning I woke up next to you in the cabin that if I ever got a life of my own, I wanted a million mornings like that." He noticed her breath quickening with the rise of her chest. "But only if you wanted me too."

"Only a million?" She asked with a smile, then with a little more hesitation, "And if I changed my mind about taking things slowly? What would you want?" Roland let that hang in the air. Inside he was doing backflips and cheering from the mountaintops.

"That depends," He smirked at the cracking control on her poker face, "Do I have to fight off the dogs for a spot to sleep when we are ready to cross that bridge, or should I go buy a queen for us?" The smile on Catarina's face was breathtaking. Standing there in her dirty gym clothes with no makeup, messy hair, and an ear-to-ear grin filled a hole in his heart he didn't even know was there.

"The fact that you think a queen will be sufficient is comical." She walked across the bathroom and kissed him. "But it's my turn to shower, so I'm kicking you out." Roland stood and grabbed his things. He winked at her before leaving.

# Chapter 5

Catarina scrubbed her body in the boiling water not caring about sore spots or the scar that ached on her side. She was walking on cloud nine. He wanted her, not for a night, not for a week or a month or a year. Sure, they would see what happened in that time, but right now he wanted her, and she wanted him too. She toweled off outside of the shower and made sure to dry the scar.

When Daniel had fired the gun at her, Sam had jumped in front of it, but the bullet tore through his throat and clipped her side. It went through tissue and muscle and out the back without hitting bone or anything important, but the scar would stay with her forever.

She wrapped the towel around her and walked down the hall to her bedroom. Jacob and Katie laughed downstairs like this was their life. Four people sharing a home without a care in the world. She was opening her door when the one down the hall opened. Roland was holding a bundle of clothes, probably on his way to the washer and dryer. The dogs were hanging out downstairs. When their eyes connected, she gave him a shy smile. Walking into her room, she left the door open in a clear invitation. There was a soft thud of clothes hitting the ground. She had barely made it to the bed when the door clicked shut. Her heart was hammering when she turned to face him.

"Do you want this?" Roland's voice was husky. "I know this is something you've not had good experiences with. We can wait."

"I don't want to wait." She sounded strong in her own ears. "If we need to stop, I will let you know."

Roland nodded and gradually walked forward. Deliberately slow, watching her face for any sign of hesitation. He looked over her shoulder at the bed and smiled. Rather than reaching for her towel, he peeled his own shirt over his head. Her heart was hammering. Leaning down, Roland kissed her. It was tentative at first, like he was asking again, and when she didn't pull away, he dove in.

She could feel the nerves and tension beginning to melt. His strong musky scent surrounded her as he pulled her close. Roland's body against hers was warm and welcoming. When they crashed onto the bed, she reached under herself. He froze, misinterpreting it as hesitation. She smiled up at him and tossed a chew toy onto the floor. Their hands were everywhere again as passions flared. The towel disappeared, and she heard his pants hit the floor. She never knew it could be like this. Despite the fervor, he made sure that every movement left her feeling safe and treasured. They had just found a rhythm that made her heart soar when the dogs started barking outside in the hall.

"Ignore them." She demanded, not wanting this to end.

Roland was laughing when it was cut short. The door flew open. Jacob and Katie both screamed. Retreating into the hall, they began shouting their apologies. Roland collapsed on her, and she buried her face in his shoulder.

"We thought something was wrong!" Katie yelled from the hallway.

"The dogs were barking!" Jacob tried to explain.

"Go away!" Catarina yelled back. Roland rolled off her, laughing hysterically. She knew that the moment was over for the both of them. "Why didn't you lock the fucking door?"

She tried to be mad but was laughing too hard. Once again, the entire house had seen her naked. She rolled over and buried her face in the pillow sure she would die of embarrassment long before Tobias ever got her. Ten minutes later, they were both downstairs. Jacob and Katie were in the kitchen digging into the takeout.

"We heard the dogs barking and we thought Roland was throwing laundry in! We thought something was wrong." Jacob explained.

"If you idiots would've looked down the hall, you would see a pile of clothes on the floor!" Roland grabbed a box, checked the contents, and handed it to Catarina.

"Couldn't wait long enough to put your clothes away or lock the door?" Katie looked impressed. Catarina wanted to crawl in a hole.

"Now that you have all seen us naked, Jacob can live his dream of being a nudist." Roland threw a fortune cookie at him.

"No nudity in my house unless its behind closed doors!" Catarina laughed. She got the dogs fed and continued to eat at the island with everyone else. Roland grabbed two glasses of water and gave her one. She liked him like this. He seemed so casual, and in his own element. At the cabin he was always on alert, but here, his smile lit up the room.

"Hey so I was doing some research," Jacob pulled his phone out. "There's an aquarium around here, do you think we could go?" He showed her where it was.

"Yeah," Catarina recognized it in a heartbeat, "I can get us discount tickets. When do you guys want to go?"

"We will get the tickets," Jacob offered smiling at Katie, "Your first date is on us."

"You know, for ruining your first...." Katie let that trail off with a wink and Catarina threw a crumpled napkin at her. They cleaned up, bought the tickets, and let the dogs out to play. Katie went out with her to clean up after them.

"I'm really sorry." She repeated. "We really did think something was wrong. I can't tell you how bad I feel. I mean you two just got each other back and...."

"Katie." Catarina turned to face her, the woman's face was a funny shade of pink. "If I look that bad naked, then I should've maimed Roland long ago!" That got a chuckle out of her. "We're good. I can't tell you how thankful I am for everything you've done to help us have a second chance. No blood no foul." She held her arms out for a hug. Katie took it gratefully. "It's been a while since I've had a friend like you."

"Who knows," She let go and sniffed, "We could be some serious trouble if we put our minds to it."

"Challenge accepted." They laughed and called the dogs in.

Inside the guys made popcorn and had a movie chosen. It was a thriller, but Catarina didn't mind. She leaned up against Roland squealing when he scared her. Having this moment seemed so surreal and she was trying not to wait for the other shoe to drop but she couldn't help it.

When the movie was over, the dogs had gone out, and the dishes were in the dishwasher, they all wandered up to bed. She sent off the last check-in of the evening and sealed the house when Catarina noticed that Roland hung back in the hallway. She gave him on optimistic smile.

"I'm not saying you have to move all your stuff into my room, but if you want to try mine out for a night or so, you're welcome to." She watched his shoulders visibly relax. "But why don't we wait for round 2 until later." She giggled.

"Don't you mean round one and a half?" Roland smiled and followed her into the room.

"How do you figure?" She tried not to be bashful while changing, but she stepped behind a changing screen before slipping into a satin button-down night dress. It looked like a long t shirt with all the comfort of satin pajamas.

"Well because we didn't really get anywhere that first time, I'm only marking it as a half, so when we do try again, it will be a full round." Roland smiled at her when she walked out from the changing screen. His eyes roamed over her in appreciation. "Wow."

"Unless we get carried away and mark it up to a two." Catarina smiled.

All the dogs were scattered around the room, waiting for permission to find a spot on the bed. There were a few dog beds on the floor for the ones that got hot at night or the dogs that came through that didn't like the bed. Catarina climbed in and watched Roland strip his shirt off. Roland climbed in beside her, an almost clumsy replay of memories that seemed like a lifetime ago.

She let out a quiet whisper that called the dogs to bed. Once they were all settled, Catarina turned to face Roland in the dark. A small light from one of the outlets was the only way she could see him. She had it installed so the dogs wouldn't hurt themselves climbing out of bed, but she was secretly grateful to see his face in the darkness. Moving her head, Catarina readjusted, but Roland wrapped an arm around her, pulling her against him. Their legs intertwined and she had to focus on keeping her breathing even.

She found the scars on his chest with her fingers, tracing them. He shuddered and tightened his hold. She almost missed the way he had felt back in the cabin, his hard edges now felt almost foreign to her. A small gasp escaped her when his lips pressed to her forehead.

"If you keep doing that, then I'm going to have to go back to my room." The rumble that came from him melted the nerves that had been jangling around her brain. "I want to do this right this time." Catarina pressed her forehead to his chest and giggled. Relaxing, she savored the moment with him being so close to her. The mahogany musk with hints of cinnamon and mint filled her senses, taking her back to a dark room in the middle of nowhere.

A warm breath fluttered stray hairs on her head when Roland sighed, all the tension dissolving from his body. She rested her face against the broad chest that belonged to the one person that made her feel like she could be anything in the world she wanted to be. They had a long ass way to go, but for now they held each other giving and taking comfort in a way that bonded them a lifetime ago. Roland's soft snore started just seconds before hers.

Catarina woke up to her alarm. The phone was flashing bright beside her before she dug her face back into the pillow. An arm tightened around her middle. She tensed and nearly turned until she remembered the night before. Roland's arm was just as tense before she relaxed.

"It's the boogeyman." Roland mumbled. He pulled his arm back to let his fingers trace small circles around her back. His touch was tender and lit a fire in its wake. Her shirt came halfway up her middle leaving the skin exposed to the air. His exploring fingers found the scar that was still new. "What's this?"

"It's from that night." She was glad the lights were off so he couldn't see her face color. "The doctor said that the corset had weakened from a ricochet, so when Daniel shot Sam…" The circles had stopped, and he traced the entire scar from end to end. "The boning in the dress broke off and opened up my side, so it took a long time to heal."

"Why didn't you tell me?" There was an edge in his voice.

"We were a little busy don't you think?" Catarina giggled and jerked when his touch tickled.. Snickering in the dark, he dragged her across the bed. Roland dammed near crushed her against him and she tucked her face against his neck.

"How bad was it?" He whispered.

"If you let me turn on the lights, I can show you." She kissed his neck lightly. He let her go and lay back on the bed. Catarina climbed over the dogs and flipped the switch. They were too bright, and she wasn't ready. When their eyes adjusted, she climbed back onto the bed and lifted the side of her shirt enough to show him the line that went across her side. It swelled where the metal had cut deep.

"So, the bullet pushed the metal boning through there?" Roland had rolled to his side and took a closer look. Catarina nodded. "How long did it take to heal?"

"About six months. But I was on heavy antibiotics, so it helped keep the infection out." Catarina scratched Buster's head when he rolled into her space and licked her knee.

"How did I not notice it yesterday?" Roland repeated before sitting up then shook his head and laughed. "Never mind don't answer that."

"I'm going to take the dogs out." She leaned to him and gave him a quick kiss. Catarina jumped off the bed and pulled on her robe. After she had all the dogs out the door she called out. "I will let you take care of your business with a cold shower." Cackling when he flushed and readjusted the blankets, she went to take care of her morning duties. After bringing the dogs back in, she found Katie in the kitchen.

"Hey, you guys' sleep ok?" Catarina poured herself a cup of coffee.

"Define sleep." Katie snickered into her own mug. They bustled around the kitchen getting breakfast ready. This morning they had fruit and pancakes. The guys came down the stairs when they were almost finished. Roland made a point of coming up behind her and kissing her neck sweetly. Smacking him playfully, Catarina had to take a breath, so her knees didn't buckle right there.

"So, today," She announced after they were all seated at the table and the dogs had been fed, "I've got a couple coming to interview for adopting Ralf and Frankie."

"The slobber monsters?" Jacob ticked his head to the two dogs who were doing just that while they ate.

"Yup," She smiled. "They will be here around ten. Then Rocco and Gunner will go for their training around that time too and will be dropped off at two."

"So… aquarium at three?" Katie asked hopefully. When Catarina nodded Katie leaned over and kissed Jacob. She knew this was just a temporary living situation, but she had the strangest feeling of Déjà vu.

The couple came a few minutes late, but it was easy to lose your way on the roads here. While Catarina did their interview, the others made themselves scarce. The couple was relocating their cyber security company after a former employee blundered a hostile takeover and ended up exposing an embezzlement campaign that went back over ten years and landed himself in prison. The couple seemed capable and sure of themselves, but she would see when they met the boys.

They went to the yard where the dogs were all playing. She ran through the basic commands with them and the list that the specialists she worked with would start using. They were both hesitant at first but warmed up to the dogs quickly. Frankie took a shine to the wife immediately, but Ralf was indifferent. They had a rough history, but over the next few months they would bond. The couple would come twice a week for two months to take them and work with them and the trainers. They left a while later and Catarina went up to shower, leaving the dogs out to run.

Walking into her room, she noticed there was a bag on the bed with a rose in front of it. Removing the paper, she pulled out the red polka dot wrap dress. Catarina already knew the shoes she would wear with it. She was bent in her closet when a soft knock surprised her.

"Hey," Roland poked his head in and smiled at her, "It fits! Do you like it?"

"It's perfect," Catarina got up before spinning in a small circle. Roland came in and closed the door. He had on a crème button down that looked light and casual.

"You look stunning." Roland walked up and hugged her. "I came to say we were leaving in thirty minutes, but we can go earlier if you're ready."

"I just need to put the dogs away before we go." Catarina wrapped her arms behind his neck, smiling up at him. She loved the security she felt in his arms. "Here's to second chances."

Pulling him down, she kissed him softly, tenderly, and conveying all the gratitude for the second chance that she could. His hand on her back slipped lower and pulled her leg up on his hip when he deepened the kiss. A squeal escaped her lips as he lifted her off the floor. He pressed her against the wall by the door while he locked it, never breaking their kiss that now had her on fire.

Both his arms crushed her to him while she ran her hands through his hair. He was walking and before she knew it, he was above her on the bed again. Pulling at the bow, it had just come undone when he found the edges of her dress. She was trying to undo the buttons on his shirt as he backed away, pulling it over his head and yanking his pants off.

Good God he was magnificent. The thought had just run through her mind when he pounced on her. The dress lay sprawled on the bed beneath them. He didn't seem to mind at all. His hands on her were a blur, trying to memorize everything at the same time.

Catarina trailed her kisses up and down his neck. Their bodies crashed together, pulling a moan from her. They climbed the mountain of passion together in a frenzy before crashing over the edge nearly screaming in extasy.

Breathless and exhausted, Catarina watched Roland for any regret or sign that this was too much, or too quick for him. She had dreamed about this until she thought she had been rejected. Roland laid down beside her and pulled her to him. He kissed her forehead while they tried to catch their breath. She sat up to put herself back together, but he pulled her back down on him with a snicker.

"I have pictured this a million times since the last time I walked away from you, and all of them lasted much longer than this." Roland smiled apologetically. "I will take my time next time, I promise."

"You know, even though I never thought it was going to be like this, I have no complaints!" Catarina lay on his chest and watched his eyes moving behind his closed lids. They shot open a second later in shock and she read his expression before he could say anything. "I've got the birth control bar that goes in my arm. We are covered."

"You were planning on this?" Roland looked surprised.

"No," She got up and pulled her dress back on, "It helps with other things too. Where did you throw my underwear?" She giggled when he pointed, and she saw them hanging off the doorknob to her room. "Come on big guy, we've got a date to get to. You know, since we are doing everything backwards." She left him on the bed while she went to the bathroom.

A few minutes later, the dogs were put away, and they were all loaded into the car. If Roland didn't stop smiling, she was going to have to kick him in the shin. Jacob already did a double take when Roland came down the stairs looking like he had just won the lottery. Katie gave her a raised eyebrow and covered her smile with a hand before turning to look for something.

They got to the aquarium and Catarina was getting out of the car when Roland ran around, pushed her back into the car, and closed the door, all before opening it again. He held up a hand to help her out and she took it, before smacking him on the arm. He was like a teenager, and it was a side of him she hadn't seen before. Jacob and Roland walked to the ticket counter while Katie and her went to check out the map.

"I'm glad the dress fit!" Katie said quietly, "he was freaking out." A tall man with albinism walked up and they moved over so he could look at the map too.

"It was seriously the best surprise." Catarina smoothed her hands along the edge of the dress. "I want to make sure we stop at the river monsters display." A few more people had crowded around the map, but Catarina was aware of the fact that the man was intentionally stepping closer to them without being too obvious. At one point he was nearly on top of them, fidgeting with his hands and stealing glances at them without actually saying anything.

"Ready to go you two?" Roland came up and put an arm around her shoulder steering her away. Jacob held his elbow out for Katie. Part of her was questioning if she was overreacting due to the circumstances but she wasn't sure. "It could just be me," Roland mumbled when they had put some distance behind them, "But he reminds me of Sam."

"That's what I thought but I thought I was just being paranoid." Jacob conceded.

"Everyone told me I was just being paranoid when you guys were after me." Catarina cracked.

"You're not paranoid when they really are out to get you." Katie said quietly.

They made their way through the aquarium, none of them were able to relax enough to enjoy it. They made a show of taking pictures and being cute. When they got about halfway through, they asked a passerby to take a picture for them. Catarina was sure the man was watching her now. When she watched his reflection in the glass, he glared at her, thinking no one saw. The more she observed, the more she was sure he had to be related to the brothers.

He walked like Tobias, head high with a slight swagger in his hips, but a silent walk like Sam used to. When an older woman tripped in front of him, he caught her with the same awkward grab that Sam had when they were learning ballroom dancing and she would trip over his massive feet. At one point Roland leaned down and kissed her, and she caught the reflection of the man gagging.

Roland hadn't let go of her since they confirmed the man watching. Katie pretended to take a phone call for 'work' and excused herself. Roland got a text message soon after she had returned and they all made their way out, missing the one display she had wanted to see. They were on the road and halfway home before Catarina realized there was a white envelope sticking out of the edge of her purse.

"Don't open it." Roland demanded a few seconds too late. She had read her name across the front and couldn't help herself. The note was printed on plain paper with a lock of red hair taped to the corner. The hair was a few shades lighter than Tobias'. Somehow, he had gotten a lock of Sam's hair to send. The letter read:

> *Sam was never supposed to die. I spent my life trying to save him and now his death is on your hands. You will know the pain I feel. We will spend time together before you beg to die. See you soon.*

The letter fell into her lap, and she started shaking. Katie read the letter out loud to the others, but Catarina was stuck on the lock of hair. That lock of Sam's hair brought back the last time she saw him. His throat was blown away. Sam stared up at her, his eyes pleading with her, while he spasmed silently on the floor. She spoke softly to him, trying to provide comfort while he died.

"Cat!" Katie's voice broke through the memories that flooded her. Catarina looked up through the tears. Katie's hand was on her arm. Roland was flying down the road, but she knew there were almost never any officers out this far. "Cat." Katie said again before she looked at her. "You will be fine. We are here to protect you." Catarina nodded at her while they pulled into the garage.

Roland was out of the car and around to her door before she had her seatbelt unbuckled. He reached in and pulled her to him. When the garage door was closed, they all went directly to the panic room and began a scan of the grounds. There were several small alerts, but nothing showed up on the cameras until the last one. It was the bear that had been hanging around. Roland left to call The Director while they locked the panic room. Katie took the dogs outside while Jacob walked her to the kitchen.

"Hey," he put a hand on her shoulder. Catarina looked up at him, the familiar face that pulled her out of a lot of medical shit and now had her back. "We are here to protect you. Nothing is going to happen to you." Jacob pulled a glass from the cupboard and filled it with water before giving it to her. "Roland would have to be dead to let someone take you away again."

"But Tobias wants to kill me." Catarina sniffed, feeling the panic rise.

"Actually, he wants to torture you, then kill you. That honestly makes perfect sense." Jacob said so nonchalantly that she reacted before her brain caught up with the motion, Catarina threw the water at him. Jacob blinked and spat out the little that ended up in his mouth. Catarina closed her mouth and started stuttering.

"Oh my God, I'm so sorry I don't know why I…" she set the glass in the sink.

"You're fine," Jacob cut her off with a wave of his hand and a smirk. "Emotional triggers can affect the fight or flight response." He grabbed a towel from the drawer and started mopping his hair. "We all know your go to is fight. I'm just glad you didn't throw the glass at me too."

"Alright, The Director said..." Roland trailed off when he came around the corner. "What' did I miss?"

"Nothing important." Jacob smirked. "Her fight or flight still works." Roland wrapped her in a hug. Katie opened the door, letting the dogs inside and walked up.

"What's the word?" She asked more as a general question with a separate look at Jacob who shook his head with a smile.

"Director said that they spotted Tobias and his missing relatives an hour ago in southern Pennsylvania." Roland released his hold but left an arm around her shoulders. "They were headed north and crashed the car fleeing police. A younger cousin of his died at the scene and the others escaped, still going north."

"What about the guy tonight and the note?" Katie asked while fiddling with the ends of her short hair.

"Director Johnston thinks it's one of his cousins that the family broke contact with years ago, saying he was cursed because of the Albinism thing."

"Judgmental family." Jacob muttered. "But we knew that."

"He put a few guys on it to go pick him up, but he says to do life as normal until we hear different." Roland checked his watch and sighed. "Your class is at seven, right?"

"Yeah," She tried not to let her agitation show, but it didn't work. She gave them a halfhearted shrug trying to express that she didn't want to go.

"So, we have something to eat, go to class, and come back and hunker down for the night." Roland's plan sounded simple and easy, but her nerves were jangling.

"Define, hunker down." Jacob cracked. Katie smacked him upside the head. "I was kidding!" Jacob laughed and went to the fridge. "Sandwiches, ok?"

"Sounds good." Roland affirmed before taking Catarina by the elbow and steering her to the couch. Sitting down, he pulled her onto his lap. "Hey," his voice was calming, and she leaned against him, "he's states away, and they will get him. There's nothing to worry about. He's been banned from flying, so even if he does come this way, we have time to get back here and prepare. He's not coming anywhere near you."

"I never thought he could get away." She sniffed back her tears. "I thought this was all over. It was supposed to be." She focused on the sensation of Roland's fingers brushing through her hair. "Will it always be like this?"

"If you mean you and me together then I hope so." Roland's attempt at making her smile only worked a little. "If you mean running from him and his family then no, this is just a minor setback. They will catch him." Roland lifted her off his lap and set her on her feet. "Now go get changed for the gym, then we will eat!"

Catarina gave him a hug when he stood. Something about the way he looked at her helped ease some of the worry that was scrambling her brain. She studied his face and realized that even though it felt like a lifetime, they had only spent a few days together, and she needed to make sure this wasn't just some whirlwind love that would be here and gone before she knew it. They still had a lot of getting to know each other before she could be sure about anything, but she was grateful for this second chance.

# Chapter 6

Roland watched Catarina disappear up the stairs, that dress damned near giving him a show. He would be lying if he said he didn't look and hoped. In the kitchen, Jacob and Katie were just starting to make sandwiches. They had originally planned on eating at the aquarium before the pale bastard ruined it.

"Hey guys," he whispered so Catarina wouldn't hear while he stepped around Clyde, who was the only dog begging for scraps, "I didn't want to say this in front of her. The Director confirmed that the cousin who died said Tobias knew that she was here in Springfield before the car crashed."

"Why aren't you telling her that?" Katie angrily whispered. "She deserves to know!"

"I will tonight. They were states away last anyone knew, so I want her to have a few hours to breathe before I tell her tonight." Roland aggressively droves his finger into the marble countertop. Jacob took a step forward, separating them.

"That's not your decision to make." Katie continued.

"She's right, big guy." Jacob's voice was low but clear. "If she finds out you knew and didn't say anything, she's going to be pissed, and it might ruin what you just got back."

"I'm not going to let anything hurt her!" Roland nearly seethed. "She's my responsibility and I'm going to protect her at all costs!"

"You should really listen to them." Catarina's voice echoed into the kitchen. Roland's heart hit his stomach. He didn't even hear her. She damned-near marched into the room with a scowl "Unless this is going to be one of those quick love 'em and leave 'em flings, they're right. I'm not a child that needs to be kept in the dark. I never signed up for a momentary intrigue, just to be left on the sideline after.  Or am I just another ass on a list of targets?"

"No!" Roland yelled. But when she jumped, he cleared his throat and repeated himself, more subdued. "No. Don't be vulgar, you mean more to me than anything. I was going to tell you after class so you could have a few hours of peace."

"That's not your job." Her voice reminded him of his mother, a tone that had you apologizing and realizing you overstepped all at the same time. "I make the decisions about me. Me and me alone." She turned her head and called loudly. "Boys, outside!" The dogs all jumped up and ran to the back door. Katie followed her out.

Jacob set to work getting the sandwiches ready, deliberately not saying anything while Roland fumed. How the hell could she not understand that he was just trying to protect her? The comment about this just being a fling still stung. She didn't even give him a chance to explain before she jumped right to him just being another horn dog. He knew the last year had been hard on her too, but it felt like a stab to the gut. He helped Jacob with the sandwiches, even if the ones he did looked slightly mangled. Jacob cleared his throat and Roland bristled.

"Don't say anything until I'm done." Jacob put both knives in the dishwasher. Probably a good strategic move. "You two only had a restart two days ago. You spent a year pining for her, yes," he held up a hand before Roland could do anything but glare, "you pined. But she also spent a year trying to get over being rejected after a super traumatic experience. You want to protect and safeguard, and right now all she knows is that everyone leaves. You both need to sit down and talk. This is probably going to be one of those growing pains, so you either give each other some grace, or this won't work. She's not Sofia. She's a hard ass that can match you step for step and you need to see her for what she is."

"You're a dick." Roland growled and stacked the sandwiches onto a plate. "You're not wrong, but you're a dick." Jacob snickered, making Roland's anger fizzle out. "So, what do I do?"

"You remember when we first picked her up?" Jacob took a piece of plastic wrap and started covering the sandwiches.

"Before or after she cracked my rib with the fire extinguisher?"

"Exactly." He put the plate in the fridge and tossed Roland an energy drink. "She took out three of us and made it to the car with only a few hours to prepare and not knowing what she was getting into. Then she used me as a human surfboard when she threw us out of the car and survived several hours in the snowstorm in the mountains with next to no supplies."

"You going to find a point any time soon?" Roland was only half joking. He didn't like being told shit like he was thick in the head. They all went through it together. They all suffered and went through all the emotional shit and now they were together again, and he could protect her the way he wasn't able to then.

"The point is, she is still that person. When we showed up, she had just disarmed her insane ex-boyfriend."

"The gun was empty." Roland threw his hands in the air.

"She didn't know that!" Jacob slammed a hand on the counter, surprising the argument out of Roland. "Damnit, dude. You're not hearing me. She's still the same person, whether you're there or not, she is more than capable of taking care of herself. You will only be there if she allows it, so stop treating her like she needs protecting and start treating her like a partner. You will get a lot farther that way." Jacob took a step back and held up both hands placatingly. "Brother, I will go to bat for you one hundred percent, but this isn't you. You're the best guy I know. I'm just trying to help, so if you need to take a swing, go for it."

Roland considered it. He was raging but Jacob had a point. They had been through hell and back together. Jacob never took a stand like this unless he was certain he was right. Jacob was the person to call it like he saw it, so you knew he cared but you also knew you were wrong. Running his hands through his hair and growling to himself, Roland shook his head.

Jacob lifted himself to sit on the counter, his metal leg clinking. Roland dug his fists into the marble, letting the pain sink in. A few deep breaths later he nodded. Walking over to Jacob, he held a fist up. It wasn't a submission, but more acknowledgement. At least that's what he was going to tell himself. Jacob obliged the fist bump.

"If you put her on an equal playing field, she just might protect you as much as you protect her." Jacob hopped off the counter and walked to the window. He gave a head nod. Roland walked out the back to Katie trying to calm Catarina pretty much the same way Jacob had done for him.

"He's protective, and that's ok, but if you two do work things out, then you might have to rely on someone other than yourself for once." Katie was explaining.

"So, what happens when this is over, and he leaves again?" Catarina was fuming. "I've never been anyone's first choice, I know that, but I'm not about to be dropped like a hot sack of shit when you all go back to the real world."

"You've always been my first choice," Roland closed the door loud enough both of them turned to watch him walk down the steps, "even if I wasn't able to say anything." Katie gave him a nod and let them have some privacy. When she passed him, she gave his bicep a well-meaning squeeze. She had been in the firing line of his rage a lot in the last year. That pressure had been a warning to keep his shit together. She closed the door a lot quieter than he had.

"I don't need decisions made for me." Catarina said as she threw the ball for the dogs to chase. There was a lot of force behind the throw, and it surprised him.

"I know, and that's my bad, I should've been strait with you about it." Roland left his hands in his pockets. "I need you to stop treating me like I'm going to leave you high and dry, and give me a fair chance to prove it, especially since The Director explained the consequences if I had reached out."

"That doesn't just erase the last year!" She turned to him.

"Do you think I don't know that?" Roland raged. There was a knock on the window from the house and he flipped the bird over his shoulder. "I didn't suffer the same way you did, but I did suffer too."

"I know." She sighed and it sounded painful. "I know I'm not being fair. I'm sorry. I didn't think that when stuff came up, that it was going to hit me this hard. Right now, none of my decisions are mine and I'm doing what I can to deal with it."

"If you could deal with this on your own and on your own terms, what would you do?" Roland took a few steps towards her, trying to ease some of the tension that had built up between them.

"I would wait for them the same way I waited for you the first time. Tobias was waiting by the car remember?" She smirked at the memory. Roland nodded. "But I've learned a few more tricks since then. Yes, I understand the likelihood of not making it out, but I know this house and these woods. A last resort would be to lock myself in the bunker and wait for the cavalry after wreaking havoc."

"You are a force to be reckoned with." Roland ran a hand over her shoulder and down her arm. She shivered despite the warm night. "No more secrets, I promise." Catarina stepped closer and he pulled her into an embrace.

"I'm sorry I'm so defensive." She mumbled into his chest.

"The first time we met I had you at gunpoint." He couldn't help the smile when he remembered how she stood between him and the old man. "I think you have every right to be defensive."

"You remember when we were locked in the cell together?" She sounded like she was laughing.

"It wasn't a cell."

"It was a cell." She leaned back and looked at him. "You knew how to get out the entire time didn't you?" Her stomach gurgled loudly before he could answer, and she sighed.

"It helped you get used to me, didn't it?" Roland brushed her hair out of her indignant face, "Lets get you some food and we can discuss you pushing me in front of a bus later?"

"Oooo," Her expression warmed to a mischievous smile. "Trying to butter me up then?"

Roland leaned down and gave her a kiss on the cheek. He enjoyed watching her blush. They walked arm in arm back to the house before she called the dogs. They ate their food and checked all the cameras again when the alarm went off. Roland finally caught sight of the bear that he thought Catarina had been making up to make him feel better.

A large cub ran into the view of the camera followed by its mother. Shit. Their den must be nearby which was a good thing for intruders but bad because of the dogs. Catarina explained how all the dogs except Clyde had perfect recall, but he was the newest one at the house. The fence was electric near the top so no animals would climb over, but that didn't mean the bear couldn't get a good swipe or two in through the lower half.

They got the dogs locked up and headed to the gym. Tonight, was Maui-Thai and Roland was excited to get his shorts out again. He used to train in MMA before he signed up for the army. He was halfway through his second service when he was injured. Katie hadn't done any MMA but she loved swimming, so the full body workout would work to her benefit. Jacob could still do it with him mechanical leg, so they didn't need to worry about him.

The class was full and although they had cleared up everything with the class the day before, some people hadn't gotten the update, so they explained again what had happened. Most of the class accepted the explanation readily. There were a few familiar faces from the class yesterday, including that kid Jeff. When they had partnered up, Thomas tried to find someone else for him before Roland told him it would be fine. Thomas didn't look convinced.

Jeff showboated for the first part of class. When they started combinations, he was doing great and suddenly missed a few, hitting Roland in the gut. Roland watched the kids barely hidden smirk and planned his revenge. They added kicks to the next combination and Roland held back severely. Jeff loudly announced that he didn't need to hold back and to kick with some effort. After getting the go ahead from Thomas, Roland gave a monster of a kick, sending Jeff flying through the air and taking out another sparing duo.

After everyone else picked themselves up off the floor from laughing, they switched sparing partners. This time he was with a police officer. A medium build, unassuming guy that looked like a small-town average Joe. He was funny and they talked through the rest of the class. Roland got a hug from Catarina as they were getting ready to leave. Jeff, who had been working himself up after the encounter, walked up for a confrontation.

"That kick was bullshit." He was puffing his chest out. Cute. "You owe me an apology!"

"You know, sport, I think it's time you head home." Roland watched his eyes blaze.

"Jeff," Thomas was storming up, "Get your shit and go! This is your last chance, don't screw it up by being an idiot!" Everyone stopped to watch, Jacob and Katie sat by their stuff while the class finished.

Thomas reached down to get the bag when Jeff made his move. He stepped in, going for one hell of a right hook, but Roland blocked it easily. Grabbing his jacket, Roland hip swept him and drove him into the ground using his fists. The wind left him in a huff. Roland didn't waste any time picking him up under the armpits like a child and walking him to the door. His feet dangled inches above the ground. Thomas was silently running after them.

"Now here's the deal sparky." Roland turned and sat him down on the curb. "You've got an amazing group of people here that most people wish they had as a support system. You have great teachers and everything to build a kick ass life most people would be jealous of. You're doing a spectacular job of pissing that away." Roland squatted down in front of him and watched shame color his angry face. "Thomas said this is your last shot. That little stunt in there would've gotten you locked up with anyone else. Your life would be over. Take this as your last chance kid. Don't fuck it up." Roland stood and walked calmly back into the building. Several people stood around watching Jeff grab his bag and speed off.

"Hey," Thomas marched up to Roland, "I'm sorry about him. You didn't deserve that." Roland held up a hand cutting him off and smiled.

"I was almost that kid. I got turned around just in time, so let's hope he gets his shit strait." Roland lowered his palm to shake Thomas' hand. "You're doing everything you can, the rest is up to him. No hard feelings." Thomas gave him a grateful smile and shook his hand.

Catarina held his hand the entire way home and Roland had to fight to keep the grin off his face. He probably shouldn't have slammed the kid down as hard as he did, but he landed on the mat, so it helped a bit. Jacob and Katie, both gave him a supportive pat on the back. Three years ago, he would've put the kid through the window.

When they got home Catarina went to let the dogs out. Roland went into the kitchen and started getting ingredients out of the fridge to make spaghetti. Part of him was hoping that using his grandma's recipe for rigatoni with prawns and muscles would help smooth over any ruffled feathers. He brought out four glasses and the chilled wine that he requested specifically for this meal.

"Smells amazing!" Catarina said when she came into the room, she was eyeing Rocco and Gunner suspiciously.

"What's up?" He covered the pan and walked over to peek outside. Everything looked normal so he closed the door. Catarina was feeding the dogs.

"Nothing, I think. Rocco and Gunner were just sniffing around the fence, but they don't normally. There's not been any alerts though, which is strange." She pulled her phone out and started messaging while Roland finished putting dinner together. "I'm going to ask their trainer what the alerts are and let him know what they did, in case something is throwing them off."

"Smart." He pushed a glass towards her. Jacob and Katie came down the stairs with wet hair. "If you two nuts still have energy after that class, then I want whatever you're taking!"

"The last time I gave you what I had, you woke up a week later in Cabo!" Jacob laughed. With dinner done, Roland started filling a serving dish.

"You didn't say it was John's version of Adderall!"

"You didn't need to destroy two bottles of Woodford Reserve and the rest of the melatonin to try to sleep, but that's how you woke up in Cabo!" Jacob took the dish to the table. "And I tried to tell you!" Roland followed with dinner.

"'You're going to be productive' isn't a warning!" The girls brought the wine and glasses in. "I mean you weren't wrong, but it wasn't a warning!" Katie and Catarina looked at each other and snickered.

While they were eating, Catarina got a message back from the trainer basically telling her to disregard the dogs unless they gave a clear alert. They all enjoyed dinner and decided to end the night watching a comedy. Roland intentionally grabbed a smaller puzzle from the bookshelf, and they all worked on it while the movie was playing.

When it was over, the dogs were let out, and everyone had gone to bed, Roland pulled her against him under the blankets. The dogs weren't entirely ok with him being a regular thing in the room, but they left him alone when they started kissing. It was supposed to be a quick kiss good night but that went up in flames just about as soon as it started.

Their clothes practically evaporated, the dogs vacated the bed, and Roland had to let them into the hall before they got defensive. He explored all the curves and hollows that made up Catarina. It was still a surreal experience to have her in his arms. He savored every second of committing her to memory. Sometime later, Catarina got up to let the dogs in and dipped into the bathroom. Roland readjusted the mattress fully back onto the bed, fixed the sheets and blankets, and pushed the beds back together against the wall.

Laying down in bed, he waited for Catarina. He was here with her after counting the seconds, every day for too long. The novelty was still shiny and new, but he was aware that if he wanted any chance at a life together, now was the time to prove it. He could live forever, but if she wasn't with him, he didn't want it.

Catarina walked back into the room and hung her robe on the door hook. He had felt the flimsy robe earlier. It was pretty but she deserved better. He would have to message a friend of his. Roland lifted the blanket so Catarina could crawl in beside him. Her body was warm and soft against his. She was asleep almost instantly, but before he dozed off, he imagined them this same way in sixty years, old, wrinkled, and sitting side by side on a porch swing somewhere.

He woke before she did. She had managed to sprawl across the bed the same way she had done back in the hotel room the day everything changed. He kissed her shoulder and pulled the blanket over her. After using the restroom and tying his hair up, Roland took the dogs out. It was still early, and he was a little bleary eyed. It was nice though, the air was cooler.

He cleaned up after each of them and called them back when they went too far. Gunner and Rocco kept running up and down the edge of the fence sniffing and whining. He tried calling them back repeatedly until they laid down, looked back and barked.

"Fuck." Roland growled. That was the signal from their training. There was a body in the woods. Roland pulled his phone out and Called The Director. He picked up on the first ring.

"I'm listening." Director Johnston stated.

"Boss we've got a problem. I was taking the dogs out this morning and the two that are being trained as Cadaver dogs just dropped and barked. They were acting strange yesterday, but this is definitely a signal." Roland walked up to the fence to look around. "There's a bear and her cub in the area that we've caught on camera a few times but not much more. Wait." He caught sight of an unnatural color just through the trees outside the view of the camera. "Boss I've got a body."

"Damnit." The Director sighed. "Let the others know. I'll make some calls. Keep everyone and the dogs inside. Don't let anyone inside unless they know the mission code."

"Any word on Tobias or his family? Or the guy from yesterday?"

"The man from yesterday was confirmed to be a cousin of Sam and Tobias named Isaak, but he took his mother's last name after being turned away from the family. Isaak Howard disappeared after he left the aquarium. The agents I sent have not been able to locate him. Tobias and the others have stolen and ditched several cars going several different directions to evade police. They were last seen in Pennsylvania."

"That's closer than I would like." Roland tried to keep the icy tone out of his voice.

"Agreed." Director Johnston said dryly. "I will call with instructions after I hear from the coroner." The line went dead. Roland got all the dogs inside. Catarina was in the kitchen making eggs and toast. Her smile fell when she saw his face.

"Let me get the others, it's going to get busy here quick so if you want to change fast, do it now." He said while walking. "Keep the house locked down unless we hear the code." She ran to the front door and engaged the house lockdown. Running up the stairs ahead of him Catarina went to change. He took the steps two at a time and pounded on Jacob's door before walking in.

Sheets and blankets went flying, bare limbs flailed, and everyone started screaming. Roland ducked back out of the room when a book clattered against the door. He leaned back in before being cut off.

"Get out!" Katie squealed trying to cover herself. Jacob stood up with no shame.

"You guys need to…" Roland started.

"Get out you psycho!" Katie sounded mortified. Roland's inner two-year-old won out. He stepped into the room, dropped his pants, and stood proud while Katie nearly had a stroke. Pulling his pants back on he held his hand out in what was more or less a shrug.

"There, now we've all seen everything. Happy?" Roland started walking and yelled over his shoulder. "Put some clothes on and meet downstairs!"

"What's going on?" Jacob yelled after him.

"Shit's about to get really busy really quick!" Roland called from the bottom of the stairs.

He nearly sprinted into the kitchen to try to save breakfast from burning. Catarina had already gotten it all done. He turned on the TV's and the security feeds. You couldn't see the body from any angle. Everyone came downstairs in a rush.

"OK," he started, not waiting for anyone to get settled, "I took the dogs out this morning and Gunner and Rocco alerted to a body. You can see it from the fence, but not on any of the cameras. I've already called The Director. The police, the coroner, detectives, and agents are all on their way now. No one gets in without the code. The Director will call with more information after he hears from the coroner." He watched Catarina's face twist in horror.

"Is it the guy from yesterday?" Katie asked.

"No, and he's in the wind right now. Tobias and the others were last spotted in Pennsylvania doing circles and switching cars to evade police." He turned to Catarina when a small gasp escaped her lips. "Evading takes time. That means more time for them to make a mistake."

"But that's only twelve hours from here!" Catarina squeaked. "And that's IF they are driving the speed limit!"

"And if they don't get caught first." Roland completed.

"That's time to secure out position and prepare!" Katie had a hard look on her face. She was one of the big minds that helped the team strategize when shit got tight. He was confident that she would keep a cool head.

"How long will the food storage last for four people?" Jacob asked.

"But the dogs!" Catarina looked like her mind was going in every direction at once. If he didn't calm her down, she might just have a fit.

"You have an emergency plan for the dogs if you can't be here, right?" Roland put a hand on her arm, hoping the touch would help center her.

"Of course!" She looked incredulous. "What kind of a question is that?"

"Cat," Katie said her name with enough force that Catarina whipped her head around to face her, "One of the biggest effects of long-term trauma is that in the middle of an event when everyone else is losing it, you can maintain a clear head, but with something moderately stressful or inconvenient you could lose clarity and freak out a bit." Catarina blinked a few times while that sank in. Roland had forgotten that fact. He and Jacob shared a look and shrugged.

"Oh," Catarina breathed. "Sorry guys. I didn't realize..."

"We're all here for you. We have four minds just in this room working out all the problems, so nothing gets missed." Jacob gave her a smile while wrapping his arm around Katie. "You're safe with us!" Roland secured her in a hug. She was tense and it bothered him.

"I just got you back, Catarina, I don't plan on letting some ginger with a revenge complex take you away." Roland gave her a small kiss on top of her head.

"Oh, goody," Catarina smirked at him. "Because I thought you were going to get all mushy and then I would have to kneecap you."

"I mean I can think of a few other things we could do that I know I would enjoy more." Roland snickered.

"We've all pretty much seen everyone here naked anyways so why not just go for it and start shagging on the couch." Jacob's voice dripped with sarcasm. Katie winked at him like they planned on doing just that.

"God damn Grandpa," Catarina scrunched her eyebrows at Jacob. "Who the hell still says shagging anymore?" Roland barked out a laugh before he could stop himself.

"Back in my day…." Katie faked an old lady's voice. Jacob put a hand over her mouth to silence her.

The laughter was tense and charged. Roland ran a hand over Catarina's shoulders trying to ease some of the anxiety. She looked up at him, searching his face. He didn't know what she was looking for, but he hoped she would find some comfort with him beside her. Roland would move heaven and earth to keep her safe. He wanted her forever, they just had to get through this first.

# Chapter 7

Catarina put the dogs in their kennels while they waited on the calvary. The first set of officers and the county conservation agents showed up quickly and gave the right codes to be buzzed in. The coroner came about thirty minutes later. Catarina walked them around her property on the outside of the fence with Roland glued to her side.

The body was identified as a friend of Isaak's who was doing surveillance on the house, which means they knew exactly where she was. He had been hiding in a ghillie suit that when laid out, blended into the long unkept grass on the neighboring plot of land. The Conservation Agent was pretty sure he was hiding when the bear got close, and they scared each other. The bear lashing out, then the man attacking with a knife. There was enough blood around that the agent went looking for the bear's den.

He came back a while later shaking his head. The bear had been gutted before trying to run and the mother was nowhere to be seen. Catarina waited inside for more information. With nothing else to do she spent her energy training the dogs in the finished basement. When she took them outside, they all behaved, even if Clyde did need an extra reminder or two. A few times she had gone outside with disposable cups and a giant mug of coffee, offered to anyone who wanted it.

It was nearly four before the officers had collected everything they needed and left with the bodies. Catarina had most of her nervous energy out. She was too wired to sleep but no one felt safe leaving the house just yet. Jacob and Roland teamed up for dinner. Katie asked if she had a swimsuit. Catarina let her know that sitting in the hot tub outside was a terrible idea.

"No," Katie encouraged, "I don't know about you, but I could use some relaxing." She grabbed a bottle of whiskey from the cabinet, and they walked upstairs. When they were both in swimsuits and the bathtub was filled with bubbles, they climbed in. It was more than big enough to accommodate the both of them, but they kicked their legs over the side anyways.

"I can't believe he was there, and we never saw him." Catarina mused when she had finally had enough of the whiskey to make her face warm.

"Don't blame yourself!" Katie took a sip of her drink and winced. "None of us did and it's not like we were looking for him, let alone someone who was clearly prepared."

"I know, I just thought after everything, I would've been better prepared to spot anything out of place." Catarina tucked a loose strand of hair back into the knot on her head.

"You're not psychic, Cat." She winced when Catarina raised her eyebrows at her. "Catarina." She amended.

"Oh, ppfftt." Catarina waved a hand to dismiss the nickname before taking a drink. "No one is psychic, but not a lot of people have been through a bank robbery and then abducted either. I just thought that would give me a little more insight." She sighed and Katie laid her head on Catarina's shoulder like they had been friends for years.

"You are insane though." Katie giggled when Catarina gave her a playful nudge with her elbow. "I mean it! Name one person who could get through this completely unscathed, and here you are making it look like a walk in the park!"

"I'm still going to therapy for this bullshit!" Catarina laughed then choked on her drink. "Fuck, I forgot I have therapy tonight!" She looked at the clock on the bathroom wall. "I've still got two hours. Nothing like a little liquid courage to confront your demons!"

"I'll drink to that!" Katie clinked her glass with Catarina's. A knock came at the door before Roland and Jacob walked in.

"I think I had a dream like this once." Jacob laughed when Katie flipped him the bird. "Dinner is ready if you guys are." Catarina held a hand up to Roland.

"Help me up?" She wiggled her eyebrows at him. Roland was reaching for a towel when she stopped him. "Not those, grab the bright ones in the closet." Roland brought it over and pulled her up until she was sitting on the edge of the tub. She wrapped the towel around herself and handed him the glass with her whiskey. Roland held her hand while she stepped down from the tub platform.

Changing quickly, she met the others at the table. After eating, she let them know that she had her therapy appointment. She watched the way Jacob sat as close to Katie as possible, while still remaining in his own seat. If she laughed about something, he would watch her smile with one of his own. His love for her was all mushy and when he caught Cataria smiling at them, he went a little pink in the face.

When seven o clock rolled around, she was perched at the desk in her office with the doors closed. They weren't soundproof but it made the session feel more private. When the video chat started, a man with midnight skin and gorgeous bone structure in a polo filled the screen. His smile was bright and familiar.

"Hey Tyrese." Catarina greeted him.

"If it isn't she hulk herself!" Tyrese laughed a big toothy laugh that warmed the room extensively. "Your video is all over the place!"

"What video?" She asked.

"Roland said it was when Trent showed up, and you disarmed him. Apparently, someone caught it on video, and you are trending!" Catarina pulled out her phone. "Type in 'Girl disarms man with gun.'" She watched the video that popped up with a news article. "I can't say it's good if you're trying not to be detected but your technique is flawless!"

"Damnit to fuck." Catarina swore when the news article tied her to her dog training business. The whole world had known where she was, and she had no clue.

"Hey, it's fine. You're in a reinforced safehouse with some of the safest people in the US!" Tyrese's soothing tone dismissed the danger. "Speaking of those people, how did the reunion go? You know, after the bit some people caught on camera."

"Oh sure," She rubbed her face with both hands, "because they couldn't have left that part off." She smiled when Tyrese snickered at her. "Do you mean before The Director told me everything, or after?"

"Whatever you feel like sharing." Tyrese gave her the smug grin that told her therapy had begun.

She went through the last few days and tried to skim over the nights they had spent together, but she should've known Tyrese was going to ask about it.

"You two have been intimate already?" His tone was careful. She nodded and blushed. "How are you feeling about that as a whole?"

"I mean it feels real. I don't feel like I'm going to wake up one day and this will just be a dream." She sighed. "I feel like it's faster than I'm used to, but I feel like there aren't any pretenses. There's a lot of getting to know each other and who we are as people but if we are working backwards, I guess it feels right for us."

"Are you ok to have him join us?" Tyrese sounded casual, but she saw in the set of his shoulders he was tense.

"Sure." Catarina nodded slowly. Pressing a button, she spoke on the intercom. "Roland, could you come to the study?" Releasing the button, she said to Tyrese. "If you don't take a breath, you're going to stretch out your polo." He chuckled, getting called out despite his casual demeanor.

Roland poked his head into the office, and she gave him a small smile. She waved him over until he was in frame of the camera.

"Thanks for joining us Caveman." Tyrese jabbed.

"Nice to see you too, Skellington." Roland kneeled so he could see the screen better. "This guy came to basic looking like a real-life Jack Skellington."

"You weren't much better!" Tyrese prodded before becoming professional again. "Now that the two of you are here, I need you to listen with an open mind. I have worked with both of you for almost a year. Yes, you both had very different experiences and have worked on a lot of different aspects, but I need to be clear." He leaned forward and his voice was strong, driving the point home. "Just because you went through what you went through together, does not mean you have to have a romantic relationship. IF that's something you both want then I see no reason, with open communication and a lot of understanding, that it wouldn't work. But I need to stress that if you don't want to, or if you feel like down the road that it's not what you both are wanting, then you don't have to do it just because of the experience you two shared."

"Why are you bringing it up now?" Catarina asked. She could feel Roland shift uncomfortably.

"Because so many people go through traumatic experiences and feel guilty if someone related to that specific event wants a romantic relationship. They feel like they have no choice, because if they don't there's feelings of abandonment. That's not the case. I've gotten to know both of you, and I want you to know that you both have a choice. This way if you do decide to continue the romantic relationship, then you won't have to question if the other person is staying only out of obligation."

A weight felt like it lifted off her shoulders. She never hinted or said anything, but this mind-reader said the words that she didn't know she needed to hear. Next to her Roland let out a breath that sounded painful. Oh God. He felt obligated to be with me. The weight on her chest came right back, and she felt like she couldn't breathe.

"Hoeft," Tyrese spoke after what felt like an eternity of silence. "Do you have anything you want to say?" If that wasn't the most loaded question she had ever heard. Roland sat back on his heels and cleared his throat several times before he found his voice, and by that time she was struggling to keep the tears from falling.

"If you have ever felt like there wasn't a choice, or like you had to pick me, then I'm so sorry." He took a steady breath and continued. "I knew you were everything I was looking for when you threw yourself and Jacob off the side of that damned mountain, and I thought I lost you." Roland brushed his knuckles down the back of her arm. "If this is too much or you don't feel the same, I'll be ok. If you are safe and happy, then that's all I can ask for."

"Did you wake up and smash your head against a brick wall for shits and giggles?" She choked out a laugh. Tyrese and Roland both stared at her, not sure how to react. She bumped him lightly with her elbow, but he lost balance and landed on his ass. "If I wanted to say no, then I wouldn't have let you help with the dogs that first night." Roland's eyes flooded with tears when he burst into a smile. It was a nice smile that warmed her heart. He climbed back onto his knees. "Can you, of all people, look me in the face, and tell me that that I would stay out of obligation if I wanted out?"

"Since you two have a lot to discuss, I'm signing off. It's good to see you both together again." Tyrese's screen went black.

"No one could tell you not to do something you wanted to." He brushed a lock of hair out of the way. "But guilt can be a bitch."

"That goes both ways!" She pointed out, "For all I knew you were here feeling guilty after getting me pulled into a multi-government shitstorm. I thought you were here trying to 'repair' any damage that it caused." He was shaking his head before she finished.

She could feel the tears of relief running down her face, and they matched his. She hadn't seen him cry before and it moved something in her. She wrapped his arms around him before he pulled her off the chair and onto his lap. He kissed her softly. It wasn't like any they had before, it was full of promise and longing. The kiss deepened and he laid her onto the floor behind the desk. And that's the exact moment the doors to her office opened.

"Guys?" Jacob's voice echoed in the small room. They were invisible behind the massive antique desk. They both responded at the same time.

"Yup?" Roland called.

"We're here." She raised her hand and gave a slight wave at him over the desk.

"Seriously?" He sounded somewhere between amused and horrified. "Director is on video call."

The doors closed and they broke into a fit of giggles like two teens. Roland pushed himself up and sat back on his heels, before lifting her to her feet in one quick motion. They made their way out of the office after straightening disheveled clothes and fixing hair. The Director stared at them as they walked into the room.

"I would express my apologies in interrupting your... meeting, but I pride myself in being an honest man." His tone was dry. "Now that I have your attention, Tobias and his family were spotted in Louisville, Kentucky. Now I understand that this is not the news you wanted but we have many assets in the area, and we are closing in on him. If we don't have him in custody by seven tomorrow morning, we will have an asset at the house to collect the dogs for safekeeping. You four will be going to a privet airfield and off to a secondary location. I will send the coordinates if it comes to that. Agent Evans, is your pilots license current?"

"Yes, Director." Jacob's answer was short and to the point.

"Then I will send you the coordinates when the time comes. Try to keep this one in the air for longer than an hour Jacob." The Director smirked and the screen went dark.

"Would we be safer carrying C4?" Catarina snickered.

"It was one time!" Jacob threw his hands in the air.

"It was twice." Katie teased him.

"And there was almost a third!" Roland laughed.

"Anyone know where to get C4?" Catarina rounded it out and they all started laughing. Catarina and Katie took all the dogs out. She didn't feel at ease outside anymore and that bothered her. Every rustle in the trees had her heart racing. The dogs had been acting odd for a few days, but they never alerted anyone in the woods.

"We'll be ok." Katie came up after washing her hands. Throwing an arm around her shoulder, Katie looked at all the dogs. Gunner ran up to her and begged to be picked up, to which she obliged.

"Where's home for you?" Catarina asked. She threw a ball for the others to chase.

"I grew up in Texas, but I had a thing for forensics, so I followed that all the way up to the FBI."

"So, I have to ask," Catarina threw a slobber covered ball again. "Correct me if I'm wrong, but there seems to be an awful lot of red tape missing from what little I know about the government."

"You're right." She smiled when Catarina mis-threw the ball, and it bounced off a fence in surprise. "So, when the whole Daniel thing came around and everyone was fighting to get a shoe in the ring, Director Johnston had a closed-door meeting with the President, and they set up a team with the freedom to take care of problems like that, where red tape would do more harm than good. We answer to the President and The Director. If there's a reason, they need to shut it down, only a few people will be displaced instead of hundreds."

"Where did the money come from?" Catarina waved to the house behind her. "Because this is more than I could ever hope to have on my own."

"While they were hunting down Daniel, they did a few massive drug busts and a few other things, then The President used those to provide funds. But as it turns out, Daniel had a lot of money stashed away state side that were seized."

"That's a lot of power to have." Catarina muttered to herself.

"That's why they do in depth psych screenings every year. Unless someone is acting fishy, then…" She let the words hang in the air. Catarina nodded her affirmation. "Any-who, how are things with Roland?

"They're fine." She shrugged and winced when she caught Katie giving her a bewildered look. "It's all hot and intense right now, and we're still getting to know each other. Like really know each other. I'm just mentally taking it slowly because I want this to last. All our contact has been in the thick of it, so I'm just hoping he is taking it as seriously as I am for the long run and not just for the moment."

"He used to take things WAY too slowly." Katie said and it was her turn to explain to Catarina. "There was this girl in Spain when he was first starting his undercover stuff. Her name was Sofia. He literally dragged his feet, and she died on one of the missions. She was an informant." Katie gave her a side hug for comfort. "He said he loved her, but he never looked at her the way he looks at you."

"What the hell is that supposed to mean?" Catarina laughed and gave her a hug back.

"He always was protecting her and treating her like she was fragile. But with you, yes, he does some things the same, but it's so different. When you're not looking, he smiles at you like he's actually found peace. When he was counting down the days, I would ask about you. He would go on and on about how you weren't afraid to talk back, or run, or how sassy you were. He said he had never met someone who was so singularly their own person, that had a strength and will power to put anyone else on their ass."

"If you get any mushier, I'm going to have to throw you into the woods." Catarina smirked. Katie laughed and they called the dogs back inside. Part of her was still on the fence about believing everyone, but she figured if it was all just a ploy, she could enjoy the ride while it lasted. She was pretty sure it wasn't, but time would tell.

Jacob was getting things ready to make popcorn in the kitchen, and Catarina gave him a wave while she went upstairs. She grabbed clothes and walked into the bathroom without knocking. Roland peaked his head out from the shower. She held a hand up before he could say anything.

"If you're ok with it, I would like to join you, but with no expectations. If something happens later then that's fine. If it's not ok with you, I can go use the other bathroom. No hard feelings." The pain she had been trying to mask pounded in time with her heart. Nothing was physically wrong she didn't think, but all the baggage she was trying to sort through was getting hard to bear.

"Your love language still physical touch?" Roland asked.

"You remembered that?" She snickered, surprised by the tears the suddenly burned her eyes. He held out a hand to her. Leaving her clothes in a pile on the floor, she stepped into the warm shower with him. She moved him out of the way of the second shower head, and turned a handle on the wall. The cold water made goosebumps rise before it warmed.

"I'll have to remember that." Roland smiled.

The shower was comically big, and even with the two of them in there, they still had room to move. Leaning her head back into the water, she made to wash her hair, but Roland stopped her. Handing her a soapy luffa, he massaged shampoo into her scalp. Catarina cleaned the days stress off her body.

They didn't say anything because nothing needed to be said. She was surprised, watching him wash his own body at how extensive the scars were. They somehow made him seem more human, more real. The feeling that resonated in the room was a brief moment of peace in the jumble that was the last few days. They drank in each other's curves and lines in a long hot kiss, before toweling off. Roland pulled her to the counter and ran several serums through her hair before applying them to his.

"What are those?" Catarina asked.

"They are actually a gift from John." Roland smiled. "Johnathan."

"Wait what?" She sputtered. "John is Jonathan? I thought he was just one of the government's resources."

"And Katie's second cousin." Roland laughed. "You remember Jenny? That FSB Agent with the super curly caramel hair and blue eyes?"

"She was the one in the pink dress?" She remembered the lean spunky woman damned near burned Daniel at the stake when she was brought to the stand. "She was cool."

"Glad you like her. That's John's wife." Roland smiled. Catarina sat dumbfounded. "John IS actually a designer. He is also a tech guru that makes a ton of top-of-the-line gadgets for us and a chemical whiz. He works exclusively for The Director on undercover missions. Their paths crossed, they fought over which knife is better for a concealed weapon and throwing, then they were married a year later."

"That's a left turn." Catarina laughed. "Wait didn't he drag her upstairs at the hotel and beat her when she dropped that tray? She was red after!"

"There are so many ways for someone to be flushed with red marks...." Roland flicked an eyebrow at her in the mirror with a devilish smile. Catarina had to look away when the room was suddenly too hot. She heard him trying to hide a chuckle. "Thanks for the example." Her eyes shot to the mirror in horror. A scarlet flush darkened her suntanned skin. Wonderful.

"Ok, Romeo, let's get down to watch the movie before they wonder if we've turned in for the night."

Later when they were curled in bed together, his head on her belly, and his body between her legs, they shared stories about growing up, life experiences, and exploring each other on a deeper level. He traced various scars on her body, and she ran her hands through his hair. His head bounced comically when she laughed. Somehow, she never remembered falling asleep.

The alarm that morning went off too early and she wasn't ready for the day. Roland was wrapped around her, and she tried shaking him awake. He groaned holding her tighter. The dogs started shuffling and getting off the bed with the familiar drill. Gunner came up licking her hands.

"Come on big guy," Catarina gave another weak attempt at leaving the bed, "I've got to fart, and I'm not above giving you a Dutch-Oven today."

"Did I tell you how sexy you sound when you talk like that?" Roland grumbled before rolling over.

"I'm happy to hear you think I'm sexy." She opened the door and let the dogs sprint downstairs. "Would you grab my suitcase out of the hall closet?"

"What for?" Roland sat up and scrambled out of bed.

"Did you hear if they got Tobias?" Catarina called over her shoulder while running downstairs to let the dogs out. Buster stayed close to her, sensing her rising panic. She was aware that he would most likely not be able to come with her, so she made a mental note to grab a personal bottle of whiskey just in case. She watched the dogs closely when they went outside. If anyone was near, none of the dogs alerted.

Back inside, Katie was getting coffee put on. Her bags were by the front door, and even though she looked put together she looked exhausted. Catarina waved while getting all the dogs fed. Returning to the kitchen, Katie greeted her with a steaming cup of coffee.

"You hear anything?" Catarina asked, her hope was hanging on by a thread.

"Not yet, and that makes me nervous." Katie took a drink.

"I mean abduction isn't that bad…" Catarina snarked.

"You know out of context, your story, abducted by five men and held in a cabin in the mountains, sounds like the start to a bad smut novel." Katie laughed when Catarina spit her coffee all over the counter.

"Or a great one." Catarina choked out. Both their nerves were all on edge and that one joke made them crack. They collapsed on the floor, laughing until tears ran down their faces. One look, and they started back up again. They both turned when another set of feet came thundering down the stairs.

"What happened?" A shirtless Jacob was looking at the coffee on the counter. The girls started cackling again.

"Nothing." Catarina was trying to get her feet under her. She grabbed paper towels and started mopping up the mess on the counter. The laughing should have helped calm her but now she was just on edge.

One text, and an hour later, their car was packed up. They were loading the dogs into a van that would take them all to a backup trainer's house. Tears were running down her face as she said goodbye to Buster. If anything happened to him while they were trying to evade the Morgan family, she would never forgive herself. When this was all over, she would have him back, but she didn't know when that would be.

Roland held her in his arms while the van pulled away. The trainer had promised emails full of pictures. The dogs had the same setup when the groomer picked them up, so they were all relaxed. Walking back to the house, they got the last of their things.

Katie was replacing her insulin pump and putting all her supplies in a bag that matched her designer purse. She had an extra in her bathroom bag, but this one would always be with her. They went through the house and turned everything off. Catarina had grabbed what she deemed were sensible clothes for a safehouse. With the warm weather, she had decided on jeans and a tank top.

Roland helped load the bags into the car on top of the ammunition and firearms. The airfield was a little over half an hour away.

Roland sat beside her in the back of the SUV, and they headed off to the airport. Katie kept her eyes open from the passenger seat. Catarina never let go of Roland's hand. They were heading out of town, slowing to make a right-hand turn, when another SUV crossed the median and hit them head on.

Her seatbelt held her in place while glass went flying around them. Airbags expanded and the crash rang in her ears. Someone was screaming and she wasn't entirely sure it wasn't her. Before she could take a breath, the car lurched sideways. Roland screamed next to her. People were moving outside the car. Sucking in a breath she tried to focus, her vision that was going in and out of clarity.

"Here!" Someone yelled.

"They're on that side!" A second voice yelled.

"Fuck!" She groaned.

"Damn the Gods!" The first voice raged. "They both have brown hair!"

"Take them both!" The second voice sounded much older. Hands grabbed at her. She looked over at Roland whose face had gone pale. He was gripping her arm like a vice. His other one was reaching for the gun on his ankle. Something orange appeared out of nowhere on his thigh.

"NOOO!" Roland's voice raged. He pulled and pulled, trying to reach his gun after a few seconds, he lost movement in his hands and unconsciousness slowly took him. Looking forward at Jacob, she realized he was already out as well. Katie's body was being lifted from the passenger seat, an orange dart sticking out from her shoulder, but her supply bag was still buckled around her body. Turning to the hands on her, she saw a young red-haired man, much younger than her, removing her seatbelt.

She hit him with her elbow and his nose burst into a bloody mess. Lunging at him, she tackled him to the ground. He hit his head and nearly went slack. Jumping to her feet, Catarina sprinted after the man who was setting Katie in the back of a windowless van. The second he sat her down, Catarina leapt at him, smashing his head into the side of the door. The impact stunned him, and she unleashed a hail of strikes. The man's arms went up to defend his face.

A sharp pain jabbed her thigh when she reached for Katie's limp body. She stole a glance and then did a double take. The orange dart surprised her so much all she got out was a harsh laugh before her vision went black and she felt herself falling.

# Chapter 8

The blackness around him felt thick and made his thoughts slow. At first, he thought he was in bed next to Catarina, but when he reached out for her, something stopped him. The crash came rushing back. The first hit came when they were preparing to turn. The crash was enough to stop them and kill the engine, but he felt fine. The second impact dug shards of the door into his leg.

Catarina's eyes were unfocused and confused. He remembered grabbing onto her arm. She looked at him before they darted him. He tried to hold onto her, but the blackness came too soon. Pulling harder to free his hand, he heard a gasp and his eyes shot open. The brightness of the room nearly blinded him. There were at least two people near. Ripping at the restraints, his rage tore from his chest in a sound that was animalistic.

"WHERE IS SHE?" his voice echoed off the walls between yells. "Get this shit off me and fight me like a man you bastard!" Another howl echoed off the walls and his vision started to focus. More figures burst into the room and his eyesight cleared. "WHAT DID YOU DO WITH HER? I'll tear you all to pieces if you've touched her!"

"AGENT HOEFT!" A shorter bald man with a voice like an explosion pushed past the people in the doorway. Director Johnston held both hands up placatingly. "Do you know where you are?" That shocked him into reality. Roland looked around at the monitors and tubes, then back to the nurses and doctors cowering in the doorway. Security loomed near the back of the crowd.

"How long?" he asked.

"Hours. I have teams on their trail now, and when you're given the green light, you can join the hunt. That is not negotiable. I will lock you in a cell if I need to." Director Johnston's green eyes blazed. There wouldn't be any arguing. "If you can calm yourself, we can get you out of those restraints. You were trying to fight everyone while coming out of it." Roland relaxed as much as he could, turning to the others, he nodded.

"I'm sorry, I can be an asshole sometimes." He wasn't sure what exactly he did so that was the best he could offer. One of the doctors walked up. He reminded Roland of Wesley Snipes but much older. Director Johnston ducked out of the room.

"You had low levels of ketamine in your system." He shined a small light into his eyes. "What do you remember?" The doctor nodded to the nurses and waved a hand at security.

"The crash, and the second car pinning me in. I was trying to hold onto Catarina when they darted me. The old man smiled while taking Katie away. I think they drugged her too. The younger one was cutting Catarina's seatbelt off when I blacked out. I was holding onto her, and I couldn't do shit!" Everyone froze at his rage. He held up the hand that had been released. "Sorry, I'm in control."

"It just happened, so anger is reasonable." The doctor said. "You have two options, we can clean out the shards and disinfect your leg and send you on your way to 'join the hunt', or we can take out the shards, disinfect, and wrap it with a soft cast and an ointment so it will stay clean. The first means you have to watch for infection or you could lose your leg, the second will take a little longer. But you can focus on your job."

"The second." Roland agreed, "If they knew where they were, we would have them by now."

The doctor nodded and rattled off instructions to the nurses. They swarmed him, removing metal and glass shards, and stitching up his arm where a piece of glass had cut him deep. A man hobbled into the room on crutches with one leg gone.

"You ready for the hunt brother?" Jacob made his way into the room.

"Where's your sidekick?" Roland noticed Jacob's high-tech prosthetic was missing.

"Crash snapped the foot off, but Boss-man has one on the way here while you're getting finished up and a prototype from John coming." Boss-man strode back into the room, and Jacob colored.

"Surveillance cameras in the area caught the getaway van picking up Isaak Howard north of Springfield." The Director spoke before either of them could move. "It looks like they are going north for now, we have cars following them already. You will be flown into the last seen location when you are cleared, and your equipment that was salvageable will be going with you. It appears that Katie's insulin bag went with her, so there's one in the win column."

"Was the second vehicle an accident or intentional?" Jacob asked.

"It appears to be intentional. All vehicles involved were reported stolen this morning. Roland took the brunt of the hit, and if it hadn't been one of our vehicles, you wouldn't have been so lucky." The Director smirked at him.

"Feeling lucky Boss," Roland winced when a particularly long shard of metal was pulled out just below his knee cap.

"I have seen all the footage from the safe house Gentleman." The Director said. Roland and Jacob looked at each other letting that sink in. "Both Ms. Madison and Ms. Stone are assets and in the 'family', so to speak. Hear me when I say this attack is personal and we have been given the green light by the president. When you've been cleared, happy hunting boys." With that he strode out of the room.

Three hours later, they were armed to the teeth and headed to a private airfield to the last known location. They had both been given enough medical equipment and pain killers to get them through their mission.

"How are you dealing with this man?" Roland asked Jacob who had a sheen of sweat on his face.

"Shitty." Jacob snapped. "I saw that car cross the median! I watched it hit us! It was a kid driving and I thought he was going to correct! I could've avoided this entire thing and now Katie and Catarina are gone!" He hit the steering wheel.

"I would've thought the same thing." Roland tried to ease Jacob's conscious. "They will be focused on Catarina. The first time I met Katie, I thought she was an accounting intern fresh out of college."

"What the hell is that supposed to mean?" Jacob spat.

"She looks like the person you don't have to worry about, someone who can't defend herself." Roland clarified. 'That was also the mistake we made with Catarina the first time around."

"Let's hope Tobias hasn't wised up any." Jacob said. "Why aren't you losing it about Catarina?"

"Because I've seen what she's capable of," Roland practically growled. "And if I lose it now, I might not be able to protect her when the time comes. The note said he wanted time with her, and as much as that makes my skin crawl, that mean's he won't kill her on sight."

"Where would he take them?" Jacob was thinking more like an agent, that was good.

"Elliot is digging through their stuff and will find something." Roland passed along the message that Director Johnston left when Jacob was getting his replacement leg on.

Elliot was the computer genius that put a large number of hackers to shame. He was more book smart than street smart, but he had a snarky attitude that only appealed to a small few. Roland frequently offered to feed the man to alligators and Elliot told him to go die in a ditch. At home he was a nudist of epic proportion and managed to convince the city to let him build a fence, higher than the city code allowed just so he could remain nude outside, without having to pay for the neighbor's therapy.

"Have we looked into family properties or past family land that's not being used?" Jacob skidded to a stop beside the hanger. A small-town farmer looking man with hunched shoulders and a shotgun, leaned around the side of the barn. They cracked one window of the truck. This vehicle was the equivalent of an armored tank, but he wasn't.

"Delta!" Roland yelled through the crack.

"Tango." The old man's voice was surprisingly clear and strong.

"What's the name of the man who called me?" The old man didn't let up.

"Director Johnston, or he had Elliot call." Roland watched for a tell, but this guy was good. "He would've told you Agent Evans is a gimp," Roland threw a thumb at Jacob then at himself, "and Agent Hoeft is covered in obvious scars and is a hard-headed asshole." The old man pulled the gun up over his shoulder and stepped out.

"The barn is this way." He pointed down a small bare trail and started walking. They looked at the empty hanger, then at each other and shrugged. Jacob pulled the car up beside him.

"You want to jump in?" Roland had rolled the window down. The old man jumped onto the hoop-step of the truck and held on like he was half his age.

"Follow this path to that patch of trees." He pointed with his shotgun. "This about that guy that escaped on his way to prison? The ginger?" He watched Roland's face. When no one answered, the man set his mouth in hard line and nodded. "Park on the side and leave the keys so I can hide the truck." He jumped off before they even stopped and walked through a door on the barn after he unlocked it. The loud door shook when he opened it.

A small plane shined where the sun hit it. The old man helped them pile all their equipment in and used a small tractor to pull it out to a suspiciously level and clear patch of greenery. Jacob tried to leave the guy some cash for his help, but he refused to take it.

Once they were in the air, they got a message from The Director. They got a lead about plots of family land across several states that had been passed down throughout generations. The center point for all of them was in Sioux Falls, South Dakota.

Even if they had broken every speed limit and avoided the officers, Tobias's family still would not have made it that far. They were ordered to set up a home base in a small local hotel near the airport. Roland growled in furry that the news wasn't better. Jacob flew them into the airport, and they were met by a few of the agents they had worked with on this case.

Once they landed, runners took the luggage and equipment to their rooms, while everyone else set up in the conference room. Dry erase boards were set up with profiles for Tobias, His Uncle Abraham, Abraham's son Isaak, and another cousin named Simon. Across the aisle they set up boards for Catarina and Katie.

Roland stopped and stared at the photographs. She stood there in nothing but a small black bikini, her bruises and injuries on display. The pictures at the cabin from the evidence left her body in full view for just anyone to walk by and see. Her face was puffy and terrified. He saw red and launched himself onto the board.

"Hey!" a set of hands grabbed him before he could tear those images down. He turned his rage to whomever grabbed him, but it was doused immediately. Tyrese let go of him. "Let's go over here a sec."

"Did you put those pictures up?" Roland erupted. "You had no right!" Tyrese held his hands up trying to calm the situation.

"Do they make you mad?" His lanky form looked deceivingly nonconfrontational but by the set of his feet, if Roland attacked, he would end up on his ass.

"How stupid are you to ask a question like that!"

"It makes everyone else mad too!" Tyrese marched over to the board. He didn't need to yell because everyone was pausing to watch the chaos unfold. "Everyone here is trying to get these two back!"

"Those pictures don't need to be there!" He was barely holding it together. "What happened is in the notes! No one needs to see those!"

"Agent McNeil." Tyrese called out, but never broke eye contact with Roland.

"Sir?" A short podgy man answered.

"Did you read the mission notes about everything Catarina went through?"

"Yes, Sir. Everything." The young kid flushed.

"Was there a difference when you read the notes and saw the pictures?" Tyrese folded his arms.

"The pictures showed the person we are working to get back. She's not just a name on a page. Catarina Stone is family. Sir." Agent McNeil was fidgeting. Roland could practically see the man's blood pressure rise under his glare.

"The pictures are there because she survived." Tyrese pointed to the board. "You all survived. Everyone here knows your story. That is what she survived, and the pictures show that she's a fighter. It's a huge part of her profile. They are up there because they need to be. Now grab the maps and start hanging shit up! They don't have time for us to sit around with thumbs up our asses!"

Roland made a mental note to punch him later. Jacob, who was normally the more collected of the two, stood like a statue in front of Katie's board. He wasn't studying it or looking over the information. He was frozen on her picture.

"Jacob." Roland called while he picked up a stack of documents. "Evans!" Jacob blinked slowly. Roland set the stack down. Walking over he grabbed his friend's shoulder. That snapped him out of it. "Hey, we'll get her back. "

"It's my fault she was taken." Jacob was visibly fighting to keep it together. "None of this would have happened if I'd paid more attention." Roland gave his shoulder a sympathetic squeeze.

"No one can convince you that it's not your fault unless you believe it." Roland picked up a stack of paper and handed it to him. "She was with us because she can handle her own shit. Between the two of them, Sam's family doesn't know what they signed up for." Jacob nodded and followed him to another whiteboard.

They started with the grandparents and worked their way down from there. Ira and Leah had both died nearly ten years ago. Their families along with two others had started their own community away from anyone else a few generations before. There was already a history of mental illness in the family including alcoholism, schizophrenia, depression, and multiple personality disorder.

The community had picked apart different religious manuscripts and chose certain parts that supported their life choices. A popular belief in the family, was that they received guidance from various gods that swayed their decisions. Sam and Tobias believed the same, which ultimately led them to protect Catarina before Sam died.

After several generations of limited genetic variety, several mutations began to repeat in the family. Several members were infertile, and others had hemophilia. Only two of them had died from it but the family was consistent in discarding children that were short or weak. Tobias and Sam were kicked out at eighteen for being short, but they shot up a year later, towering at six foot seven.

Ira and Leah had four children: Jonas, Abraham, Elaina, and Malaki. Jonas and his wife Miriam had two boys: Tobias and Sam. Abraham and his wife Martha had one boy named Isaak. Martha died in childbirth and Isaak was the first case of albinism in the family. Elaina and her husband Silas had one set of twins, but both Elaina and one of the twins died of hemophilia. Silas and his son Simon were still living in what was left of the family land. Finally, Malaki and his wife Gia had three children that ran another part of land in another state. Their kids Obadiah, Aliya, and Cecelia were all healthy.

Several cousins and family members lived on plots of land that were in the family across Montana, North and South Dakota, Minnesota, and Iowa. The only ones in the family that went off the grid were Tobias, Abraham, Isaak, Simon, and Obadiah. Obadiah was the one who died crashing the truck that freed Tobias.

"OK," Jacob sighed when they got everything hung up. "You three," He pointed to several agents, "Grab another board and start pinning current and past family land. You two," He pointed to another pair, "Find any and all vehicles that anyone in the family, or even the community, has owned along with all stolen car reports, narrowing down which ones could be our guys. Find what direction they are going and maybe we can head them off." He pointed to a single agent who was left. "Name?"

"Agent Tina Hernandez. Tina is fine." She said.

"Tina," Jacob reached into his pocket and handed her a card, "Open this app on a laptop that will have no other purpose. This is my login and password. Your priority is to monitor Agent Madison's glucose levels and report any changes to me, I don't care how small." Tina took the card and bolted.

"Ok," Roland took a breath knowing that Jacob was back in the game, "So far there were two crashes to get what they needed, and they used ketamine to sedate us so they are organized."

"I wouldn't be surprised if they planned all this while he was in jail."

"But the calls are all recorded. Someone would've reported it."

"Hey," Jacob called to the agents working on the family land, "One of you, I don't care who." A short young-looking agent raised his hand. "Good, you go through all the communication Tobias had with anyone." The agent scurried out of the room.

"We know Tobias blames Catarina for Sam's death. Do you think his family knows what actually happened? I didn't see any of them in court." Roland studied pictures of Sam and Daniel's bodies. Even with the blood cleared away, Daniel's mangled face made him nauseous. Part of his jaw and cheek had been blown to pieces. Sam's throat was torn out by a bullet from Daniel's gun.

"Tobias told his family to stay away, but I wonder if his lawyer knows anything." Roland walked over to a file and opened it. He found the lawyers number and continued over to the improvised video call setup. Handing the number to the operator, he stood on the floor marker . A fat old man that made his skin crawl popped up on screen.

"Agent Hoeft, I was about to leave for the night, I don't know where my client is." His voice was gruff. Charlie Walsh was a third-generation criminal defense lawyer that criminals loved, and anyone with a conscious hated. He looked like the grime people scraped off their shoes.

"Mr. Walsh shut up and listen." Roland knew his tone was out of line, but no one could blame him at this point.

"Agent…" Mr. Walsh bristled.

"Charlie, he's got Cat and our forensic scientist Katie Madison. They are going to die if we can't get to them first." Roland slammed his hand on the desk in front of him. The fat man stared in shock, but he didn't open his mouth again. "Tobias and his family have gone off the grid."

"I'm so sorry Agent Hoeft. I don't know where they would have gone." He pulled a file from his desk and flipped through it. "He mentioned several properties to me, but he never spoke to his family."

"Did he ever have you pass along any messages?" Jacob stepped into the frame.

"Just one to his aunt Elaina. I have a copy of it here I can fax to you." Mr. Walsh read over the letter.

"His aunt Elaina died five years ago in a car crash." Roland had committed the family to memory. Mr. Walsh dropped the paper he was holding and scrambled to pick it up again. "Her husband Silas too. They were going to leave the community, but no one could prove that it was anything more than an accident."

"Dear Aunt Elaina," Mr. Walsh read, "By the time you read this I will be on my way to prison. Don't mourn for me. I've done a lot I'm not proud of to protect Samuel. The girl who was involved got him killed. I know there's no bringing him back, and I hope that one day we will all be together again like we used to years ago. Let

Abraham know that I'm sorry I couldn't protect him. One day I will make the girl pay. Pray for my soul at church. Yours, Tobias."

"Nothing but apologies and a threat." Roland growled.

"Wait," Jacob grabbed his shoulder before Roland could fly off the handle. "They don't have a church building, do they?"

"Not that I know of." Mr. Walsh said, digging through a few more papers. "Their original family land was purchased by a Historic restoration company and has been fenced off as private property for years. The other pieces of land could have a church building they have used since."

"Please go through all your information," Jacob had regained control of himself, "His cousin, Isaak got close to her and slipped her a letter from Tobias."

"What did it say?" Mr. Walsh's color looked bad. He was scrambling through his stacks of papers.

"He said: 'You will know the pain I feel. We will spend time together before you beg to die. See you soon." Roland gritted out. He half wondered if he needed to call an ambulance for the lawyer when his face blanched.

"Agents, it's going to be a late night at the office for me. The second I get anything I will send it your way." Mr. Welch nodded at the camera. "I hope you find her soon."

The screen went black. Roland tried to take a breath, but he felt like he had a piece of rebar lodged in his lungs. If that bastard did anything to her, Roland would destroy the entire family in a very biblical way.

"Agent Evans?" Tina called.

"Jacob is fine." Jacob jogged over to the computer.

"Katie, I mean Agent Madison…"

"Listen up everyone!" Jacob called out with a huff. Not one person moved. Roland knew they had become the success story of the year, but now everyone was all formal and it was pissing Jacob off. "We're a team working towards the same goal! Knock it off with this formal Agent crap unless The Director is here. I'm Jacob, this is Roland, and we are all looking for Catarina and Katie. This attack was personal! They will regret hurting our family!" He turned to look at the screen with Tina.

"Get a move on!" Roland called out when no one moved. Agents jumped into motion. Roland leaned over the screen and joined the hushed conversation.

"Her levels have been pretty steady," Tina scrolled through the last twenty-four hours. "Except here when it dropped the night before they were taken."

"Don't worry about that. I know what that is." Jacob's voice was clipped, and Roland hid his face when Tina blushed, reading between the lines. "Then there is a spike here immediately following the crash. Then the numbers were almost in normal range before they spiked again."

"If they are giving them repeat doses, that would explain the spikes." Roland said. "You think they will listen if she tells them she's diabetic?"

"Only if she throws Catarina under the bus." Jacob looked at him. He could see in his friend's face that he hoped that would happen.

Roland couldn't even blame the guy. If he was in Jacob's shoes, he would be doing the same thing. They had known each other for years, but suddenly they were on opposite sides of the field. Roland damned-near felt his blood pressure go up. Jacob watched his barely controlled rage.

"Listen man." Roland dropped his voice and watched Jacob tense. "This whole situation sucks, and I know it. I'm not angry with you for how you're feeling, I would do the same. I'm doing everything I can to keep my shit together."

"You and I both know we're going to get pissed at each other because of all this bullshit." Jacob matched his tone. "I'm pissed at you right now for getting her dragged into this last year."

"You know Daniel listened in on the police scanner!" Roland stood up straight. "I'll move heaven and earth to protect her!"

"Even if it means I lose Katie?" They were both nearly shouting.

"No, you idiot! I'm going to bring them both home safe, even if it's the last thing I do! I would expect you to do the same for Catarina! That doesn't mean I don't hate you right now, but your still my best friend, even if I want to kick the shit out of you sometimes!"

"Good because I really want to beat your fucking face in!" Jacob roared.

"The feeling is mutual!" Roland matched his energy. They both nodded, acknowledging each other's anger, and leaned back to the computer where Tina was nearly hyperventilating. Roland looked up at the room that was again frozen.

"What the hell is everyone standing around for?!" Roland yelled. Everyone suddenly burst into motion.

"Don't mind us. It's been a while since we've been pissed in an office setting." Jacob soothed the poor woman who had gotten caught in the middle. Tina was still trying to get herself put back together. Roland got impatient and walked over to the pallet of water that had been wheeled in. Everyone was muttering when he grabbed one. Tina took it gratefully and Jacob seemed to have calmed her down a bit.

"This family has no clue what they're messing with." Several of the agents thought they were safe to start speculating.

Roland's specialized hearing implant helped him hear what they were saying.

"Seriously!" Someone else responded. "They'd be better off taking on the kraken!"

"If Agent Hoeft gets his hands on someone, do you think he can stop himself?"

"It would be horrible to get her back only to go to prison." One of the newer agents whispered.

"Despite what you think," Roland said loudly. The group jumped, one of them spilling the papers in her hands. "I am in control of myself." Two of the agents dropped to pick up the files that had fallen. "Angry doesn't mean out of control."

"Didn't you pump that guy full of lead?" A kid asked pointing to Daniel's picture. Roland wasn't sure he was even old enough to be here."

"I didn't even have a gun in my hand." Roland tried to keep the sneer off his face. "I was covering Cat from the gunfire."

"How many of you watched the footage from that night?" Jacob stepped up behind Roland. No one raised their hands. "I suggest you all take a few minutes to watch it. We don't need mistakes being made based on assumptions." Jacob patted his back, and they walked back to the laptop to analyze Katie's chart.

# Chapter 9

Catarina's head was spinning. She could feel herself fighting the urge to throw up. A soft hand checked the pulse on her wrist. Vaguely she remembered fighting someone. That's all she needed.

She grabbed that hand only to realize her own were tied. Rotating her body, she successfully smashed her head against a wall, while pulling the figure on top of her. Her eyes shot open, and she grabbed the neckline of the kid's jacket. Pulling his face against her chest, she redirected his head, forcing it

into the wall. Using her other hand, Catarina reached as far back as her tied hands allowed, on the other side of the collar. Sinching down, the kid was now being strangled by his own clothing.

He pulled his head back while trying to scream. The motion killed her wrists, but it locked the jacket choak in and cut off his ability to make any noise. The panicked eyes bulged, and she hesitated.

"Sam." She whispered confused. He looked so young, her eyes filled with tears. The kid flailed and his feet hit the wall.

"Let him go!" A harsh voice broke the silence. In the main room a tall man with a few days growth of a beard pointed a gun at her. She would've been shocked at the gun, but from the top of his hair down to his sandaled feet, he looked like he was carved from alabaster. A light behind him gave the illusion that he was glowing. She knew his face but couldn't place it.

"Isaak," The kid flailing against her wheezed out. Isaak. She knew that name. He stormed up to them and thrust the gun in her face. Catarina let go, holding her hands in view. Isaak grabbed the now wheezing teen and pulled him off the bed and into the main room.

She realized they were in a camper. The whole container lurched, and she looked past the two to see a glaring pair of eyes in a rear-view mirror. RV, she corrected herself. The upholstery was dated at best, and it was small. Catarina watched Isaak unlatch and open the fridge door. Taking a bottle of water, he tossed onto the bed at her feet.

"I've seen you before." Catarina mumbled looking at his incredibly blue eyes.

"Drink." He was cautious, as opposed to his counterpart who was guzzling down his own bottle of water with his back to her. "It will help you clear your head."

"Darting me would probably be an easier way to drug me." Catarina smirked and it all came back to her in a rush. Sitting up, she gasped and looked around. Katie was still asleep beside her. She scooted over and checked for a pulse.

"She's fine." Isaak stepped forward and leaned against the doorframe. "I've kept an eye on her sugars, and she will have access to her supplies as needed."

"You know about diabetes?" Catarina looked skeptically at him.

"Oh, yeah. Figured it out right around the same time we discovered fire, and the wheel." Isaak's voice dripped with sarcasm. Catarina rolled her eyes.

"So, you want your revenge for Sam." Catarina huffed after she wiggled to a sitting position.

"Don't say his name!" The younger one turned and rushed the bed, only stopping when Isaak put his hand up. "Don't you ever say his name! You're the reason he's dead!"

"SIMON!" The man driving the RV yelled. The kid flinched and backed up a bit. He wasn't exactly a kid, but he couldn't be older than twenty-four. Simon looked so much like Sam that she had to blink a few times.

"He never said if she had diabetes or not," Isaak murmured. "Only that she had long brown hair." Simon grumbled to himself and went to sit towards the front near the kitchen area.

"What will happen to the person that's not her." Catarina kept her voice low. Isaak seemed to have a level head on his shoulders so far, but that could change at any time.

"The whole country is looking for us." Isaak sat on the end of the bed, keeping her in sight. "We aren't stupid. Whoever is not the one we are looking for will be dropped off safely in a spot where we can get away without a fuss."

"And I believe you because?" She let the last word trail off.

"Because right now I'm the only one trying to make sure that's, what's left of the family, doesn't act too quickly."

"What will happen to the one who was involved?" Catarina examined his face. Isaak wasn't overtly hostile just yet besides the gun, but she was choking Simon, so she couldn't blame him.

"Well," He rubbed the back of his neck and watched her face. Simon sat down in the kitchen area. His back was to the older man that was driving, but they looked like they were having their own conversation. "I guess that's up to Tobias. I'd rather not have to run for the rest of my life, but he was there, and I wasn't. So, it's not up to me."

Catarina's heart sank. She was extremely aware of the situation, but she had hoped that the time they had spent together would give her a little leeway. Katie groaned on the bed beside her. She scooted to her friend.

"I think I'm going to..." Katie mumbled before gagging.

"Here," Isaak spoke up. He handed them a large bowl. Katie propped herself up on one elbow after Catarina set it beside her. They made it just in time. While Katie threw up stomach acid, Catarina held her hair back the best she could.

"Thanks," Katie mumbled.

"Got vomit!" Isaak called to the two in front. The RV slowed. Catarina tried not to fall over but it was a lot of work with her hands tied. When they stopped, Isaak took the bowl and washed it in the sink. Simon and the older man made their way back after putting up a screen across the front window. The older one grabbed Catarina, dragging her off the bed.

"I don't know which one of you is Catarina," His voice was velvety but firm. Simon was pulling Katie out of the bed. "You should know that we were warned about your antics. Nothing will happen to you if you behave yourself."

"Sounds riveting." Katie grumbled.

"Have her brush her teeth then bring her here." The man said. "Isaak, you're going up."

"It's my face, isn't it?" Isaak sneered at the man.

"Yes, it is!" The man lifted Catarina into his arms and shoved her onto the bunk above the driver's seats in front. "Would you just do what you're told for once? Stop asking questions."

"Why don't you just say what you're thinking, Abraham?" Isaak grabbed Katie and hoisted her up to the bed beside Catarina. "My skin is a curse, and you wish I'd never been born!" He climbed up and pushed Catarina against the wall.

"I'm your father and you will address me as your father!" Abraham peeked out one of the windows.

"When you start acting like one, I might consider it." Isaak grunted when he pushed Katie right up against Catarina then climbed in beside them like a trio of sardines. "You kicked me out, so why don't you hold your breath until that happens."

Abraham and Simon started packing blankets on the edge of the bed to block off the three of them from viewing the door. Simon grabbed what looked like the edge of a few suitcases. They had been cut and glued together into a makeshift wall blocking them from the rest of the room. When he placed it just right, the final illusion would appear as if the bed was full of luggage and blankets.

"I've always wanted to be a sandwich." Katie snickered. "Somehow I imagined it differently."

"You think your man would be up for it?" Catarina kept it up.

"Giving the fact that everyone has pretty much seen everyone else naked at this point, I think he could handle a lot more than we give him credit for." Katie gave her a warm smile.

"Shut up." Isaak demanded. He was lying on his side, facing them. In one swift movement, he unzipped the cloth ceiling above them and peeled it back. A detonator surrounded by wires and what looked like clay mounds were attached to the ceiling. "If anything happens, we can all go see Samuel together." He closed it up again.

They heard the doors open then close, and waited in silence. Catarina studied Isaak's face up close. His jaw was more defined than anyone else in the family that she'd seen. His nose was wide like his family's, but it emphasized the other sharp facial features. Her thoughts were cut off when the door to the RV opened.

"Well, my boy here, spilled his water all over but we got it cleaned up," Abraham was sporting a thick Alabama drawl. "But come on in, take a look around." Three sets of footsteps rocked the RV.

"I appreciate it." A young voice rang out in the silence. Catarina stared at Isaak, his arctic blue eyes bore into hers. He raised a finger to his mouth, demanding silence.

"Bed is back there," Simon matched Abraham's twang. "I sleep up there."

"No worries," The officer said. "There were two young women that were abducted quite a way south of here and we're all on high alert. You had me worried when I saw you pull over."

"Sorry to get you all worked up officer." Abraham chuckled. He sounded so at ease it made Catarina anxious. "We've still got a long way to go before we get to our fishing hole in Grand Forks. If this is how the trip started, it makes me glad I packed an extra of everything."

"Good to be prepared." The officer said. "I'll leave you to it." The vehicle swayed slightly when the three of them walked out and the door clicked shut. Isaak relaxed enough that his jaw stopped ticking, but Catarina could still see he was ready for them to spring into action at any moment.

"Try it." Isaak said quietly. "See how well it goes for you." He made eye contact and she colored.

"You think we're afraid?" Catarina asked him.

"Not yet." He smiled like a cat that had just cornered its' prey. "But you will be."

The others climbed back in, and they took off again. They stayed like that for a long time. Catarina tried not to dose off but at some point, they hit a bump and she twitched. Katie looked at her and gave a small smirk. She didn't look good.

"Hey," She whispered. "You, ok? You look awful."

"I thought it was just the drugs." Katie said. "My sugars are low."

"Hey, shit for brains, you have any food?" Snapped Catarina. She made to climb over Katie, but Isaak pushed her back.

"Simon, you wanna move this crap?" Isaak called. After some shuffling, the wall of items moved and Isaak crawled out, dragging Katie with him. Catarina rolled to the edge of the bunk to supervise. She had no clue what she would do if something happened. They gave Katie her bag that had all her supplies in it and untied her hands, so she could test herself. She looked concerned.

"How bad is it?" Catarina asked.

"Not too bad if I can get some food quick." Katie shrugged while putting everything back. "Really bad if it takes more than ten minutes."

"We'll stop for food here in a few." Isaak said after he glanced at Abraham, who was driving. "I've got a travel size trail mix, if you want. That could hold you over." Isaak was being much nicer to Katie, and Catarina didn't miss that fact.

"Thanks." Katie nodded.

They got her the snack and put the both of them back in the bed at the tail end of the RV. Catarina made a mental note of every item that could be used as a weapon. The window had been boarded up with a white PVC board so they couldn't signal to anyone. They stopped in what looked like a parking lot where Simon and Isaak left to get food. Abraham stood in the kitchen area with a gun ready.

"We will drop you off with cash and your supplies when we are able." He said looking at Katie. "I just need Tobias to confirm what I already know." His harsh eyes turned to Catarina. "He told us you had fight in you. He didn't say you were stupid though."

"Stupid?" Catarina let out a choked laugh. "Nothing says stupid like organizing a traffic accident and kidnapping two women that are under the protection of the government."

"I think you mean stupid like running to fight the very people trying to abduct you, to save someone who is going to get out alive and unharmed anyways." Abraham shot back.

"At this point my life being in danger is just another Tuesday." Catarina shrugged. "Sam had more fight in him than you idiots did." The gun in Abraham's hand leveled at her.

"You don't get to say his name." Abraham snarled. "You're the reason he's dead."

"You sure about that sparky?" Catarina felt her eyebrow twitch. Abraham studied her face for a few seconds before stepping towards her.

"Tobias told us everything." He growled. "You won't be able to lie your way out of this."

"You sure she's the one that's lying?" Katie piped up. "She tried to keep Daniel's attention on her to keep the others out of danger." Abraham's face softened when he looked at Katie.

"I admire your loyalty to your friend dear, but this no longer concerns you." His glare came back when he looked at Catarina. "As for you. If you cause any trouble, you will suffer the consequences."

"Don't threaten me with a good time." Catarina smirked. Abraham sneered, winding himself up for what she assumed was going to be a decent fire and brimstone speech, when the door opened. Isaak and Simon walked in with their arms full of food.

"Remember what Tobias said, Abraham." Isaak smirked when his dad growled at him. "When it comes to fight or flight with that one," he nodded at Catarina before putting the bags on the table, "you better put up your dukes."

"I told you to call me father." Abraham growled. Simon set his bags down too.

"And I told you to hold your breath." Isaak started sorting through the bags.

"I bet even 'Daddy' would suffice at this point." Katie snickered. Isaak's eyes bulged, he dropped everything he was holding, and flushed profusely.

"What does she mean?" Simon asked while looking back and forth between them confused. Katie and Catarina were trying to keep their laughter quiet.

"Don't worry about it." Isaak was suddenly incredibly interested in sorting out the food they had acquired. "It's just a corrupt world joke." Abraham rolled his eyes before grabbing what he wanted from the bags and isolating himself in the driver's seat.

Simon brought a few bags to the two women. Catarina wasn't sure if it was expectation or kindness, but he opened the burgers for them both. Katie ate hers quickly before Simon returned with a bottle of juice. He kept stealing glances at Catarina when he thought she didn't see him. Abraham pulled the small RV back onto the interstate before Catarina had decided to call him out.

"If you have a question, spit it out before you combust." She smirked when Simon flushed.

"Tobias told us everything that happened when you were with them the first time." Simon stated while gathering up the trash and putting it into the bag in an attempt to not look at her. "Did you really use a guy as a body-board when you jumped out of a moving car?"

"Oh yeah." Catarina smirked at the memory. "So, you know I'm Catarina?"

"We're all pretty sure, but we have to have Tobias confirm it." Simon sat across from Isaak at the table. "When you did that, what were you thinking?"

"Fuck it." She smiled.

"Language!" Abraham shouted from the driver's seat.

"Eat me!" Catarina shot back. Abraham glared in the rear-view mirror at her, nearly driving into a semi in the process.

"Gross" Simon crinkled his nose. "We're not cannibals." Catarina watched Isaak's face go red.

"Different meanings, buddy." Katie laughed at his confused face. The vehicle settled into silence for a long time before Isaak pulled Katie's bag from one of the cupboards. He cut the zip ties on her wrists but leveled the gun at Catarina.

"Do what you need to, but any wrong move and you can say goodbye to your friend." Isaak's voice was casual as he tossed Katie's bag in her lap. Katie didn't wait to open it and check her blood sugar with practiced confidence.

"How long until we get to where we are going?" Catarina groaned. "I need to piss, and I highly doubt you're going to let me out of this van."

"A little over seven hours if we drive straight through." Isaak looked at a clock that was mounted on the wall. "You can use the bathroom here." He pointed to the closed door beside the bed. "If you break anything, I start breaking bones, starting from the feet, and working my way up."

"What is it with bad guys getting sensitive over shit getting broken?" Catarina looked at Katie, who handed the bag back to Isaak.

"I don't know, but I'm going first." Katie laughed. Isaak cut the zip ties from her ankle and stood back so she could go into the bathroom. After the door clicked, he leveled the gun at her again. Catarina rolled her eyes, bored with the gesture.

"You've got a gun aimed at you and you're not afraid?" Simon scoffed in disbelief. "There's no way you're sane."

"Simon," Catarina smirked while listing the events off on her fingers, "in the last year, I was the victim of a bank robbery, kidnapped, beaten, frozen, strangled, used as a hostage, shot at, then my ex tried to abduct me with a gun, and now you nuts have managed to do it." Simon's smirk slowly faded as she continued. "The bar for kidnapping isn't all that high to begin with. You idiots have literally accomplished the bare minimum."

"So why haven't you tried to escape?" He asked. Isaak smacked the back of Simon's head.

"The second she is safe," Catarina nodded to the bathroom door, "is when the real fun begins, and I'll show you my definition of a good time."

"Doesn't your idea of a good time involve impaling someone's eyeball with the barrel of a gun?" Katie walked out of the bathroom and plopped on the bed. Catarina held her arms out for Isaak to cut her loose.

"That was one time." Catarina laughed. Isaak cut her restraints, but never took the gun off of her. Once in the bathroom she quietly took stock of anything she could use as escape, or to send out a signal. There was something lightly flapping against the top of the RV she hadn't noticed before. It looked like something purple was jammed in the lip of the ceiling vent. She took care of her business and exited the bathroom, put out at the fact that she still didn't find anything.

"We need to stop for gas." Abraham growled from the front seat. Simon dug through a bag on the table before retrieving four sets of flex cuffs. Catarina sighed and held her arms out to be secured.

"Under normal circumstances," Simon commented, "This would just be a precaution." He secured them both with deft movements.

"Aww," Katie teased. "He thinks we're exceptional!" Isaak walked up with a handful of water bottles. Opening each of them, he passed them out. Catarina realized how dry her mouth was and drank almost as quickly as Katie. Isaak stopped them and took the water back with a smirk. Catarina only noted the taste after it was too late. She wasn't watching for it because she heard the seal break when he opened the bottles. The RV teetered and swayed as the drugs took effect. There was a soft thump when Katie passed out, and Catarina got one last insult in as everything went dark.

"You dick."


The swaying her body was doing had her wanting to puke up everything she had eaten in the last decade. It took everything in her, but Catarina threw herself to the side before dry heaving. Someone grabbed her hair and used it to drag her down the bed. Holding her face over the trash can, Abraham mumbled to himself.

"Weak women." He smelled like he hadn't showered in days. Catarina didn't throw up, but when he released her hair, she laughed.

"You might want to be careful," She rolled to look up at him, the last of the drugs lingering in a subtle euphoria, "some people get all hot and bothered being dragged around by their hair." Abraham jumped back and shook his arm like he had been electrocuted.

"Not funny!" Isaak called from the front of the RV. "You'd better watch what you say before it gets you hurt!"

"What time is it?" Katie muttered.

"Almost ten." Simon's voice chimed behind her, and Catarina jumped. Simon was testing Katie's blood sugar and noted. "Down to ninety, let's get you some food." He removed the flex-cuffs from each of them and plopped back down at the table when he was finished.

"How much longer, until we get to Tobias?" Catarina asked. "I'd like to spend what time I can trying to summon dark entities." Silence and shocked faces filled the RV.

"We don't joke about that." Abraham's voice was strangely subdued. Catarina flicked an eyebrow at him. "Another three hours if you two behave." Catarina groaned.

"I get it from my grandma." Catarina snarked while making a cute face.

"The sass or the fight?" Isaak asked while driving.

"Both!" She laughed. "She was locked in a concentration camp and survived, so I'd say it's a safe bet." Reading the room, she realized everyone was staring at her. The subtle euphoria seemed to be silencing the filter in her brain.

"Don't stop there." Simon was leaning forward, excited for the story.

"Well," Catarina decided the short version might be better. "She was born in the states, but her family went back to visit their grandparents that weren't doing well. They got to see them for two days before they died, and in the process of cleaning out the house, they were taken into custody for nothing more than being in the wrong place at the wrong time. She was the only one that made it out. She was in there for four years and just turned twenty-two before getting back to her old home in America."

"That's crazy." Simon whispered. Catarina felt her heart ache, he looked so much like Sam that she kept having to stop herself from tearing up.

"The strongest ones in each of the bunk houses were sent to the river to get buckets of water. It was Grandma Cat's turn to get the water and she saw a soldier following her. Rape was such a regular thing there, that she was warned about it the day they got there. Her dad ran the combat school back home, and he taught her a few things. She had just set the buckets down when the soldier grabbed her and dragged her out of sight. Just when the bastard thought he was safe, she yanked a knife out of his boot, and cut the artery in his thigh. Grandma jumped on him and cut almost clean through his neck to stop the scream. Moving a bunch of rocks in the river took some time, but she moved his body into the hole and weighed him down. No one ever found him, and he was labeled a deserter." Catarina shrugged.

"What about the blood?" Isaak asked. "You can't kill someone like that and avoid getting blood on yourself."

"She washed it off in the river," Catarina called up to him. "She was beat up a little in the process, so what she couldn't wash out, everyone just assumed it was hers."

"That's the picture hanging in the hall at your place?" Katie asked.

"Yeah," Catarina smiled. "The letter was a letter of apology from the monarchy because her family was taken."

"Catarina….. Cat." Abraham spat the name and shook his head. "Named after an animal, acts like an animal, and it's continued through the family line." He began laughing loudly to himself. "You're basically rabid! The women in your family were insane, and your murderous grandmother should've died there! The women in your family should've been slaughtered like dogs!"

He had been leaning against the back of the booth next to the table and was completely caught off guard when she lunged at him. She grabbed a grate from the stovetop and swung it when he sprang into action. It caught him on the browbone, snapping his head back with a sickening pop. Blood was still spurting from the wound when he blindly tackled her. He was pulling the grate out of her grip, and she kneed him in the groin when the RV slowed rapidly. Catarina thrust her hips up and rolled when Abraham finally buckled. With one hand, she ripped open a drawer and grabbed a knife. Abraham's face was still contorted in pain when she pressed it hard against his throat, and he froze. They were both breathing hard while blood gushed from his head.

"We don't joke about that." She pressed her forehead into his, forcing him to look into her eyes, and see the barely contained insanity that lurked there.

Two pairs of hands dragged her off him, but only Simon had the sense to disarm her. She smiled triumphantly down at Abraham, who still hadn't moved. The expression that passed on his face was a mix of confusion and alarm. It was clear that even though they had been warned, he didn't take the advice seriously.

"Clearly," Abraham climbed off the ground and Catarina was satisfied to see that he pissed himself. "We've underestimated you." He took a towel from a drawer, pressing it hard to the cut and raised a finger at her. "That was your only chance. Next time, I will apologize to Tobias for killing you before he could."

"Like I said," Catarina sneered back, her eyebrow ticked with a threat, "Don't threaten me with a good time. It just might be a check that you won't be able to cash." Abraham nodded at the challenge before stepping to the side and letting Simon and Isaak put her back on the bed. While they were busying themselves with first aid and pulling back onto the road, Catarina whispered to Katie. "What did you see?"

"Simon is the type who hesitates while Abraham is a little more….. reactive." Katie kept her voice low too. "Be careful though, it looks like Isaak is always watching." Catarina stole a glance at Isaak, who was in fact, monitoring their every move. "I think I have an idea."

"Great!" Catarina whispered, trying to keep her face resigned and calm.

"I'm starting a fire." Katie informed her.

"God damnit." Catarina looked at the small woman who was smiling.

# Chapter 10

Roland kicked the pads the other agent was holding so hard, that the kid went sliding backwards on his ass. It had been hours and they were no closer to finding the girls. Jacob was with another agent, burning out energy on the wrestling mats that had been brought in. They were all sweating profusely, but at least the risk of a blowup had gone down.

Director Johnston had flown in to oversee the recovery of their team members. Tyrese had a meeting with him behind closed doors, resulting in orders for Roland and Jacob to start an hour of intense exercise. That hour was almost up, and Roland was itching to get back in the game.

"Sorry agent." Roland apologized to the kid who was slow to get back up. Roland gave him a hand.

"Don't worry about it." He accepted the offer and stretched before holding the pads up again. "And call me Noah, it saves time." Noah braced for impact while Roland unloaded a flurry of punches.

"Sounds good." Roland said when he finished. The doors burst open, and Elliot walked in. Elliot was one of the most impressive tech experts he had ever known. He had partnered with Jonathan to build Jacob's leg. Standing at five foot ten inches, he could destroy most of the department in hand-to-hand combat.

He was also a nudist in his personal life, a fact that was only known by his close friends, but he and Roland were far from friends. Roland thought Elliot was a self-righteous asshole with a useful brain, and Elliot thought of him as a brainless ape who should've been cast as Sloth in the movie Goonies.

"Guys, we got a lead!" Elliot called out. "It's not much, but it's something."

"Anything right now is a good thing." Jacob hopped to the edge of the mat and put his leg back on. They were barreling through the door to the next room a few seconds later. Director Johnston was standing in the center of several tables with files scattered across them all. Beside him a tall black man was speaking low beside him.

"Tyrese," Roland shook his hand. "Been a minute."

"I need to pick your brain later, but right now, The Director has some information for us." Tyrese took a half step back, opening the floor.

"Boys," Director Johnston nodded in greeting. "Katie had a tracker placed under the surface of her skin before this mission started. Only a handful of people knew about it." He pointed to several yellow pins on the map in front of them. "It's not an exact location, but it signals to the closest cell phone towers."

"Why haven't we deployed all of our resources?" Jacob asked with barely concealed fury. "If you know where they are, then what are we doing here with our thumbs up our asses?"

"Agent Evans." The Director held up a placating hand. "Let me finish. The signal has only blipped on the radar for a few seconds at a time. Which means the chip has been damaged, or they are being transported in a modified vehicle that the signal cannot transmit through."

"Like a faraday cage?" Roland asked.

"Exactly, and at the speed they are moving, I'm thinking they're in a large vehicle. Could be a van, RV, SUV, or even a box truck." Director Johnston stepped back from the group and called out to a group of agents on computers. "Pull all the camera footage for the areas where Agent Madison's tracker pinged and compare all the vehicles. See if you can narrow it down at all."

"Wouldn't we be better off going to the last point that her tracker registered?" Jacob jumped on that point. "Or at least the general area."

"We are getting everything packed up." Tyrese informed him. "The air force is up the road, and they will assist in transport to Rapid City Airport. It's not the last place on the list, but it looks like they are headed in that direction, and it's in the center of several plots of land they own."

Tyrese started walking and signaled for Roland to follow. When they got into the next room, they planted themselves in a set of chairs, and sighed, Tyrese jumped right in.

"Jacob met with me already, but you've been avoiding me."

"Is there a question in there somewhere?" Roland snapped.

"I would ask how you're doing but I can see it." Tyrese sat back in his chair. "While they are all packing, we are going to talk, or I won't recommend that you continue onto South Dakota." Looking at his watch, he continued. "You can't make packing go any faster, and if you could, there's likely to be damage to the equipment. Talk."

"I'm pissed that I couldn't stop them being taken. I hate Daniel for not killing Tobias too, if he had, we wouldn't be here. And I'm pissed that we can't find her!" Roland was doing his best not to yell, but he wasn't doing great. Tyrese just directed Roland to sit. After they were both planted in the chairs, Roland continued. "If I had been paying more attention, I could've done something!"

"So, what you're telling me, is because you were distracted, and only focused on her, that you let your guard down?" Tyrese asked.

"No!" Roland was straining to keep calm. "I just got her back! I was watching everything! Every turn, every car behind us, and every person we passed on the street!"

"Roland, you need to understand one thing." Tyrese leaned forward and pressed his fingers together. "You could've had x-ray vision, and still not prevented what happened. Understand?" Tyrese waited until he huffed before continuing. "You can kick yourself into the next life, and that's completely reasonable. Do it later. Right now, you have two people who aren't waiting around for us to find them. They need us to meet them halfway. Whether that's finding them running from a building after they've killed everyone inside or kicking in the door while they've held that family at bay. Sort the rest out later."

"Fine." Roland smirked at Tyrese. "I'll put it on a shelf, but we will dissect this again."

"It's a date." Tyrese smiled. "Now, how did your conversation go after her last session?"

"It was good." Roland sighed, the memory relaxed his racing thoughts. "We both were upfront about wanting whatever this is without feeling required to be here. We know that since everything about this is backwards, stuff is going to come up out of order, and we need to have a lot of understanding and be willing to talk through shit."

"Well, that's..." Tyrese sounded unsure, "healthy." He readjusted in his seat a few times before continuing. "I know she went to years of therapy after she left her ex-boyfriend."

"Abuser." Roland quickly inserted.

"Exactly." Nodded Tyrese. "Just promise me, that if you two make this a long-term thing, that you two might try couples therapy if the need arises." Holding out a hand, he waited. Roland stared at it for a few seconds before accepting.

"You're not the pain in the ass I thought you were when we first met." Roland said when they climbed to their feet.

"Funny." Laughed Tyrese. "You're still a hot head. Might want to see a therapist about that." They walked back into the main room.

Half the equipment was being packed up but there were still a few agents working on laptops. The Director was on the phone across the room. Roland walked over to Jacob who was still attached to Tina.

"It looks like there was another spike here, and it's been steadily going down over the last several hours." Jacob mused out loud. Roland walked over to a group of agents that were packing up boxes of files.

"Any updates?" Roland's voice was calmer than he felt, but one of the agents jumped.

"Well, not an update, but maybe something useful." The Agent with glasses said. "There are four separate parts of the family as a whole." Roland followed him over to the board with the family lineage displayed. "The four families that started the sect expanded and separated even farther. Each set of families cherry-picked their beliefs and customs until they became their own individual sects. Does that make sense?"

"Basically, religious zealotry that disintegrated into four separate cults." Roland confirmed, before crumbling a blank piece of paper and throwing it at Jacob. Jacob picked it up and threw it at the back of Roland's head while walking over.

"So, we have no idea what this one believes." Jacob studied the family trees.

"Exactly!" The Agent confirmed before pointing to another sect. "So, we know where these two are, Levi and Rebecca. They only have a landline, but they had been communicating regularly with Abraham. Abraham is the last one alive out of his brothers and sister, so now he's the one in charge of their portion of the cult. He stopped all communication right before sentencing."

"You think Levi and Rebecca know where they are?" Jacob sounded hopeful.

"It's a possibility, but they also have children, grandchildren, and great-grandchildren scattered on plots of land throughout the same few states as Tobias's family." The agent took his glasses off to clean them. "Director Johnston will have him waiting to be interviewed when you two arrive in Rapid City, South Dakota."

"Everyone, be packed and loaded into the Humvees out front in thirty minutes, we fly out in one hour." Director Johnston's voice boomed from the center of the room. "Anyone that's late gets to drive to Rapid City, and I will expect a ten-page essay on why being punctual is of the utmost importance."

The room exploded in movement. Roland and Jacob booked it back to their room, throwing their belongings into bags, and were some of the first out to the vehicles. They dropped their bags with the transport units and left to help cart the rest of the equipment out. They were across town and in the air in record time.

When they landed in Rapid City, Roland's nerves were damned near shot. He wanted to punch someone, and Jacob didn't look much better. The other agents gave them a wide berth. Director Johnston was delegating tasks to get their new headquarters in the new hotel set up and running. He told Roland and Jacob to find a sparring partner and burn off some energy before the 'interview'.

They turned one of the rooms beside the conference room into a sparing arena. Roland had to focus on not overexerting himself. He thought about the look on her face in the park when he finally found her. Her laugh played over and over in his mind like a broken record. He felt the rage fueling his strikes, seeing her face in the car wreck nearly doubled him over.

"Hey!" Jacob's voice boomed behind him. Roland whipped around, ready to attack. Tyrese, Jacob, and his combat partner were all staring at him. They were tense, but no one was reacting to any threat, so he relaxed his posture and stood tall. The oscillating fan in the corner passed him and Roland noticed his face was wet. Pulling the end of his shirt up to wipe the tears away, Roland nodded.

"What's going on in your head?" Tyrese asked. The two agents got the hint and left the room.

"I'm angry." Roland divulged as soon as the doors closed. "This should've never happened. I know we can't change that now, but I want every last one of them to rot away in prison! I want Cat back! I want Katie back. I want to go back to the other day where we were all together and safe."

"Same." Jacob confirmed. "Get it out of your system now, or shove it down deep and we will get it out when this is all over." Tyrese looked like he was going to object but gave up with a shrug.

"Director Johnston has new information." Tyrese said before leading them back into the main conference room. Roland grabbed water from one of the buckets of ice on the way by. Jacob diverted to the table of food to grab a few protein bars. Handing one to Roland, he returned the nod Director Johnson gave him.

"Alright everyone," His voice boomed in the silence, "we have Levi and Rebecca in the conference room down the hall. No one talks with them unless myself or Tyrese are present. Right now, Katie and Catarina have been gone for fourteen hours. The agents that were tracking Tobias Morgan lost him. In some stroke of dumb luck, he was caught on a traffic camera on the way through Box Elder. Officers in the area are on alert and ready to catch him."

"How can we help?" A well-built man in his fifties strode into the room, followed by four associates. He had long brown and grey hair that was pulled back into Viking-style braids. Dark Pagan tattoos covered his arms and climbed up his neck. He stopped beside Roland and Jacob, holding out a fist to each of them to bump.

"Thank you, Brandt." Director Johnston continued. "Agent Brandt Hagen is our expert on religion, psychology, and terrorism. He will be watching the interviews. The rest of you split into four groups right now." He paused while the room split. Jacob reached out and grabbed Tina by the arm, placing her in the center of their little circle. "Group one, you will continue the traffic camera search for any sign of Catarina and Katie or the vehicle they may be in. Group two will be sorting through all the land owned or previously owned by any of the families to find where they might have been taken. Group three will do research on the members that were involved, and then all the families that have any reason to help Tobias. Group four will comb through the financials of the family and find anything out of the ordinary. Move people, these girls will be brought home alive and well!" The room burst into life.

Roland, Jacob, Tina, Brandt and Brandt's group followed Director Johnston out the doors and down the hall. They marched into the room where an older couple sat together at the end of a long table. The man's head was shaved, his face was weatherworn and hard. The woman wore a hair net around her bun with her head was slightly bowed. They wore plain clothes that were pressed to within an inch of their life.

"Hello Mr. and Mrs. Martin. My name is Director Boone Johnston. Under normal circumstances I would have more cordiality, so please forgive my curt behavior." The Director sat in the next chair, everyone behind him following suit and finding their own. "You've had frequent phone calls with Abraham Charles Morgan and that stopped abruptly. We can't track the phone he was using, and we don't know where they have gone. The lives of two of our agents are at risk and we need all the information you have about them."

Levi's face contorted in confusion while he looked around at the others in the room before settling on Roland and Jacob. He leaned back in his chair and sighed. Roland kept his gaze locked with the old man. The eye contact was a challenge, and Roland wasn't about to lose.

"Ira and Leah's boy." Rebecca leaned sideways and whispered to her husband. His eyes nearly glittered in recognition.

"You're after that bitch that got Samuel killed." Levi smirked. "Tobias told us everything. How she tricked him into loving her, how she made sure that he was standing in front of her to take the bullets, and even how she laughed when he died." Rebecca shuddered beside him, disdain written on her face. "She's going to suffer for what she did to Samuel. I don't care if our families are feuding, we are rooting for them."

"It seems like you don't have the entire story." Director Johnston said. "I have the footage from that night," he nodded at the whiteboard on one wall, and a projector lit up, "tell me what you think the real story is."

The night that everything fell apart played out in front of Roland. He watched Daniel drive the knife into Tobias. The camera in the hall was just clear enough to capture the satisfaction on his face. Three other images split the screen when the agents filled the hall. Roland watched Daniel's face contort when he realized Catarina never really loved him. Spittle flew from his lips as his brain fractured, and he screamed.

Rebecca flinched in her seat at the threats, but Levi smiled. Everyone watched when Daniel brought the gun up, Sam lunged at him, and Jacob missed grabbing him by a hair's breath. Roland had dragged Catarina to the floor, shielding her with his body. Gunfire echoed in the room and stopped as soon as it started.

Rebecca looked green at the gruesome scene while bits of Daniel's face was blown to pieces.

It was only a few seconds of silence before Daniel, by some miracle, took a step towards Catarina, and the room erupted again. They watched his body disappear out the window. Catarina's scream echoed in Roland's ears. No one moved as she crawled over to Sam's thrashing body and crooned softly. Roland felt tears welling up in his eyes as he watched the woman he loved, whispering soft soothing words to a dying man that no one could've saved.

The lights flipped on, and Roland realized he wasn't the only one blinking back tears. Two of the agents with Brandt looked pale. They were probably from the new recruits that made it past the vetting process two months ago. This video would've been new to them.

"So, as you can see," Director Johnston said, "there has been a misinterpretation in what events transpired."

"Are you calling Tobias a liar?!" Levi roared. Rebecca ducked her head lower and folded her hands in her lap.

"Not at all." Brandt's voice was confident. "Tobias spent his whole life protecting his brother. Daniel was a mass murderer that got close to Samuel and used that trust to betray them all. Because of how traumatic that event was and losing his brother, Tobias's mind fractured to protect himself. The person who killed Samuel is dead, but that rage is still there. Tobias's mind altered bits and pieces of his reality to cope with the trauma. He didn't lie because he doesn't know what his own brain did to that memory. He wholeheartedly believes it's true, which is why we need to find him before he hurts anyone else."

"You make a lot of sense for a devil worshiping abomination." Levi sneered at Brandt, eyeing his necklace that clearly had Thor's Hammer shining in the light. Brandt smiled and nodded at the insult, taking it in stride. "If that's true, then whatever he's planning, he's not expecting to live through it."

"Is there any way you can get in contact with him?" The Director asked.

"No." Levi said with a smirk. "Not until it's too late." He sighed and shook his head. "There are too many places he could go and not enough time to get to them all."

"Is there anywhere that stands out?" Director Johnston urged. "Abraham, Isaak, and Simon are all complicit, so it would need to be somewhere that could house at least six people."

"They included that cursed fool, Isaak?" Levi's lip curled and Rebecca shook her head slightly. "They are doomed to fail." Rebecca lifted her head enough to look at him from the corner of her eye. Their tempers had calmed but now they looked almost sad. Roland could practically hear the silent conversation between them, and he wanted to combust. They had information and were deliberately hiding it.

"If you have anything that might help," Jacob leaned forward, "we will get him the help he needs. He's not in his right mind."

"It's not much." Levi sighed and leaned forward, holding out a hand. "If you get me paper and a pen, I can tell you where they won't be. Our families kicked him out for a reason." The items practically appeared, and he began writing.

"If they keep that demon-child with them, they won't be welcome on most of the properties." Rebecca spoke up. "That boy was a curse from the moment he took his first breath."

"Quiet." Levi muttered. Rebecca immediately stopped and folded her hands in her lap again. Levi finished writing and pushed the paper back to the center of the table. "Here are the loyal members of our community that will let me know if they've crossed paths with him or if they show up, they will chase him off their land."

"Thank you." Jacob inclined his head before taking the paper and walking out. Roland was hot on his heels.

They pulled people from each group to start adding the new information to the profile. They eliminated any families or land that were more than three hundred miles east of the last known location. Not only were the residencies considered, but the farmland was too. Each member of the family was in charge of various acreages of either corn, hay, wheat, or barley. Nearly all the business was run with cash, and they didn't keep much in the bank.

Over the years they bought and sold land. A few times during bad years, they lost a few smaller plots of land to the bank. The home Tobias grew up in was part of that group. The land had been bulldozed and turned into a warehouse, so there was one less property to search.

"Hoeft, Evans!" Director Johnston marched back into the room. "You two have the first two rooms down the hall. While we narrow down the search, you two go get some shut eye. We need you alert and ready when we roll out."

"Director." Elliot called as he hung up his cell phone. "An officer was conducting a traffic stop on the west end of box elder when the driver took off. It's Tobias Morgan."

"Are you sure?" The Director asked.

"Body cam footage confirmed it." Elliot nodded. "They're following him all over Rapid City right now, but he hasn't left city limits. My guess is he's trying to avoid leading us back to where they are holding our girls." He pointed at the map. "We have roadblocks on all roads leading out, but they are boxing him in as we speak."

"Alright," Director Johnston said, "see what we can do to help on that end. Roland and Jacob, as hard as it is, I need you two to get some sleep. We have enough people on this right now, and you'll both be more pertinent later." They knew arguing would only get them benched, so they made their way down the hall.

Roland wanted to scream. Everything in him was raging that laying down and sleeping was the wrong thing to do. He walked into the small room and collapsed on the bed. His brain raced through all the information they had so far, trying to find the answers that weren't there. Sighing, he got up and took a shower.

The burning water had him gasping for air. Roland thought back to the safe house. He was so stunned when Catarina just walked into the bathroom, until he saw the look on her face. He could see her struggling to keep it together, but the cracks in her composure ready to do anything to help. The small shower seemed so empty without her next to him and he hated it.

Toweling off, Roland dressed in his clothes for tomorrow. He repacked his bag and put his boots back on. The last thing he wanted was to be woken up to a go order, and still needing to get packed and get his shoes on. Leaving his feet hanging off the end of the bed, Roland let the exhaustion pull him into sleep that was damned near comatose.

Hearing voices, he grumbled. Reaching out for Catarina brought the rest of the memories back like a hurricane. The voice behind his wasn't familiar, but he wasn't worried. Roland saw a young agent waiting for instructions.

"WHAT?" Roland snarled. The guy flinched but didn't move.

"Director Johnston said to wake you." He took a step back when Roland sat up. Every muscle in his body screamed in agony and an audible groan escaped him.

"What time is it?" He tried to stand but his body objected, and he decided to wait a minute.

"A little after six." The agent started back towards the door. "Your medication and pain killers are on the bathroom counter by the water. Also, extra bandages and creams for your injuries are in the go bag beside them. Breakfast is in the main conference room. There are grab and go options for anyone rolling out, but The Director wants to talk to you and Agent Evans before you go." He nodded and left the room before Roland could ask any more questions.

On his way to the bathroom, he felt like every part of him had been backed over by a Seven-Forty-Seven... Repeatedly. He cursed every member of Tobias's family back to his ancestors. The medication went down fine, and he checked the bandages. Reapplying some cremes and wrapping his leg in new dressings, Roland kept the rest in his go bag.

He marched into the conference room and spotted Jacob building a stack of food on his plate. Roland waved to Tyrese, who was still wiping the crud from his eyes while talking to Brandt. They both returned the gesture and continued in their musings.

"Hey man, did you sleep at all?" Roland clapped Jacob on the shoulder and started scooping his own meal.

"Yeah," Jacob groaned at the impact. "Is it wrong that I feel like a bastard for getting a few hours of shut eye?"

"No." Roland started to dig in. "But they know that we will have to rest sometime, and so will they." It didn't take them long to inhale their food. By the time they finished, Brandt and his associates nearly ran into the room.

"Hey, we just got another update." Brandt pulled his phone out his tablet and read the report out loud. "Twelve-oh-five am: Suspect drove off the road, avoiding the spike strip and continuing onto the residential area and officers lost sight. Three-forty: Vehicle found empty and submerged in the river. Four-fifteen: Dogs picked up suspect's scent. Five-fifty: Suspect spotted in local bakery. Six-oh-nine: Suspect barricaded inside abandoned office building."

"That was minutes ago!" Jacob pulled his go bag on.

"Hold on!" Brandt raised a hand, stopping the man mid step. "They have the building surrounded and have caught glimpses of him in the windows on various floors."

"Why haven't we gone in yet?" Roland was baffled at the thought of the officers just waiting around.

"Because the building is a popular spot for meth and drug users. He could take hostages." A mousey woman with braids and plain glasses offered. "We are getting thermal readings on the building in the next half an hour, and he won't be able to leave."

"Alright, let's go." Roland picked up his bag and they made their way out. As long as Tobias was pinned down, Catarina and Katie were safe, in theory. He knew that they would try to escape, and that meant trying their captor's patience. They needed to be found, and quick.

# Chapter 11

Catarina struggled to catch her breath. At the moment, she was tied to the metal frame of a twin bed. Katie was in the one next to her. The sunrise gave her enough light to get her bearings. She had been pulling at the frame, trying to get loose and get the both of them out of there, before anyone in the house woke up.

They had gotten to the cabin late at night. There was a realty sign posted out front, so their odds of being found plummeted. Katie had burns on her hand that needed first aid from the fire, so her hands had been treated and wrapped.

Katie had managed to get her hands on a battery and a gum wrapper. After thinning out the middle of the wrapper and pressing either end to the battery, the middle got hot and started smoking. She had a paper in her pocket and got a flame going. Katie tossed it over to the curtain divider by the wardrobe, spreading quickly. Since it was by the stove, they blamed it on the old electrical system.

Simon immediately ran off and stole a van to finish the journey. The smoke and debris from the fire extinguisher left the RV unusable. They were bound and gagged, then tossed in the back like luggage. Abraham started a small fire in the bed of the RV before they sped off. Catarina kept waiting for the explosion that never came.

They bounced around in the back while the elevation changed drastically. Catarina felt her ears pop and had flashbacks of going up the mountain the first time she had been abducted. There was a screwdriver beside her head that she managed to slowly move down to between her and Katie. Taking the hint, Katie helped work the screwdriver into the rope and slowly loosen the knot enough to get out.

Around one corner, when the van slowed, they pressed the button to open the trunk and took off running into the sunset. Katie had ahold of her supply pack, and Catarina had enough presence of mind to grab a bag full of food. Abraham, Isaak, and Simon all started yelling at once. Catarina scooped up a rock, and mid stride, chucked it back, nailing Simon in the knee, sending him ass-over-end into the gravel.

Isaak sprinted like a freaking track star when he finally got the van put in park. He grabbed Catarina by the hair, but she posted her feet, sliding atop the gravel and tucked her body, thrusting her shoulder into his hips. Isaak's long frame went flying over her and skidded on his ass into a tree beside the primitive road. Abraham was doing his best to keep up with a loose jog, but it was pitiful at best. He had watched Catarina chuck the rock at Simon and copied the strategy.

He was an old bastard, but he had an arm like a rocket. The first rock hit Katie in the shoulder, knocking her to the ground. Catarina sprinted to help her up when the second hit her in the side, knocking the wind out of her. The third and final rock was much smaller but still grazed her temple, sending the world spinning around her. She was able to get her arm up enough to protect her face from the gravel, but the road rash that ran up her arm was awful.

They were loaded back into the car as far from each other as possible. They were running out of time, and she knew it. In a last desperate attempt, she lunged at Abraham who was now driving. She had been sitting in the seat behind him and tried to get him to crash. Isaak was beside her and pulled her back into her seat before elbowing her in the face, turning all the lights off.

She woke up about five minutes before they pulled onto the road that led back to the cabin. All the injuries were cleaned, and they were taken upstairs to a small room at the end of the hall. After being tied to their individual beds, they fell asleep quickly. They would need their rest if they were going to make it out of here alive.

Katie groaned quietly. In the last half an hour or so, Catarina managed to get one foot out of her bindings and was working on the second. Her wrists and ankles were raw and tender, but she didn't plan on dying tonight.

"You up or just having wild sex dreams?" Catarina teased.

"Isaak should've hit you harder." Katie groaned. "I'm good, but I can't move, and I think my sugars are low."

"How low?" Catarina's foot just slipped out of the last loop. Folding her legs over her head, she rolled until she was squatting on her pillow. It felt like someone took a sledgehammer to her ribs. "Are we in a danger zone yet?"

"Not yet, if I can get something to eat." Katie tried to readjust but the bed creaked. They both froze and listened intently, but after a few minutes they didn't hear anything except the low rumble of someone snoring in the hall. There was a burlap bag that had slouched over, spilling fruits and snacks on a small bed, at the other end of the room beside the door.

"Give me a sec, I've almost got it." Catarina whispered.

"There's a set of scissors on the floor by your bed." Katie had lifted her head and was staring at them. Catarina crab walked down the bed and felt around with her feet while Katie gave her instructions. "Left, down a little."

"Got it!" Catarina struggled to pull herself back to where she had been before. The pain in her side was awful and for the first time, she felt serious guilt for hitting Roland with the fire extinguisher when they met the second time. Awkwardly rotating the scissors to a spot where she could grip them, she angled them back and began cutting the rope.

Creeping across the room, Catarina felt around for any area of the floor that might creek. She was going to pick up the bag, but the springs started to squeak. Under the bed, a collection of books were stacked next to their shoes, so she gradually removed the snack bag and replaced the weight with the books Indiana Jones style.

Back across the room, she popped a few grapes into Katie's mouth while she cut her bindings. As slowly as they could, Catarina helped Katie roll to her side. Every time the bed began to squeak, they slowed to an almost unmoving pace. When Katie had a hand and leg on the floor, the snoring from the hall stuttered. They froze, waiting for someone to burst into the room. After a few seconds that passed like molasses, Catarina let out a breath and helped Katie off the bed.

Cautious of the noisy floor that seemed to be itching to give them away, Katie sat and ate as much as she could when they got their shoes on. Catarina was inspecting the window for alarms. They looked old enough to still have weights inside the walls. She unlatched the window and lifted it as carefully as she could. She wanted to cry when it opened silently, until it got stuck halfway.

"Here." Katie whispered through a mouthful of crackers. She came up to the window, lowering it slightly, then lifting it with equal pressure on either side. It finally opened all the way. Katie would be able to fit out the window easily, but Catarina would have some trouble with her 'God given birthing hips' that her mother always commented on.

"Ok, here's the plan," Catarina whispered. "You'll lower yourself out the window and hold onto the frame while I hand you the bag. Drop to the ground and run, I won't be far behind."

"Are you stupid or actually insane?" Katie retorted.

"I mean it's Wednesday, so probably a healthy mix of both." Catarina pointed to the window. "You've seen my entire ass, and there's no way that we are both fitting out the window at the same time."

"Yes, I have, and I also know that they are going to hear when I hit the ground, and you won't have time to get out the window. I'm going to hang on until we are both ready to fall and then *we* take off to find a place to call Director Johnston. Jacob and I do rock climbing regularly. I can hang on just fine."

"Fine, but we have to hurry, or this won't work." Catarina waited while Katie stuck her legs out the window and shifted her hands sideways, giving Catarina room to exit. Catarina handed the bag to her lean friend and followed her out the window. Katie winced when adjusting the bag. Her shoulder was probably aching after getting hit with the rock. Despite the burns on her fingers, Katie held the inside frame of the window like a pro.

"On three." Katie whispered. Their feet were braced against the house, right above a large window. Just to the left was the rear door and if anyone was downstairs, they would be screwed. "One, two…" They heard a large piece of furniture moving on the other side of their door. "Three."

The drop wasn't bad, and they hit the ground rolling backwards to disperse the impact. It was still jarring, but both of them got up and ran awkwardly like you do when your body has had no time at all to warm up first thing in the morning. They had just made the tree line when Abraham yelled from the window.

"They've escaped!!" His voice held so much rage, he damned near shook the trees.

"Well, that didn't take long." Katie laughed. They ran towards the sunrise, hearing the window slamming shut. Catarina's side was killing her. She didn't get a look at her face, but without ice she knew both of them would be bad. Katie popped grapes into her mouth while running and smiled at Catarina.

Behind them, the door to the house rattled as it was yanked shut. Katie changed direction to hide them in the thicker area of trees. They listened but didn't hear any motors running. Catarina was damned near gasping for air, the pain in her side was horrible. Katie kept looking at her over her shoulder and slowed.

"We need to find a way out of here or stand and fight." Katie huffed.

"You go, they only want me." Catarina hated it but it was the only solution she could think of. "Go get help and I will stay alive until then."

"Screw that. Let's just set a fire and evade until help comes." Katie was collecting rocks while she jogged. The movement was fluid and graceful, unlike Catarina who was practically gasping for air.

"I'm pretty sure setting fire to a forest is a federal offense."

"Class four." Katie smirked, leading the way to a cluster of boulders next to a downed tree. They threw a rock into a small crevasse to make sure no animal had it occupied before climbing in. Katie started eating fruit and breakfast bars by the handful while Catarina attempted to start a fire. It was only a few minutes before they heard someone running close by.

"I lost the trail!" Simon yelled, his voice was too close.

"Spread out!" Abraham bellowed, he was farther away. "Don't hurt the thin one, she's done nothing wrong. If Catarina is injured, we will atone to Tobias later."

The footsteps faded away quickly, and Catarina looked around for anything she could use as a weapon. Several yards away, a few trees had died and fallen over. She was sure there would be a branch that she could use as a bat.

"Stay here." Catarina whispered. Katie had leaned back against one of the rocks and was looking pale. "You keep eating and sit tight. There's water in the bag, make sure you drink some." Katie gave a weak nod.

Looking around, Catarina crept out of their hiding place and made her way to the fallen trees. Testing a few of the thicker branches left her feeling defeated. On the other side, there was a branch that didn't appear to be attached to anything. She stepped over the tree and reached for it when a distinct rattle echoed in her ears. Less than four feet away, a huge rattlesnake was coiled and watching her.

It had been hidden by the fallen tree, but now that she was close, it was ready for anything. Trying to calm her breathing, Catarina leaned back from the branch and stepped back to the other side of the tree slowly. As she retreated, she watched the snake loosen before slithering away quickly. When she was checking around the fallen tree again, two alabaster arms yanked her backwards.

Isaak pulled her away in a bear hug. Catarina flared her elbows and dropped. Immediately after her ass hit the ground, she swiveled on it and grabbed his heals. At the same time, she leaned back and threw her feet up into his diaphragm when Isaak leaned forward. The force of the kick coupled with Catarina yanking his heels, sent the man flying backwards. The thud when Isaak hit the ground was sickening. He was gasping for air and making too much noise.

Running over, Catarina wrapped her left arm around his neck before tucking Isaak's against his own face, and sitting into a nice arm triangle. He only flailed for a few seconds before going limp. She threw a rock down the hill and scurried back into their little hideout.

Katie's breathing was better, but her color was still bad. Two sets of footsteps came running before she could ask anything, but only one followed the noise away. Catarina winked at Katie and peaked over the rocks that were hiding them. Simon's small frame was bent over Isaak.

Catarina climbed noiselessly to the top of the rock and leapt just as Simon turned. He grunted loudly when his face hit the hard ground underneath them, but he rolled onto her. His hands closed around her neck, clamping down desperately.

"SHE'S HERE!" Simon's voice echoed off the trees around them. Isaak was stirring beside them when Catarina crossed her arms on top of Simon's. Locking his forearms to her chest she thrust her hips up and to the side. Simon crashed onto Isaak. Rolling forward, she yanked Simon's hands off then punched him in the liver. He dropped like a sack of potatoes.

She climbed to her feet while Abraham was closing in, stopping only feet away. The left side of his face was black and swollen where she had hit him with the stovetop grate. A long knife glimmered against the sunlight in his hand. Isaak and Simon were both no help on the ground. Catarina side stepped, creating distance and putting her back to the rock where Katie was hiding.

"Come quietly so we don't have to do anything……regrettable." Abraham threatened.

"A knife?" Catarina giggled, stepping to the side again where a small mound of loose dirt sat. "If I didn't know any better, I'd think you're flirting with me."

Abraham looked like his brain short-circuited, and she took the opportunity to kick the dirt into his face. When his arms came up, Catarina gave a mother of a front kick to his diaphragm, Spartan-style, sending him backwards. That was the exact moment when someone kicked her own feet out from under her. The world spun and she hit the ground so hard she couldn't breathe.

Isaak sprawled on top of her, pinning her to the ground. While scrambling to get into a better position, Catarina could hear herself gasping for air. Blackness began to close around the edge of her vision, and she started to panic.

Isaak's ice blue eyes bore into hers, but the rage she expected wasn't there. He put one fist against her diaphragm and pushed. The air rushed out of her, and she was able to suck in enough breath for the darkness to fade. Grabbing Isaak's shoulder probably seemed like a gesture of gratitude until Catarina knocked their heads together. In an impressive display of resilience, the blow only stunned him for a second, despite the blood that now poured from his nose. It was enough. She wrapped an arm around his neck and propped his own up in a second arm triangle.

Catarina had just kicked his weight off herself, when Simon grabbed her thighs. Taking a fistful of her own hair with the same arm that was wrapped around Isaak kept the hold tight. Using her now free hand, Catarina reached down the back of Simon's pants. That shocked the kid into stillness that only lasted a few seconds until Catarina ripped his underwear up his back. Letting go while screaming and flailing was more than she had hoped for, but she was pleasantly surprised when it happened.

Isaak's fighting was getting weaker quickly, but Catarina's window to escape was fading fast. She shoved him to the side and rolled in the other direction. Catarina stood up and stumbled. Abraham was running towards her again with the Bowie knife in hand. Someone hit her from behind and she fell towards Abraham. He made to catch her, but mis-stepped and disaster struck.

Searing pain coursed through her when the knife bit into her arm. The knife was just underneath the skin on the outside of her bicep. It was either the luckiest or unluckiest outcome, depending on who was asked. Catarina screamed with pain. The white-hot agony left spasms ripping through her body. Her brain couldn't fathom the foreign object protruding from her, and the longer she stared, the less sense it made. Rolling to her side, with her eyes locked on the knife, she struggled to sit up.

Abraham took ahold of the handle. Before she could string a clear thought together, his dark callous hand ripped it out of her arm. She didn't have enough air to even scream. Blood poured from the wound and in the back of her mind, she watched her hand and fingers moving. If she could move them, then it might have missed most of the important bits. A boot hit her in the chest sending her into the dirt. That seemed to shock the sound out of her. Gritting her teeth didn't muffle the scream and the sound echoed off the forest around them.

"Tie her up." Abraham's voice boomed over her groans of pain. Catarina rolled in an attempt to run, but both Isaak and Simon threw themselves on top of her before she got anywhere. "Get her back to the house and secured while I search for the other one."

"I can't believe you stabbed me, you bastard!" Catarina's voice was jarring even to her own ears, despite being face down in the dirt. Isaak was climbing off her but as soon as he was out of the way, Abraham's boot nailed her in the side. She groaned and coughed while Isaak tied her hands behind her. He wrapped his overshirt tightly around the stab wound that had been bleeding freely while Simon secured her ankles and knees.

"Take her back to the house." Abraham ordered. "If she is smart enough to keep her mouth shut, get her food. If not, let her starve." He turned his back and marched into the trees.

"You're lucky that's all he did after a comment like that." Simon mumbled. Isaak pulled her to her feet before tossing Catarina over his shoulder.

"She won't learn, boy." Isaak said, his voice sounding so similar to Abraham. "This one will fight until she's dead."

"Tobias is going to kill me anyways." Catarina grunted through the pain. Her blood was coloring the shirt on her arm. She caught a slight glimpse of Katie peaking over the rocks and gave her a slight nod. "If I'm going to die for something I didn't do, I might as well earn it."

They made it back to the house in relative silence. By the time she was unceremoniously dumped onto a sofa, Isaak was damned near drenched in sweat. She struggled to sit up while Isaak pulled a bag out of the closet under the stairs. Simon started preparing breakfast.

"Can you get my stuff?" Simon asked while he cracked eggs into a pan.

"You, ok?" Isaak froze, staring with alarm.

"I think I'll be fine if I handle it soon." Simon shrugged. Catarina jumped when Isaak sprinted up the stairs like his ass was on fire.

She heard a door open and close seconds before he returned with a reflective yellow bag. Isaak took over cooking while Simon gave himself an injection. Catarina took her opportunity to take stock of anything she could use as a weapon.

A shadowbox above the back doors held six knives of various shapes and sizes. They were clean and shining in the dull light. Something about the way they laid on the leather cushion made her skin crawl. If she could find anything else, she would make it work. There were the standard kitchen utensils, wall decorations, and the legs on the kitchen chairs and table. She had plenty of options.

Simon took over the cooking again and Isaak cut the bindings on her legs. Catarina jumped to her feet but froze when Isaak wrapped one arm around her front. She would've fought but his other hand pressed the sharp end of a knife to her side, right over her kidney.

He stared down at her, his cool eyes shimmered like he was laughing. Grabbing her bicep, Isaak steered her towards the kitchen table, plopping her down next to the first aid kit. Simon kept glancing back at her over his shoulder.

"I'm going to bandage this up, but we don't have anything for the pain." Isaak muttered as he untied the shirt on her arm.

"What did he take?" Catarina ticked her chin towards Simon.

"It's a clotting agent." Simon answered, raising his voice in a way that let her know that he didn't appreciate being spoken of like he wasn't there. "We've got a family history of hemophilia."

"The royalty disease." Catarina narrowed her eyes at him. Simon lifted his head haughtily, misinterpreting her realization as reverence. The reason it was named the royalty disease was because years of inbreeding among the royals resulted in a laundry list of genetic mutations. "Close family relations then?" A white hand wrapped around her throat, cutting off any other comments.

"You," Isaak gave her a small shake, but she flicked her eyebrow at him with a challenge, "don't get to talk about our family."

"They were the ones who kicked you out, not me." Catarina whispered back. He released her to clean and bandage the wound. She didn't bother trying to keep silent when he flushed the pocket of skin the knife had made. The only other sounds in the house were Simon's cooking. The eggs would probably have smelled amazing if the pain hadn't been making her nauseous.

"When will Tobias be here?" Catarina asked. Isaak was finishing wrapping her arm back up and shrugged. He dropped the metal tools he had used into a huge cup that he had filled with rubbing alcohol.

"The police had him pinned down but that won't last long." Simon stated with an abundance of pride. "They were never caught because Tobias is the best under pressure."

"That's great for him." Catarina caught sight of movement at the edge of the trees where they had come from. Looks like it was now or never. "Sucks for you though!"

She leaned back in the chair, and kicked Isaak in the chest, toppling him and his chair. Grabbing the cup with the rubbing alcohol, she stood and threw it at the open flame on the stove. The fire that ensued was spectacular. Turning, she grabbed the chair she had been sitting on, and used it to beat Isaak. Simon was busy with a fire extinguisher behind her when she dropped the chair back on its legs and used it to climb onto the table.

Launching herself in the air with her hands still tied, she grabbed the shadow box, and it came toppling off the wall. Isaak dove under the table to avoid the glass shards, and Catarina hit the door sprawling into the deck when it opened. With the ropes pulling at her wrists, she climbed to her feet, getting ready to run.

"Go ahead and run!" Abraham called out to her from across the yard. The bag of food was hanging on his arm and Katie's limp body was thrown over his shoulder.

"What did you do to her?" Catarina tried not to panic. She took a step and Abraham pulled a knife from his hip. She didn't miss the threat. Someone yanked her by the hair, pulling her backwards into a body. The sharp blade of a knife cut into her stomach slightly and she jumped.

"Uncle," Simon came out of the house holding the fire extinguisher, "You'd better come and see this." Abraham looked at Simon's worried face, then scowled back at her.

Walking up to the back of the house, his anger escalated until Catarina nearly saw steam coming out of his ears. Katie's limp body hit the ground with a thud when he dropped her. He started raging incoherently. Abraham beat his arms against the side of the house, threw chairs from the deck into the yard, and in a final fit, ran up to her with his arms outstretched. Isaak rotated her to the side in a statement, staring down his father.

"Do you know what you've done?!" Spittle flew from Abraham's lips and Catarina turned her head away. "Those knives are worth more than any life here! Not yours, not hers, not even mine!"

"We will make sure she pays." Isaak soothed. "Simon, take the other one inside and tie her to her bed. This one will clean her mess." Simon immediately picked up Katie and disappeared into the house. Isaak began walking Catarina to the doors. The box had hit the table but got hung up on two of the chairs. Glass was everywhere.

"You're lucky great grandfather Ismael wasn't hurt." Abraham seethed. "Your punishment would be a lot worse if he had." She was going to ask what he meant but the knife bit deeper into her side.

Catarina watched the old man gently round up the odd-looking knives and set them delicately on the table beside the box. He took so much care that if she hadn't known any better, she would've written him off as a defenseless old man. Resting the box on the table, Abraham lifted out the strange leather pillow the knives had been sitting against.

"There you go grandfather." Abraham muttered while wiping the glass off. Tattoos covered the dark leather pillow. The intricate black lines wove in and out of a mural. Flaming corpses and limbs scattered in grotesque horror on the leather-like material. Realization stole her breath when the dots connected, the pillow was made from human skin, and she gagged audibly.

"Don't..." Isaak started, but it was too late.

"Tie her to the post!" Abraham shouted before reaching back into the box. Isaak dragged her down the steps to a burn pile a little way from the house. Just feet away from it was a large metal post that stood straight out of the ground. Simon came out of the house with a handful of ropes, jogging down to where they stood.

"I can't save you from this." Isaak whispered while tying her hands to the ring far above her head. "Try to breathe. It won't kill you, but you will want to die."

"Ten lashes for your escape, the injuries you've caused, and damaging the ceremonial box. The other will receive her four for the escape when she wakes."

"No." Catarina looked over her shoulder at Abraham. An old whip hung from his hands. Cat O' Nine Tails. Fuck me running. She swore to herself. The next words were out of her mouth before she had a chance to think them through or regret her decision. "She's diabetic, and you can't guarantee that she won't get infected. I'll take hers. She wouldn't be here if it wasn't for me. I'll take 'em all." She turned back to the post and leaned her forehead against it, waiting for the blow.

Heavy footsteps walked up behind her. The distinct scent of mildew and pepper wafted over while Abraham sliced down through the back of her tank top, her exposed back prickling at the warm air. With one swift movement, he unclasped her bra. Tears blurred her vision at the impending pain.

"You're not brave." Abraham seethed in her ear. "Fourteen lashes, you will break." Desperately, she took deep breaths, trying to find enough oxygen when he stepped back again. Focusing on a scratch in the pole, she tried to mentally escape while she could.

Then the whip cracked.

# Chapter 12

Roland followed the agent around the dark corner. The old building was abandoned after the owner took out a number of loans and 'disappeared'. There were a few rumors that hinted at mob dealings, but no one ever claimed the building. There were eight teams of three that were clearing it floor by floor and separate teams covering each of the exits.

Director Johnston had already reached out to law enforcement in each area where it was possible that the women were being kept. So far, they were dead ends. While they were going over the plan for this raid, Roland couldn't help but notice how the infiltration team avoided eye contact and kept extra distance when they did talk to him.

Roland waited for the signal before kicking the next door open and barging into the next room. A few people were laid out on soiled mattresses and some just laid where they fell after shooting up with whatever their drug of choice was. A glint of red hair disappeared around the other side of a filing cabinet, and he had to stop himself from sprinting after it.

"On me." Agent O'Brien called, rushing to the spot where the hair disappeared. Roland made sure to clear every corner where someone could be hiding. Rounding the edge of the cabinet, their flashlights lit up the curly hair of a young woman with her hands up in surrender.

"What's your name?" Roland asked. The woman couldn't have been older than twenty. Her dirty clothes hung loose on her small frame, while her pupils were dilated wide with obvious drug use.

"Ava." She said, turning her hand over in the light, enthralled by the sight. "Do you have some Molly? I'll do anything." She giggled like she didn't understand the severity of what she was suggesting. Her face was flushed shining with sweat.

"No." Agent O'Brien answered. "Have you seen someone around here that looks like you? You know, the red hair?"

"Oh," She held both hands over her mouth with a gasp. "You've lost someone? Here," she waved a hand for them to follow while she led them to a door, "there's always a few people that stay in the tunnels if they don't want to be bothered."

"Tunnels?" Roland asked. "What tunnels?"

"Easy," O'Brien warned, "you already look like you're going to blow a gasket." They continued following the woman down several flights of stairs, always checking people and spaces.

"Is that why you all have been avoiding us?" Roland grumbled. Ava waited patiently while they cleared a broom cupboard, like she was used to guiding paranoid people. Finally, they reached the basement.

"Just you." His voice was casual but to the point. Shooting a quick glance at Roland's enraged expression, O'Brien continued. "It's not personal. You look like you could walk through an atom bomb," he paused to clear a doorway, "and right now you're on edge because your girl is gone. Everyone is waiting for you to combust or Hulk-out or something and no one wants to be in the way when it happens."

"Glad to know self-control means jack shit to your company. I'm not that scary." Roland came around a corner to see someone lying on the floor. It looked like the man had been dead for a while. Roland cleared the rest of the small room.

"Everyone is afraid of something." They reached another set of stairs.

"What are you afraid of?" Roland asked.

"Someone saying some funny-ass-shit while I'm playing dead." O'Brien smiled before following the girl down the stairs. Roland liked him, he seemed like he was good company.

They continued down several twists and turns before their radios squelched an all clear for the building. They radioed back the new information about the tunnels. Ava had slowed significantly and was singing softly to herself. Roland's heart sunk when they came up to a section that forked off into three tunnels. They had gotten the news about this building over an hour ago and no one had seen Tobias, so he had to be down here somewhere.

Ava sighed and sat down on a pile of cushions that looked like they were caked into the dirt. It was likely that this was a storm drain the city had overlooked when doing renovations to keep people from taking up residency. Roland made a note to point that out later.

"Get two more teams down here." O'Brien ordered into his radio. "We are taking the left and right tunnels."

"Who said we were taking those ones?" Roland argued while making his way to the tunnel on the right.

"I did, because people are statistically more likely to choose one side or the other rather than going straight up the middle. " He stated, holding his middle finger in the air with a smile and a nod. Roland smirked at the dig, then they split up.

Roland had to focus on not sprinting through the tunnel and remember the check everyone he passed. The blackness ahead and behind him was eerie. When he thought he heard footsteps following him, Roland pressed himself against the wall, and shut his light off. The last thing that he wanted was to be blindsided. The second ticked by in what seemed like an eternity. When a light started to shine around one of the bends he had passed, he stood in a low ready.

"Who's back there?" Roland yelled and the light stopped moving before anyone rounded the corner.

"Rapid City S.R.T., Sargent McCombs." The voice boomed around the corner. "What's your name?"

"Agent Hoeft, and I haven't Hulked out yet." Roland responded. "You're clear to catch up." The light moved forward followed by three bodies.

"It's nothing personal." Agent McCombs nodded, and they continued. "The center tunnel stopped about a thousand yards in. "You should've waited. Just because we got orders to allow you on the raid doesn't mean you get your own special rules." His voice was gruff. "You're just in the way and would be better off anywhere else."

"We're all special in our own way Sargent." Roland had to bite back a laugh when the tunnel stopped. Roland started to climb the rungs up to the manhole cover above. "You should be proud of yourself," he called back, "lots of windows in that building and I didn't see you licking one!"

Someone snickered below him and several blows followed. Roland made it to the cover and braced his body to push it up just enough to look around. In the back of his mind, he could hear the others muttering to themselves waiting for him to fail.

"You're not going to lift that, it's too heavy." McCombs mocked. "Even for someone like you. I've tagged our location and we can come back here above ground." Roland ignored him. After checking the vicinity, he lifted the cover aside and climbed into the street.

"You coming?" Roland leaned back over the drain. It was a small side road and there were no cars coming. "There's a store across the way, here, and I'm pretty sure they've got glue you can huff. Maybe even spray-paint if you're into that." They were all climbing up the rungs now.

"Anyone ever tell you?" McCombs climbed onto the street beside him. "You're asking for a beating, rude fucker."

"I didn't get almost eight years of successful undercover work in my resume by being cute." Roland went chest to chest with the man. "If you need your ego stroked, then join the Airforce." Roland deliberately turned his back, leaning down and replacing the manhole cover. "If you can work on a team and your balls aren't weighing you down, you're welcome to join the rest of us on a hunt for a fugitive. Just wave if you get your tongue stuck to another flagpole," he started walking up the street, "some one's bound to come piss on it for you."

They spent the next hour canvassing the area and checking cameras. The other tunnel led to the southeast of town into a residential zone. Someone had caught Tobias on a doorbell camera. Director Johnston had the local police doing grid searches and called their teams back to the hotel.

Roland showered quickly when he got back to his room. It was about seventy-five degrees out but in all his gear, the pressure he was under, and the running, he needed it. The cool water helped calm a fraction of the day's stress, but Catarina and Katie were still missing.

A box was waiting for him on the bed when he went to grab his clothes. The black card with gold lettering told him exactly who it was from: John. Roland opened the box, pulling out several shirts. They were thicker and more ridged than he liked, but they were still the same T-shirt style he was comfortable with. A note fell onto the bed and Roland scooped it up.

*Roland,*

> *Cute that that's what you're going by now. You owe me a phone call when this shit blows over. Wear these until then. Elliot and I have been experimenting with a new body armor and came up with this ugly-ass-shit. I'll use small words to explain it for you. It's a mix of synthetic spider-silk, Kevlar, and liquid armor. Wear the padding inside the shirt for my benefit. It's meant to stop a bullet and disperse some of the foot-pounds of impact. If you still can't understand that I will send you a dictionary next. Elliot said to use your brain before your muscles because only you would waste his genius using this to run through walls. Wonderful to see you two still getting along. Bring our girls home safe, and make sure Cat calls me when you do. I have a few things for her.*

> *John.*

Roland laughed for the first time in the last twenty-four hours. Under the shirts was a pile of what looked like light padding. He knew it was deceivingly thin and anyone not looking for it wouldn't see it. Underneath those were several loose button-down shirts. Roland got dressed and headed out to the makeshift bullpen.

Jacob was bent over a file wearing a similar overshirt. He looked like lasers were about to shoot out of his eyes. If Roland didn't intervene quickly, the paper would probably burst into flame. Jacob didn't even hear him walking up.

"What did you guys find?" Roland pitched his voice a little louder than needed, but Jacob snapped out of his trance. A few heads turned and several of them closed in to see what piece of the puzzle had fallen into place.

"I'm not sure." Jacob kept studying the file before moving towards one of the whiteboards. "What health issues did we find in their family history?" He looked up and two of the agents had their hands raised. "This isn't preschool, call it out."

"Hemophilia, cleft palate, and albinism." One agent answered.

"Infertility and tumors." Another agent nodded.

"A few cases of scoliosis." A third chimed in.

"Of those," Jacob started shifting through one of the piles of paper, "Only a few of them require pharmaceutical use for symptoms, pain management, or treatment."

"And someone has one that requires a regular refill, we can narrow down the search area." Roland chimed in. Jacob found the file he was looking for.

"It looks like Isaak just has albinism, and the occasional migraine, but no CT scan to see if there's a tumor or not. Abraham might have scoliosis, but there's no medical history besides a broken arm and sprained ankle after a fall from a ladder seven years ago."

"And we're sure it really was a fall from a ladder?" Brandt walked up. "There's a history of family brutality: missing fingers for stealing, beatings for disrespect, and even whipping for more serious offenses."

"The hospital report says that he was helping paint his cousin's dining room and the step on the old wooden ladder broke." Jacob flipped a few more pages. "There was fresh paint still drying on his clothes when they patched his arm up, and primer dried under his nails."

"What do you mean more serious offenses?" Roland's mind was stuck in a loop with Brandt's revelation.

"One of Abraham's nieces, Cecilia, was watching several children while they were doing a tattoo ceremony. The second youngest in that group, Rachael, snuck away while the children were playing and drowned." Brandt's eyes traveled over the papers pinned on the boards while he spoke. "Rachel was only three. Cecilia was fourteen and was supposed to marry her cousin Obadiah."

"He was the driver during the original crash to help Tobias escape." Jacob walked over and pointed to the picture that was pinned beside the crash photos. "He died on impact. What happened to Cecillia?"

"Um..." Brandt was a man known to never be uncomfortable in any situation. Roland watched this man explain to a jury, in graphic and explicit detail, a human trafficking initiation involving mutilation, amputation, and exploitation of involved parties. Right now, standing in front of Roland, this man was sweating, and deliberately avoiding eye contact.

"What happened to Cecilia?" Roland could feel his own blood pressure rising. Brandt looked at him and shook his head slowly. Roland knew what he was going to say before it ever left his mouth.

"I'm telling you as a friend, don't torture yourself with the what if's. You don't need this added onto your mental load." Brandt took a step forward with his palms up, waiting for Roland to lash out.

"Don't tell me what I need." Roland was barely concealing his anger. "What happened to Cecilia?"

"We can handle it." Jacob came to stand between them, using his body to try and diffuse the tension. Brandt started to fidget with the rings on his hands.

"She was tied to a post and received eight lashes every week until she turned eighteen." Brandt's stated the facts in an even tone with no emotion. "Then she disappeared. Other members over the age of eighteen have had their fingers, toes, tongues, eyes, and ears removed depending on the infraction, and the severity. Burn by fire, boiling water, or oil, were also pretty common. Because she was under eighteen and unmarried, she was spared something much worse."

"Where did we get the information we have on them?" Jacob's voice cracked. "It's not like we can infiltrate their group, how do we know the information is accurate?"

"Some of the younger cousins ran away and were in the system for a while." Director Johnston said. "We could never bring up a case because none of them were willing to testify. We don't know what they do with their dead since there has never been any formal paperwork drawn up. We suspect though, that there is some sort of ritualistic burial in tune with their individual belief system."

"So, we have no evidence and no idea what's happening to Katie or Catarina?" Jacob seemed somber, but Roland could hear the edge in it.

"Actually, I'm having one of the cousins flown back here as we speak to get more insight." The Director looked at his watch and sighed. "She will be here in the next half an hour. Her name is Sarah. She was thirteen when her and her sister escaped. Her twin, Ava, fell off the grid a few months ago…"

"Ava?" Roland interrupted and everyone stilled around him. "Director, do we have a picture of either of them?"

"Throw it up on the screen." Director Johnston called out without breaking eye contact. Roland could see him holding back any questions.

"It's her." He confirmed. Director Johnston waved an agent over. "I saw her in the building when we were clearing it. She was a lot thinner, but it was her. She asked for Molly, so she probably dropped off the grid on a bender." The Director whispered instructions and the agent ran off. Roland redirected his attention to the folder in Jacob's hand. "What were you saying about the medical history of the family?"

"Oh yeah," Jacob shook his head and looked back at the board. "There was a file in the hospital at Elgin, North Dakota, on a John Doe that matches the general family description from about two years ago. Red hair, green eyes, and freakishly tall. He did a brain scan and paid in cash. The notes in the file state that John Doe had severe hemophilia along with a rare brain tumor at the base of his skull."

"How do they know it's connected to our case?" Brandt asked.

"They didn't." Jacob stated. "One of agents sorting through all the hospital information has some sharp eyes and flagged it as important." Jacob looked at one of the agents typing away on a keyboard in the 'research' section of the room. "Hey, will you bring up the Emergency Room footage in Jacobsen Memorial Hospital on November Fifteenth, two years ago at two-thirty pm?"

"Why two-thirty?" Roland asked. "And how do they have all that footage this long?"

"Because it can take up to three hours to be seen and they were checked in at three. They were part of an experimental project to keep all their records digitally uploaded to a cloud server and only cleared every seven years. Stop there!" Jacob called out. Walking through the doors of the hospital was a tall red-headed kid with an older man they all knew. "That's Abraham."

"What's the rest of the diagnosis?" Roland asked. "Brain tumors will have a lot of paperwork."

"Well, it looks like he was given less than three years to live. He is on several pain killers and antibiotics. Basically, trying to give him a decent quality of life for as long as they can." Jacob flipped through a few pages and stopped. "His last prescription was maxed out and he probably doesn't have a lot of time left. If he dies, that might set the rest of them off."

"We need to talk to Sarah the second she gets here." Roland's voice was on edge.

"Hold it." Director Johnston's voice boomed. "It's almost five and you two haven't eaten since this morning. I will not have this operation blown because you two idiots got lightheaded deciding that food was beneath you." He threw a thumb over his shoulder. Jacob and Roland damned near ran out of the room.

The dinner that had been provided was the equivalent of a cookout. Brats, burgers, hotdogs, chicken, fruits, and various salads. There was a small line forming, and they waited just like everyone else. Tina was in the line too.

"Hey, Tina." Jacob waved to get her attention. The poor woman looked surprised and started stuttering.

"Oh! I.... um.... the laptop...." She pointed to the doors, "I have someone on it... It's not been left... I mean... someone is watching…"

"Hey, hey, hey." Jacob held his hands up. "I know you've got it handled. I just wanted to apologize."

"We both do." Roland pitched in.

"Freaking out right next to you and dragging you around by the arm isn't ok and I'm very sorry. If you want to find someone else to cover the monitoring, we will completely understand."

"Oh," Tina visibly relaxed, "No, I'm good. I mean with the legacy you guys already built, then the first time meeting you, I thought you were a no excuses hard ass. I thought you were coming here to chew my ass for not being with the laptop every second."

"God no!" Jacob laughed, it was harsh and probably more tense than he meant it, but it was a laugh. "I just want to apologize for everything and tell you what a great job you're doing."

Tina gave a grateful nod and got her food. Roland and Jacob couldn't find the energy to talk, but they made their way through the line and got their food. There were several tables all around the room, but they found their own near the back. Basically, inhaling his, Roland thought through the new information and how that changed the situation. If Catarina and Katie had any chance of surviving, they would need to either sit tight or fight like hell.

When they finished, they found The Director and made their way to the conference room where a healthy young red-head sat at the desk. Sarah was the spitting image of Ava. The Director sat across from her while Roland and Jacob sat on either side of him.

"Director Johnston, right?" Sarah stood and held out a hand. Her voice was soft and delicate. Roland thought she would have the perfect voice for reading to children.

"Correct," Director Johnston took it and pointed to the others. She sat with a nod. "This is special Agent Hoeft and Special Agent Evans. They were on an undercover operation for over five years where they encountered Tobais and Samuel Morgan, your second cousins."

"The trial on TV." Sarah shuddered. "I saw that Tobias and a few other prisoners escaped. How can I help?"

"During their undercover operation, a civilian was abducted and used as leverage for one of the events." Director Johnston was clear direct in the way Roland had always known him to be, and it eased the tension in the room. "At the end of the operation, a worldwide serial killer was taken down, but unfortunately Samuel was killed in the crossfire. Tobias had what was diagnosed as a psychotic break, and put the blame for Samuel's death on that civilian."

"Oh my God." Sarah raised trembling hands to her mouth in horror. "He went after them, didn't he?" The Director nodded before he took his cell phone out and sent a quick text.

"He did," Director Johnston set his phone down on the table, "along with several other family members: Abraham Morgan, Isaak Havard, Simon Morgan, and Obediah Morgan." At the mention of Obadiah, Sarah's eyes went wide. Three things happened at once: Tyrese walked into the room, Sarah fainted, and Director Johnston leapt to his feet, catching her head before it could hit the table.

"Shit!" Tyrese yelled in surprise.

"Doctor," The Director said casually, "impeccable timing as usual. I believe our guest here will need some help getting through a difficult conversation."

Tyrese walked over and leaned her back into her seat. Roland got up and grabbed a bottle of cold water out of the mini fridge. When he got back to the table, Sarah was awake and apologizing.

"I would like to be more delicate," Director Johnston blazed on while Tyrese monitored her pulse, "but we simply don't have the time. Tobias plans on torturing and killing our friend, and we need to know where he might take her and the other agent." Sarah was sipping water and set the bottle on the table.

"Her?" She whispered. "You need to find her fast. If Tobias has mentally broken, he will be worse than his father…… His father was a monster." Roland could feel his blood pressure spike while she continued. "If they are all with him, then she won't be able to escape."

"Obadiah died on impact when he ran a crudely armored car into the prison transport bus." Jacob said it gently, but Sarah's eyes rolled back into her head and Tyrese caught her this time.

"This is going to be a long interview." The Director grumbled. It was so out of pocket for him that it surprised a chuckle out of the rest of them. Once again, after Sarah was awake and talking, they continued.

"Where have you narrowed it down to?" Sarah asked. Tyrese laid a map down and Roland waved a hand around the areas that they hadn't ruled out. "If Abraham and Isaak are working together, that's either really good, or really, really bad. I met up with Isaak a few years ago and he was still angry about being thrown out. He was determined to prove his father wrong or drag the rest of the family to hell with him."

"Prove him wrong about what?" Jacob asked.

"Abraham was convinced that Isaak's skin was a mark from the Gods that their family was cursed for what he did." Sarah was trembling while she spoke, while tears rolled down her face. "Abraham found out his wife was slowly putting foxglove leaves in his food. Not all at once, but slowly over time so he would get weak and stop hitting her. Because of it, he beat her repeatedly for a week. She became deformed and not long after, she found out she was pregnant. She died giving birth to Isaak. Normally with something like that they would just drop off the baby at hospital, but Abraham couldn't let him go. Isaak reminded him of the worst parts of himself, but Martha was the best thing in Abraham's life, and the last part of her was with Isaak."

"Do you know where they would take her?" Director Johnston pushed.

"There are a few family cabins they might be able to stay at if they keep Isaak out of sight." She sniffled. "Do you have a closer map of this area?" Jacob ran out of the room to get it. "They ruined our lives, my sister's and mine, and I haven't seen her in years. I want you to find them and put them in prison. They don't deserve anything better. My sister Ava got addicted to drugs to deal with it all, and I have been trying to find her and get her to rehab now that I have the money." She stood up straight.

"We found her this morning." The words flew out of him before he could think, and Sarah clattered to the floor under the impression that her sister was dead. Tyrese threw a water bottle at him, and Director Johnston smacked his arm with the file he had rolled into a club.

"Hoeft, I could shoot you." Director Johnston threatened but it was halfhearted at best. Jacob walked back I with a paper and Elliot on his heels.

"I told you guys that he's too ugly for the general public!" Elliot chirped with a smile. "Don't worry miss, he'll be heading back to his bell tower soon." He waved at Roland.

"Elliot, if you like this job then I suggest you conduct yourself like an adult with the rest of us before you find yourself designing a new resume." Director Johnston snapped at him.

"You're a horrible man." Sarah scowled at Elliot. Roland perked up at her dislike for him.

"Would you like some food?" Roland offered. "I would love to get you a plate."

"No thank you, but another water would be amazing," Sarah gave him a soft smile. Roland got up with a spring in his step.

They spent the next thirty minutes diving into the map and properties that they knew of and a few that they were unaware of. On top of that Sarah had given them an entire page of names that property could've been purchased with. There was a new sense of urgency that came with the information. All the locations were within a two-hour drive.

# Chapter 13

Catarina had done it. She had taken the blows for the both of them. At first, she was determined not to cry out. The initial blow knocked the wind out of her and buckled her knees. The next few were worse, and then she couldn't help it. Her agony tore through her throat and had the birds flying away. At some point she lost consciousness, then a bucket of water was dumped over her head. Tobias mocked her. When she finally got to her feet, he finished the perverse punishment. She screamed then too.

Isaak had placed himself directly in her line of sight, maintaining eye contact, but never lifting a hand to help. The look in his eyes made her skin crawl. It didn't seem like he was enjoying her pain but there was an intensity that radiated of him. No one was going to come to her rescue, and she knew it, so she didn't try to stop the tears. Catarina was sobbing and so engulfed in her own pain that she never heard Simon fall.

Isaak sprinted towards the man. Abraham dropped the whip and joined them. There was enough length in her bindings that Catarina was able to watch the scene unfold. Out of the corner of her eye she saw the whip on the ground, her own bright red blood staining the ends.

Abraham gathered Simon in his arms like a child and carried him inside the house, Isaak following close behind. Catarina's head spun while she tried to get her shit together. She couldn't reach the ring where the ropes were tied to, but she might be able to climb.

Glancing back at the house to make sure no one was watching, she wrapped her legs around the pole and tried to pull herself higher. It was like lightning burning its way through her. Every muscle in her back spasming uncontrollably and she went limp with the pain.

Footsteps nearby shocked her, but she didn't bother moving. She had forgotten how many lashes she had been through, but if more were coming, she didn't want to see. A shockingly white hand wrapped around her throat and lifted her head. Isaak stared down at her with a soft expression.

"What happens now?" Catarina's voice cracked with a sob. Isaak brushed her hair back out of her face.

"Now, I take you upstairs to clean your back and arm." Isaak said. "If you can behave, you might be able to eat later." Letting her go, he stood behind her and reclasped her bra. She managed not to cry out again, but it took a lot of effort. Then, he surprised her by grabbing the bottom ends of her shirt and tied them in a knot that kept it secured.

"Wait." She breathed when he started untying her from the post. "Has anyone checked on Katie? Her sugars were really low this morning." Isaak stopped.

"You're asking about her, when you just took fourteen of the worst lashes I've seen in a long time?" Isaak looked stunned.

"Well, someone has to live to tell the world how fucking funny I am." Catarina snarked with tears and snot still streaming down her face.

That surprised a short laugh out of Isaak, and he finished untying her. Even though he left her hands bound, she didn't try to run. Her body was still in too much agony to make it far. Every step she took was weak and Isaak held her arm to keep her from falling. He tied her face down on the bed and left for supplies.

Katie was still out cold and bound to her own bed. Her color looked a little better than it had earlier. She could hear the voices from the bedrooms across the hall, and didn't bother to wake Katie. A few minutes later Isaak came back. Sitting on the edge of the bed, he began untying her shirt and unclasping her bra. Catarina put her face in the pillow to muffle her cries of pain.

"Here." Isaak lifted her face and put a thick towel under it. "It's better at muffling the sound." He continued to clean with quick efficient hands. She could feel where her skin had been cut open and screamed into the towel when those spots were touched. Catarina was covered in sweat and shaking by the time he finished with her back. He silently moved onto her arm.

"What happened?" Katie's voice was soft in the room. Catarina lifted her head with a whimper, despite the pain that shot through her body.

"You're awake!" Her own voice was shaky. That's when she saw the bowl with the bloody towels by the bed. It looked bad.

"How long have I been out? What happened to you?" Katie begged.

"She took the lashes for both of you." Isaak said softly. "Abraham has only ever delivered a punishment that harshly once before."

"Aww, come on he's just saying that." Catarina snickered. "I'm doing great! He pulled his punches like a gentleman."

"Now I know you're a fucking lying." Katie laughed. "He found me hiding and I walked up to him with my hands up ready to surrender and the next thing I know, I'm waking up here."

"He's never normally like that." Isaak mumbled more to himself than anyone else.

"Could be that bump on his head." Catarina suggested before turning her attention back to Katie. "How are you feeling? Where are your sugars at?"

"I'm ok," Katie laid her head back down and Catarina did the same, "I'm pretty sure I'm still on the low end, so if you've got some juice or fruit that would be nice." Isaak collected his supplies and left the room. "Lashes? Like you were whipped?" Her voice was full of concern, but Catarina didn't have the energy to look at her.

"You always read about the famous *Cat O' Nine Tails* in the history books, but it's not nearly as fun as they made it sound." Catarina tried to sound funny, but the joke fell flat.

"How many times?" Katie demanded.

"I was told fourteen but I lost count." She gave a tired laugh that was filled with sadness and pain. "I need to sleep a bit. I might come up with a better plan once my brain has had time to rest."

"Cat, I'm so sorry." Katie's voice cracked. "You didn't have to take my beating for me."

"If you think I'm not going to watch over you the same way you've done for me, you've lost your damned mind. But its ok, I can roll with crazy."

"Can I do anything?" She sounded desperate.

"What I need is nothing you can provide, but thanks anyway." Catarina teased.

"Don't leave me hanging, what is it?" Katie sounded a little brighter, it was forced but it was an effort.

"Cookies and an orgasm." Catarina cracked and they both snickered quietly. Catarina's laughs quickly turned to tears. Those tears shook her endurance and with every tremor her body and mind screamed in agony. Vaguely she remembered Isaak coming back into the room, but Catarina was drifting into the safety of her dreams.

A sharp stabbing sensation in her back shocked her out of her temporary escape. Her head shot up looking around for the cause. Isaak was sitting on the bed beside her. Looking over at Katie, she was relieved that her friend was still in the room. A sniffle brought her eyes back to the man beside her. He had been crying.

"I'm just changing the dressings." Isaak said quietly. Catarina laid her head back down.

"What's going on? Somethings happened." Catarina mumbled. Her voice was groggy with her sinuses swollen.

"Simon's dead." Isaak nearly whimpered. "That tumor finally won. He's been fighting it for so long…" Isaak sounded like he was barely keeping himself together.

"I'm so sorry for your loss." Katie whispered.

"I'm sorry us being here ruined your last memories of him." Catarina added.

"You two didn't choose to be here," Isaak whispered after a pause. "He got one last adventure." Finishing up, his hands were gentle. "The ceremony will be in a few hours. I will bring some food up so you two won't be hungry while we are preparing him to meet the Gods." He laid a cool damp cloth over Catarina's back before collecting his things and leaving. Somewhere in the house they could hear Abrahams muffled sobs. They were pitiful and broken.

"What time is it?" Catarina whispered.

"It's a little after noon, maybe closet to one." Katie mused. "Are you ok? You started laughing, then crying and I'm pretty sure you passed out."

"Oh, it's just your, normal, everyday, run of the mill nervous breakdown." Catarina tried to laugh through the aching in her shoulders. "Happens every time."

"Every time you're kidnapped or beaten?" Katie made the effort to keep the mood light and Catarina was more than grateful for it.

"Meh, take your pick." Catarina sighed. "You think of anything to help us get out?"

"Sorry, I didn't." Katie mumbled. "I was thinking though, if we ever get out of here, the least I can do is make you a bridesmaid. You know if Jacob ever gets up the nerve to pop the question."

"I'm down with that." Catarina smiled. "I do have one condition though, no escape rooms." They both tried to relax for the next few hours.

At one point, Isaak came in with a few sandwiches. He untied them one at a time to eat and use the bathroom. Neither one of them tried anything though, not with the risk of death to the other.

Catarina struggled with even the smallest movements, including using the bathroom. When she got a look at her back in the mirror, her breath caught in her throat. Raised purple and red welts crisscrossed her back where the skin was still intact. Deep red gashes split her skin wide in a gruesome display of brutality. Each time she moved, several of the crevasses split and dripped crimson. Opening the door, she found Isaak in the hall waiting to take her back to her bed.

"I know it's horrific now," he said wile tying her back up, "but you're not dead yet, and that counts for something." Isaak rested a hand on her forearm with a small squeeze that could've been interpreted as just about anything before leaving again. They were quiet for a long time until the sound of heavy furniture moving around startled them.

"How much of the footage from the cabin did you see?" Catarina asked Katie.

"All of it that you were in, and everything that Daniel was in too."

"What were your thoughts on the whole thing?" Catarina sighed. "I need a distraction."

"Well, when you first got there, I thought you were for sure going to die of infection." Katie was trying to keep the mood light. "I couldn't believe you escaped as many times as you did. Between the hypothermia and the infection, a bunch of us had a bet going to see if you would successfully escape."

"I'm pretty sure whatever guardian angel I've got has a drinking problem by now." Catarina itched her nose on her arm that hadn't been stabbed.

"I thought you two were going to get caught when you broke out of the cell in the basement, and he held you."

"I knew it was a cell!" Catarina laughed. "Wait you could see that? It was pitch black down there!"

"Special enhanced night vision cameras." Katie confirmed. "You could see the regret on Roland's face when he decided to stop you. He was watching you every second he could without getting caught. Every time you clapped back at him, he fell more in love with you."

"I thought it was just the drugs blurring my interpretation." Catarina chuckled then winced with the pain in her back.

"We were all blown away that you realized you were being drugged, by the way." Katie laughed. "John and Elliot had a field day when they realized the chemical wasn't as inconspicuous as they thought."

"Oh no I thought I was losing my mind the first few days. But I started to notice the effects were stronger within an hour of the 'antibiotics', and I made the connection." Catarina admitted. "So how do you think Jacob is handling this?"

"Probably just about as well as Roland." Katie let out a huff. "They will find us. We just have to stall long enough. I'm surprised they didn't connect the RV to all this yet, my underwear was blowing in the wind when I attached it to the vent."

"Wait, that was your metallic purple underwear flapping in the wind?" Catarina lifted her head to gawk at the other woman who nodded while giggling. "Why metallic purple?"

"I forgot to wash my stuff before we were heading to the second safehouse, so that's what I had."

They talked through the next few hours about everything from life over the last year, to future plans, and family history. Outside the window, the sky changed from an azure blue, to burnt orange, and finally to a deep navy. She could feel the faint pangs of hunger starting when a set of shoes marched up the stairs.

Isaak walked into the room. He had changed into a floor length dark purple loincloth with shining gold embroidery and a cloak to match. The contrast between the clothing and his skin was so shocking, he looked like he had been plucked from a Greek fable. He had what looked like two bottles of juice.

"We don't have time to make dinner before the ceremony," Isaak said, "these are meal replacement shakes, for tonight. I will take you one at a time to use the bathroom, then you can have your drink. Witnessing this ceremony is a great honor. You will not speak, or you will be gagged. You will not scream, you will not try to escape, and you will not interrupt. We are laying our family to rest, and he deserves peace during this process." Isaak walked over and began untying Katie. "Do either of you get queasy or faint at the sight of blood?" Katie and Catarina shared a nervous look before shaking their heads. Katie drank her shake before Isaak led her out of the room.

Catarina tested her movement as much as she could. Her body protested harshly leaving her gasping for breath. She felt so useless. Last time she had been in this situation, no one had cared that she had dropped off the map. This time people were looking for her. She just had to stay alive long enough to be found, escaped or not. The door to the room opened again.

"I've got this shirt if you want it." Isaak clasped her bra again and began untying her bonds. "You have to promise not to fight or run. I wouldn't have to say that to anyone else but you."

"I'll take the shirt." Catarina's breath caught and she whimpered when she brought her arms down. She knew she would be stiff, but her body felt like she had been cast in stone. Every movement gave the sensation that shards of glass were embedded in her joints and muscles, slicing her apart bit by bit. "I think my body deserves a bit of a break before the next peak of this adventure."

He gave her the drink and Catarina downed it all in one shot. The belch that followed was horrifyingly amazing and probably should've been recorded for posterity's sake. Isaak just smirked and handed her a dark blue shirt. Catarina got both her arms into the shirt but got stuck trying to lift it over her head when her shoulders spasmed. Isaak stood in front of her, and gently pulled it the rest of the way on, avoiding her back when it was possible.

"Thanks." She muttered. Isaak nodded back before helping her to her feet and letting her have a few moments alone in the bathroom.

He led her downstairs to where the furniture had been pushed up against the wall. Simon was laid out on a shining steel table in the center of the room. His body was covered by a small cloth giving him a nominal show of modesty in death. Catarina hesitated on the step, tears blurring her vision. He looked just like Sam. Isaak took her forearm and led her the rest of the way.

Katie was sitting on a chair beside the front door, both hands secured to the wall beside her with metal shackles that looked like they were pulled from a historical film. A second chair with another set of shackles were beside her. Wood shavings that were scattered on the floor showed that this was a new addition to the house. Isaak locked her into her seat and gave her a look the reinstated the demand for silence.

Abraham walked down the stairs wearing the same dark purple loincloth and robes as Isaak. His body was scarred and marked with violence from his past, but no one would ever call him a weak man despite the signs of ageing.

Walking across the room, Abraham's bare feet crackled the huge tarp that had been laid out from one end to the other. Reaching into the box that was now on the table, he pulled the knives out. One by one, he laid them each in their own spot surrounding Simon. Isaak had gone around the room lighting dishes filled with several powders. They never produced a flame, acting like incense instead. Lavender, cinnamon, and thyme wafted around the room. Abraham and Isaak stood on either side of the table.

"Simon," they both declared together, "your life has been cut short by the gods of prosperity. It is not our right to question the gods. In life you have done all you can to honor your duties, lead your family, and died with honor. The gods now demand your body be returned to its original place. We are nothing, we ask for nothing, and we return to nothing."

They each picked up a knife and began cutting into the body. Blood pooled under Simon's pale form. There was a bucket located at the bottom corner of the table. It took a minute for Catarina to notice that the table was constructed to allow the blood to drain effortlessly into it. Thick red liquid trickled down with a clatter.

Abraham and Isaak were in the process of removing Simon's hands, degloving, and removing the muscles and tissues around the wrists until enough was exposed to remove the hand from his arm completely. They continued to the feet, repeating the gruesome actions. Moving with an eerie precision, they showed their clear familiarity with the process. Neither made a movement that was hesitant or uncertain.

When both hands and feet had been cleanly removed, Abraham and Isaak dipped their hands in the blood and began to cover their faces and bodies. It was like a scene straight out of her nightmares. Isaak's bright blue eyes damned near glowed past the red the darkened his face. Smearing the blood over their shoulders and torsos in silence of the room was terrifying,

Catarina didn't realize she was shaking until Katie's leg pressed against hers. Katie was staring intensely at her, almost begging her to remain calm. Catarina had cinched her jaw shut to keep any noise locked firmly inside. Trying to understand what was happening was beyond her mental capabilities right now. She tried to focus only on the smells of the incense and not the coppery stench that tainted the air.

Isaak took a separate knife and slashed a deep grotesque line through the throat while Abraham held the head. She couldn't mentally put Simon's name with the dismembered carcass on the table. For a fraction of a second, Abraham held the head in his hands with a gentle care that was so out of place in this mutilation. Then the second was gone as Isaak and Abraham simultaneously wrenched a knife through the remains of the neck and tore the head away. Trails of blood splattered in every direction.

Abraham set the head down on the table as they began to remove the skin from the rest of the body in strips and dropped them into a second bucket. Every time the pieces hit the bottom with a thick *plop,* Catarina's mind started buzzing around the edges more and more. By the time they had finished, she was shaking, drenched in sweat, and mentally tingling on the edge of true insanity.

A sharp wet snap ripped her attention back into the moment. That sound repeated over and over again while they cut through and removed the top of the ribcage, piece by piece. Every time that snap ricocheted through the room, Catarina flinched, incapable of anything else while her body fought the shock that was pulling her from reality.

Something bumped into her leg, and she looked down. Katie's leg was wrapped around the front of hers. Katie didn't look good. She was shaking and looked a little green. Catarina wrapped her other leg in front Katie's, trying to offer any support she could. Katie looked at her, then down at their entangled legs, then back at Catarina. With a quick nod, she demonstrated practicing slow breathing.

Catarina felt like shit. Not because of the burning wounds on her back or arm, not because her body teetering on the edge of shock, and not even because of the horrible stench in the air. She was so engulfed in her own horror that she mentally checked out, leaving Katie to fend for herself. Catarina met her eye and silently mouthed *'I'm sorry'*. Katie gave her a weak smile and shrugged. Together, they struggled to remain calm and rational.

Piece by piece, what remained of the body had been dismantled. Simon was nothing more than a meat puzzle on a bloody table. Isaak sighed heavily as the last piece was set aside. Abraham set the heart in the center of the table. That was about the exact moment that Katie slumped over in her chair.

"You disrespectful..." Abraham picked up a knife and took a step towards them.

"It's her sugars!" Catarina interrupted. "Let me get her some juice and you can finish your ceremony!" Abraham stopped, suspicion gleaming in his eyes. "I won't run. I won't fight. Please. She has nothing to do with this." Catarina's voice was pleading. Abraham and Isaak shared a look before Isaak stepped towards her.

"Quickly." Isaak removed a key from one of the jars on the counter. "Your word is your life." He unlocked the shackles and stood back.

With a nod, Catarina hurried to the fridge and pulled out a container of orange juice. After she had it in a cup, she hurried over to Katie. Catarina shook the woman enough to wake her up and had her drink most of the glass. Katie was drenched in her own sweat and had a hard time focusing. After she had finished the juice, Catarina stood with her shoulders hunched.

"Can I please get her a slice of bread, or something with carbs, so her body doesn't burn through that, and we have to do this all again?" Catarina lowered her head, giving the illusion of subservience. "Please?" The seconds ticked by like molasses in a snowstorm.

"Quickly." Abraham's voice was softer than she expected. With a nod that came across as a bow, Catarina scurried over to the counter, put her cup in the sink, and grabbed a piece of bread. Katie finished it in seconds, some of the light returning to her eyes. As soon as the bread was gone, Catarina sat back in her chair, placing her wrists back in the iron cuffs. Isaak leaned down to lock them closed.

"Thank you." Catarina whispered so softly that only Isaak could hear. She couldn't be sure, but she thought he mumbled something back. His eyes were so bright that they burned into her face. The room felt like it was a thousand degrees.

Spinning on his heels, Isaak rejoined Abraham at the table. They picked up what was clearly the heart and split it in two. Each man took half and started to eat. Catarina was doing everything she could to compartmentalize this whole thing.

Back in the cabin a year ago, Roland taught her how. She had just found out that the man who had been fixated on her was a serial killer with over six hundred lives he had extinguished. Roland showed her how to pretend that she was an actress in a complete immersion movie, and that none of this was real. It helped back then because there really were little hidden camera's all over the cabin. If she could pretend next to a murderer, she could pretend in a house of zealots.

Silently, the men gathered the parts of the mess on the table and took them outside. In the quiet, Catarina took a shaky breath. Katie's color was looking better than it had, her eyes were focused and steady. Catarina nodded trying to make sure she was ok. Katie nodded back, sure and strong. Catarina began fidgeting, trying to see if they could escape, but they were locked tight.

The minutes passed by slowly. Simon's head still sat on the table, facing away from them. The slow even *plop… plop…..plop* of blood dripping into the bucket seemed to last for an eternity. Except for a few splatters, most of the mess was contained to the table, tarp, and bucket. Footsteps coming up to the house had Catarina's heart racing.

Abraham stepped through the door, still covered in the darkening remains of Simon. Isaak was a few seconds behind him, followed by a man in a jacket and jeans. His red hair was longer than she remembered. Green eyes that had been so full of life were now sunken in and filled with anger and pain. Staring down at her brought a rush of emotions to his face.

"Tobias." Catarina tried to say his name, but it only came out as a whisper. She didn't break his eye contact because she wasn't guilty of anything. He was the only one who was mixing fact and fiction.

"Catarina." Tobias growled but didn't move. "The consequences of your actions will come, but we're still laying our family to rest." He looked like he was challenging her. Nothing she could try would change their situation, so she sighed and gave him a curt nod.

Isaak walked over to the corner and turned over a floorboard. Pulling out a black bag, he handed it to Tobias. Tobias took it and disappeared up the stairs. While they waited, Abraham, blood covered and silent, filled another cup with juice from the fridge and helped Katie to drink. This action was done in a caring, almost fatherly way, and Katie's shoulders slumped in relief.

When Tobias Returned, he was wearing the same ceremonial clothing as the others. His freckled torso was toned and strong. Jail seemed to have sharpened some of the softer parts of him. Besides a few hugs and dancing, the only contact she had with him in the cabin was when he had used his body heat to warm her. She remembered the brief moment where their bodies had been pressed together for her survival.

Without a word, they all walked to the bucket of blood and began covering Tobias the same way the other two had been. Simon's heart had already been consumed so when Tobias dipped his hands into the bucket and began to drink, Catarina had to focus on not making a sound.

Abraham picked up a few of the spices from the counter. One by one he took each and placed them inside Simon's mouth. Lavender, cinnamon sticks, and thyme filled the skull of the man who looked just like Sam. With a needle and thread, Tobias, sewed the mouth shut the lifted the severed head in the air.

"Simon Aller Morgan, The Gods of Prosperity saw fit to terminate your existence." Tobias's voice boomed off the walls. "You will be laid to rest in the tree of your choosing, watching the sun rise each morning from now until eternity. Safe travels, brother." The three men that were drenched in blood marched out the door, head in hand.

# Chapter 14

Roland was buzzing like he was sitting on a live power line. Tyrese had suggested he try decaf three hours ago, and Roland asked him exactly where he preferred to be tazed. Elliot generously offered to 'get the freakshow monster into his cave for hibernation'. Roland in turn recommended that he use some of his tech skills to pull the dick out of his personality and build himself a functioning appendage, so his privacy fence actually served a purpose. Everyone was overflowing with good thoughts and happy feelings.

They were on their way to yet another spot that Sarah had pointed out on the map. It wasn't fair to be upset with her for not knowing exactly which location they would be at, but they had been to three other locations with nothing to show for it. Other teams had various locations over several states, but the only thing they had accomplished was crossing off points on a plan.

They found a report of an RV on fire and some of the team went to get the evidence from local police. It seemed like nothing at first, but a small scrap of purple metallic fabric was found stuck in one of the vents. Jacob had confirmed that it was Katie's underwear. She had jammed them in there. The vehicle was being processed but nothing new had been found yet.

The bird was coming in low and fast. A small farmhouse in the middle of nowhere glowed softly in the surrounding darkness. Another light flipped on as they got close. The pilot gave a signal and they all braced for the countdown. At zero, the pilot had them almost at a full stop in front of the house. In less than a handful of seconds, they were out, and the bird was flying up and away.

In a well-practiced formation, they rushed the house. The porch light flipped on before anyone made it close. Diving behind anything solid, the team watched an old man shuffle onto the porch with a shotgun at the ready. All their lights burst to life, damned near blinding the man.

"This is the FBI," an officer far to the right yelled, his voice cracking in the night, "put your weapons down and get your hands in the air!"

"How do I know you're not those damned kids that keep destroying our mailbox?" The old man had a voice like an announcer. His grip on the gun relaxed a bit and the barrel tilted towards the ground.

"If you can keep that barrel on the ground, I will come show you my ID." Roland called out before lowering his gun and walking up to the house. The old man was still glaring into the now illuminated yard, but he nodded and turned the gun away.

"I don't suppose you've come to tell me that I finally won the lotto?" He laughed and held out a hand when Roland showed his credentials.

"Even I wish that were the case." Roland said solemnly, shaking the offered hand. Everyone surrounding the house lowered their weapons, but tension was still buzzing in the air.

"Whelp, come on then." the old man waved over his shoulder as he walked to the front door. "Might as well come in so yall can fill Betty in too." He stopped with his hand on the door before turning to the group waiting on his lawn. "I'll put a fresh pot of coffee on, but if any one of you drags mud onto the carpet, I'm not promising I can control my wife. She scares me." Roland followed him into the house, and he was pretty sure the old man smiled, but he wasn't going to share that information.

"Gerald, who's out there?" A small frail voice called out.

"Don't worry dear." Gerald crooned, walking through the living room and into the kitchen. The five men on his team waited expectantly just inside the front door, all weapons holstered. "Looks like the FBI needs our assistance."

"Oh my," a tiny woman pulled her robe tighter around her, taking in their new guests. Her white hair was wrapped in rollers, and she shuffled to the wall, flipping on the light. "I'm sorry I'm not more presentable, but this really is an unreasonable hour."

"We won't take up much time." Roland tried to say it gently despite his gut feeling that they were no closer to finding the women. "We are searching for two women who we believe are in immediate danger, and this house was on the list of possible locations of where they might be being kept."

"Dear God." Gerald muttered. "You're welcome to search the property, but we've lived here for the last ten years. It belonged to my father's cousin's friend before we bought it."

"Thank you." The leading officer, Schultz, nodded to two of his team members, and they slipped out the door. "Have you noticed anything suspicious on your land lately? Or did anything stand out when you got the property?"

"The pigs," Betty nodded, "they had three pigs, but they only fed them in a small lean to that fell over a few years after we moved in."

"That's right." Gerald nodded. "We were cleaning out the area for a garden, and found a few sets of shoes, glasses, and a few pieces of jewelry."

"Did you keep them?" Schultz asked.

"I believe they are in the cellar." Gerald pointed to a door just past them in the kitchen. "Down the stairs and to the right."

A few minutes later they were waiting for the bird on the front lawn. Schultz tucked the phone number for the family into a pocket. The items had blood on them, which meant DNA. No one found anything else on the small property. Roland tried to keep the horrible possibilities out of his head. This was just another useless stop keeping him from saving Catarina.

Gerald had given them a history of the property and a few names of the previous owners. They would be able to check the history of the house, but they were running out of time. Obadiah was Cecelia's brother and with his DNA they could find out if any of the items found in the former pig pen belonged to her.

Back in the air, Roland was physically and emotionally spent. A black mist of rage was clouding his thoughts. Every second that ticked by boiled raged to the surface. He needed to hit something, hard. If they didn't find her tonight, he was going to combust. One more night of not knowing would be the death of him.

A memory that he relived a thousand times came unbidden to the surface. That night Catarina had found out that he and Jacob were undercover agents. Roland and Catarina were sharing a bed to acclimate before traveling for the heist. In the dark he heard her crying, an emotional response to the pressure and new situation. He got her to laugh, and they laid there in each other's arms while she traced the scars that marred his body. That was the night that he knew he loved her. His chest throbbed, making him flinch.

She had to be close, and he knew it. They were in the center of the geographical area of the family properties, and no one had found her yet. Director Johnston had separated Jacob and Roland on the current searches, probably anticipating the impending outburst.

Touching down in the field right next to the hotel, Roland was the first on the ground. Not bothering to wait for the others, he marched inside. Director Johnston and Elliot were deep in conversation in the lobby. Roland knew Schultz had already relayed the information they recovered, so he waved as he was passing.

"Hoeft," Director Johnston called, leaving him skidding to a stop, "do you need to use the bathroom?" It was such a strange question that Roland snickered, thinking it was a joke. Director Johnston never broke composure.

"Yes, sir." Roland replied after clearing his throat. Director Johnston waved a hand to the bathroom beside the lobby. Roland was in and out in minutes, after untying his boots and slipping them off for a few seconds before exiting. The damned things weren't well broken in yet and hurt like hell. They flopped obnoxiously while he walked back into the lobby.

"Any news?" Roland asked.

He was still about three yards away when Elliot raised a bulky single barrel handgun and shot him in the chest. Looking down, a fluorescent green dart stuck out of his right peck, directly above where the armor plate was located. Roland flipped his boot into the air, caught it, and launched it at Elliot with so much force that when it hit the bastard in the face, he spun, and went crashing down on the glass coffee table. The explosion of glass echoed across the lobby, stopping everyone in their tracks.

Roland's world was spinning around him before it teetered to the side, and he fell flat on his back. Bodies passed in and out of his field of vision. He tried to clear his mind, but the room fell into blackness.

Struggling in his bed, Roland rolled to the side and vomited into a trash bin that had been well placed. His hair was tied back tightly, and it was a good thing too, because his arms were securely locked into a strait jacket.

He was still in the hotel room. Pulling his feet under himself, Roland stood and walked to the door that was currently propped open. The carpet brushed his bare feet while he walked to the conference room. One of the green agents was walking through the door, but stepped to the side, holding it open for him.

Jacob was stripping off his own restraint next to Director Johnston. Tyrese towered over them all and waved Roland over. Looking around, he saw the ass end of Elliot slipping out the far door like a fucking coward. Roland walked over to the small group, making a mental note to intercept Elliot's laundry and add a few stinging nettles.

"How'd you sleep big guy?" Jacob asked, Director Johnston turned his back trying to hide a smile. Tyrese went to work freeing Roland from the contraption.

"Hard." Roland grumbled. "Why the hell weren't we just given any warning? A surprise mutiny grades on the little trust I have left."

"Mutiny implies you're the one in charge." Director Johnston was doing his best to hide a smirk, but they could all see it. "And the day you stop trusting me is the day you wind up in an asylum."

"All you bastards will drive me to checking myself in voluntarily." Roland complained as his arms were freed.

"If you're done wallowing in self-pity…" Director Johnston cleared his throat and continued. "The two of you were well on your way to spiraling. Even if we had found the girls last night, you would've been a liability at best. You've now had twelve hours of uninterrupted, quality sleep that will allow you to be the elite team I hired you to be." He waved his hand to the doors. "Get some food and be in the conference room in five for updates."

They didn't waste any time. Roland had to admit that he felt significantly better, but not enough to resist beating Elliot to an unrecognizable pulp next time he saw the weasel. Roland's arms were stiff, and his body ached. The pounding headache that stuck with him since the crash had finally dissipated.

Once they were all sitting at the large table, plates in hand, Director Johnston started the meeting. Roland didn't miss Elliot hiding on the other side of the local detectives. Jacob was acting like he was completely oblivious to the animosity radiating off Roland.

"Alright everyone." Director Johnston called out, leaving the room hushed. "Brandt is going to go over the information we have so far. Don't wait to ask questions, this is an open operation for all agencies involved." He sat down while a display popped up on the whiteboard.

"We have completed raids on all the locations marked with red based on the information we received from Sara and the direction of travel from Tobias. The areas marked in yellow are other locations that have yet to be searched but are high on our list of possibilities. Currently we are in the process of going over them with drones doing thermal imaging scans. The areas marked in blue are locations related to the family in one way or another that are low on the list." Everyone was taking notes while Brandt continued. "Now that the two wild cards have recovered," He waved at Roland and Jacob, "we are going back through the information gathered in the house and the trial. There might be information in there that we haven't connected yet, rather than chasing our tails."

"Is there any surveillance in the room the brothers shared?" Someone called out. Brandt smiled and gave him a thumbs up.

"Yes, and we have people combing through that with the recording sped up to save time." Brandt nodded to Director Johnston. "The Director has a medical team on the way to help with Ava. She is the sister of Sarah who grew up in a different sect of the family, but they might be able to provide some insight. A team has been sent to pick up Ava. Sarah is staying here at the hotel. Right now, we need teams combing through street surveillance to find anyone that could be related to this family. Make note of anything. This family doesn't work alone, but they won't stray far from their close friends."

Turning his back in dismissal, the room burst to life. Everyone fled to their stations while Roland waited until Director Johnston was available. He didn't miss the nice shining bruise that Elliot was sporting. Roland's boot did a number on his face. It was a great improvement in his opinion.

"Boys," Director Johnston said, and Roland was surprised to find Jacob nearly attached to him.

"Yes, *Dad*?" Roland snarked, and he had no idea where *that* came from. A manilla envelope thwacked him in the face, with minimal force, thank God.

"I have a room set up," Director Johnston was barely containing a smile while smoothing the envelope in his hands, "You two are going to sit with Tyrese and go over your conversations with the brothers that could have anything to do with their location."

"And have our heads examined." Jacob complained, earning him a smack with the folder as well.

"If you two aren't completely transparent about everything, you will be flipping burgers for the rest of your lives." Director Johnston nodded to Tyrese who was leaning against the far door. "We are running out of options. Humor me until Sarah and Ava are ready for their interview. Our girls have been gone three days too many, try to unlock something useful." He walked away, leaving Roland and Jacob with no other choice than to follow Tyrese.

They went down the hall, past the conference rooms and all the way down to a small twin room at the end of the hotel. It was complete with the same obnoxious rug pattern and blackout shades as their own individual rooms. Jacob plopped down onto one of the beds, tucked his hands behind his head.

"Shrink me doc!" He jeered. Tyrese had just rounded the corner and threw his plastic water bottle at him.

"Alright you two nuts," Tyrese said as he plopped down on the armchair beside the small desk, "let's do a deep dive into the broken pieces of your brains."

"Broken?" Jacob sounded offended.

"Brains?" Roland laughed.

"Hardy-har-har." Tyrese mocked them both. "Roland, have a seat on the other bed so we can get started."

"Is this really the best idea? I mean you've seen inside my head." Roland flopped on the bed. He was acting like a child, and he knew it. He didn't want to be here, he could do so much more if they let him go scorched earth on this God-forsaken-family.

"This will help the investigation and you." Tyrese stated, crossing an ankle over his knee. "Now back in the hotel, the lase time you guys saw the brothers, did they mention anything regarding their family or their home?"

"Just in passing after we found out about Daniel's upbringing." Roland recalled, "Something about how he was glad that Sam didn't remember the bad shit growing up before his parents died." Roland had to close his eyes. The ceiling tiles were giving him a headache.

"From what we gathered on surveillance, their dad was borderline bipolar at best, with violent tendencies." Tyrese informed them. "What about before, at the cabin?"

"Honestly, nothing I can remember." Jacob said. "We were all pretty focused on convincing Catarina that she wasn't going to die." The statement left Roland drowning in a sea of memories.

The images flashed through his brain, unwanted and just as painful as when they happened. Catarina lay wet and frozen in the snow, her blue lips and glassy eyes stopping his heart. Roland could practically feel her icy skin against his own. Her pale body covered in scars and bruises, new and old, left him trying to catch his breath. He could still see the fear in her eyes when they pinned her to the table, trying to drain an infected leg that might have killed her. Her screams of pain reverberated in his mind, over and over until she went quiet. Roland had panicked, thinking her heart gave out.

When she started vomiting, he nearly blew his cover to save her. One sharp look from Jacob had him hesitating long enough for Jacob to get her on the path to healing. Roland could hear the silence in the bathroom when she hadn't come out. The relief that melted the ice in his veins nearly dropped him to his knees when they found her alive. Stubborn, but alive.

A sharp crack echoed in his ears, and he was jerked back to the moment. The ceiling was spinning, the air wasn't coming, and he felt like there was a knife sticking out of his chest. Another sharp crack left him focusing on Jacob.

"Come back, man." Jacob held him by the shirt, despite the fact that Roland was on his back on the ground. "Can you hear me?" Roland nodded when his ability to speak failed. Jacob seemed to understand but didn't try to move him. Tyrese came back into the room.

"Here," Tyrese said, handing a tank to Jacob, "The nurse also gave me this." He held up a needle.

"Thanks." Jacob took it and held a mask up to Roland's face. "Take slow deep breaths. It's just oxygen, if I need to sedate you, I will." Roland steadied his breathing, and the room slowly focused around him, despite his entire body shaking. Jacob was studying him like he was a bomb about to go off. Closing his eyes, Roland counted slowly until he could feel himself coming back down to earth.

Rage was boiling just beneath the surface of his calm demeanor. How in the hell did he allow himself to get so caught up in the past that he lost control and collapsed? In all his years of undercover work, he had never gotten close to a mental breakdown, and now he was on his ass, sucking down oxygen like a fucking child.

"Give him a few minutes and he'll burst out of his clothes and turn green." Jacob muttered. It surprised a dark chuckle from him, instantly dousing the fury.

"You would be lucky to get me out of my clothes." Roland shot back. Opening his eyes, the room stood still, and he took Tyrese's offered hand. They were all sitting in a tight circle on the floor. "You know, I know I'm a big deal and all, but if you guys are wanting to get all hot and heavy, you've got each other, cause I'm taken."

"He's fine." Jacob said while giving him a semi-friendly smack on the side of the head. "Get back onto the bed."

"How did I get down here?" Roland used one hand on the side of the bed to help himself up.

"Well, your eyes glassed over, and I'm pretty sure you were getting up to run, but you started convulsing and went down like a fat kid on a seesaw." Tyrese said it with a straight face, surprising a harsh laugh out of Roland. It damned near sounded like a cough.

"And now we've found the source of my body dysmorphia." Roland shot.

"Oh, yeah." Jacob scrunched his face, mocking Roland. "*That's* the source, and not the fact that your dad looks like the physical embodiment of the giant from Jack and the Bean Stock. You know, the Samoan version."

"That's rich, coming from you, Hop-a-long. Don't you have a stick of butter to chew on or something?" Roland said, his dark mood clearing with the banter. Jacob clicked a spot on his prosthetic, reached down to grab the ancle, and pulled it off, successfully smacking Roland on the hip in the process.

"Leave my hometown out of this!" Jacob said, shaking it at him. Once Roland brought up the New Orleans 'love of butter on everything', it generally went down hill from there.

"Ok, ok, ok." Tyrese objected when Roland stood to return the blow. Picking up the oxygen mask again, Roland sat back down. Tyrese switched gears and got them back on track. "What were you thinking about when you started to panic?"

"Catarina at the cabin when we found her in the snow, then when she almost died from the infection." Roland sighed and set the mask on the tank. "She was so fucking cold, and I couldn't do anything fast enough. Then she got that damned infection….. and I can't get her screams out of my head."

"That's completely understandable." Tyrese had slipped into his, all too familiar, therapeutic voice. It was smooth and reassuring, but slow enough to put the listener at ease. "Before all this, you had been undercover for years and had lost Sophia."

"She's not Sophia." Roland snapped. Sophia was an informant early on in his undercover days that he started a relationship with. She knew she was an informant, but they had gotten close. When Roland was on the verge of shutting down a human trafficking operation, Sophia was killed by a sniper. Roland dragged her into an alley, but it was too late. She had long blonde beach waves, a slender frame, and everything about her was timid and passive. Catarina was everything Sophia wasn't. The glow of anger burst to life in his chest.

"That's not what I'm saying." Tyrese's voice was calm and impartial. "You had just lost someone that meant a lot to you. That alone is a trauma. Then you met and abducted Catarina. She gave the five of you the biggest run for your money, that no one could've ever seen coming." He held up a hand to silence both the men who tried to speak. "I saw all the tapes, she damned-near handed all of you, your asses. She kept fighting the same way you did all those years, and you saw her nearly die repeatedly, your brain panicked. You've known she was alive this whole time but now, no one knows. So, your brain went back to its last experience that matched and tried to comfort itself."

"So, what you're saying is, flashbacks are my brain's way of trying to face the unknown by comparing it to what has happened before?" Roland clarified. The logic made sense, but he wanted to be sure. His anger was dimmed for the moment. Jacob had just clicked his leg back on and leaned forward, fiddling with his hands while he thought.

"Exactly," Tyrese sat back in his chair and crossed an ankle over his knee. "You're not broken, you're trying to cope with the unknown. Catarina is the opposite of Sophia and that's not bad. It means she's a survivor, no matter what it takes. Katie is very much the same. With the two of them helping each other, and all of us looking for them, can you really see an ending where she won't survive?"

The words sunk deep into the silence. Roland swiped at his face, trying to hide the emotions that spilled over. He had to know that she would survive. Somewhere deep in his mind he was very aware of everything she was capable of. Catarina and Katie were survivors, and they would do everything they could to save each other.

The bed shifted when someone sat down. A hand squeezed his shoulder and Roland cried harder. Reaching over, he grabbed Jacob's shoulder in return. They both sat and worked through their own overwhelming pain. One way or another, they would bring Catarina and Katie back home safe. Throughout the years, they had walked through fire together, brothers in every sense of the word. When Jacob lost his leg and thought his life was over, Roland was there every damned day to pull his head out of the black nothingness that consumed him. When Roland was recovering from his surgeries, Jacob never left his side, making sure he always had a lifeline when he was drowning.

At some point he looked up and Jacob did the same. They had been in the exact same spot before, several times. Jacob shook his head, giving Roland a miniscule shove and chuckled to himself, fighting the ironic smirk he was failing to hide. Roland brushed his hair off his own face, shaking his head. The sadness was still there, but the sudden breakdown left him feeling elated, almost like he was floating.

"Prague." Roland referenced the time they were at deaths door during a bombing while trying to rescue a team they lost contact with. They were half mad and desperate, but ready to die, and got a case of the giggles while fighting for their lives. In hindsight, they probably looked insane but neither of them could stop laughing.

"That stupid scouting tank." Jacob snorted. They were both so out of their minds that they ran up to the tank, naked as newborns. The enemy had mistaken them for two informants, only to be taken over then used to find and save the hostages that had been taken. The memory took them from giggling to hysterical.

"Two days of praying for death, and your white ass saved us." Roland was full belly laughing now.

"You looked a little cold that day, Tic-Tack." Jacob fell back on the bed holding his stomach.

"At least I still have all my limbs. You left Good-Ole-Lefty back there!" Roland was struggling to not fall off the bed. Tyrese was smiling, watching the chaos unfold, like a parent supervising a mud fight. The laughter slowly diminished to light chuckles with the occasional snort mixed in. After a long silence, Jacob sat back up and held up a fist to bump.

"Why is it, that after a mental break like that, I always feel clearer than I did before?" Roland asked after obliging Jacob's offered hand.

"It's the brain decompressing from the fight of flight response, when it's done in an emotionally safe environment. It can also be your body releasing oxytocin and other things that help your body recover. Depending on how bad it's needed, your brain can finally relax and see everything clearly." Tyrese said.

"An emotional reset button." Jacob sighed. "So, we can be ready to go when the next blow comes."

"Exactly." Tyrese nodded while walking to the door. "Let's go interview the sisters and get our people back."

# Chapter 15

Catarina was bent over the table while Isaak cleaned and bandaged her back. Struggling to stay awake, she took a drink from the glass that had been offered. Katie was replacing her insulin pump attached to her arm across the table. She looked better this morning.

Last night, after the ceremony and the house was cleaned up, Abraham got Katie a bowl of fruit. Uncuffing her hands, he also brought her supplies from her bag. With the new confirmation that Katie was not the guilty party, Abraham was going out of his way to treat her with care. It made Catarina's skin crawl to see the man that beat her so thoroughly now, treating another living human like a porcelain doll.

This morning, they were fed at the table without being tied to their chairs. Katie was no longer deemed a threat, and Catarina was too weak and injured to run. She was pretty sure something got infected between the blood-coated whip, and the sweat pouring off her. Isaak was being remarkably gentle for someone who just dismembered his cousin.

Abraham was finishing the dishes while Tobias sat with his head in his hands on the couch. Tobias hadn't said anything to her since last night. Occasionally, he would look over, studying her, but she pretended not to notice. He looked so empty. The confident, self-assured man was gone, in his place sat a man who was lost in his own mind and was struggling with reality.

Isaak finished taping down the bandages on her back and tied the back of her shirt closed. He grabbed her bicep and gently pulled her to her feet, the chair scraping against the floor. Catarina didn't bother resisting when he led her to the closet under the stairs. There were a few jackets and shirts hanging in the dark space, but Isaak reached in and pulled out a grey flannel.

Catarina kept her body slouched, and her lids half closed. The best thing for the situation was their captors believing that she was physically and mentally broken. She stayed limp while Isaak guided her hands into the sleeves and softly buttoned up the flannel.

She didn't miss how closely he watched her. It wasn't the same way Roland had back at the cabin, and it wasn't the way Daniel had either. Isaak almost put himself as a buffer between her and Abraham, but there was something more behind it that made her very nervous. She made sure to avoid eye contact with him when possible.

Tobias cleared his throat then stood up. Catarina flinched, and Isaak's hand shot out to grab her arm. It was another thing to tuck away, that yes, he was still always ready and watching. Leading her back to the center of the room, Isaak left her standing in front of Tobias. She finally looked at him and it broke her heart. He looked so broken and searching for hope.

"Looks like we've got a bit of a situation here." Tobias said softly and it nearly took her breath away. It was one of the first things he said to her when they met, back at the cabin.

"You look like shit." Catarina mirrored her original retort, pulling a sad smirk from Tobias. The others in the room had pretty much stopped breathing at this.

"We have a lot to discuss." Tobias completed the exchange and grabbed her elbow steering her towards one of the couches that faced the stairs in a U formation. Isaak sat down beside her, and Abraham and Katie took the sofa near the closet. Catarina was mildly surprised when Tobias took the recliner directly to her left. If needed, she could vault the last sofa that stood between her and the door, but she didn't like her odds.

"So, I guess you're wondering why I've gathered you all here…" Catarina snarked. Abraham leapt to his feet to rush her, when Tobias, of all people, jumped to his feet body-blocking his uncle.

"Stop." Tobias's voice held a morsel of amusement. They stood nose to nose, a small power struggle obvious between the two. "Her default is witty-one-liners under stress. Yours is violent rage." No one dared to breathe. There was so much tension buzzing between the two men that they could've set off a bomb. Isaak was wound tight beside her, ready to spring at any second.

"You said she killed Samuel." Abraham's voice was choked up.

"I said she was the reason he was dead," Tobias sighed and sat down, diffusing the situation, "that's not the same thing." Abraham scowled at Catarina before returning to his own seat.

"Why don't you start at the beginning, so we don't miss anything." Isaak offered. He looked like he had relaxed, but Catarina watched his jaw tick before he stole a quick glance at her when he thought she wasn't looking.

"Start with how you two crossed paths." Abraham seemed to have lost some of steam that had been building, he pointed to Tobias and Catarina.

"We were doing a bunch of smaller robberies to finance one big one..." Tobias continued through the events from the robbery to the abduction, looking at Catarina to fill in the gaps when he had left to go get their stash of cash.

Abraham seemed less than pleased to have to listen to her perspective on the matter. Tobias didn't miss all the small things between Sam and Daniel, even the ones that didn't seem like blatant manipulation on Daniel's part. He didn't take his eyes off a spot on the floor. When he wanted Catarina's perspective on he would wave a hand at her, and she would explain in as few words as possible.

"What we didn't know," Tobias had a few tears running down his face now, but he never sniffled, "was that Jacob and Roland were undercover FBI agents."

"What about her?" Abraham asked. Tobias waved a hand in the air and Catarina took her cue.

"I didn't know until the night I was told to share the room with Roland." Catarina felt her face grow hot. "I found out on accident, and they were pissed."

"Then she was sworn to secrecy." Tobias was struggling to keep his emotions in check. "Then we practiced and traveled to the event." His voice broke repeatedly, and his hands started shaking. "I didn't see anything wrong. E-everything was going s-s-so smooth. I should've noticed something was off. D-Daniel was a freaky b-bastard. We went through the dances, and g-got the jewelry. Roland dragged her out with us as insurance, l-like we planned. I should've been watching. We were upstairs getting our gear to go, and I was watching S-Sam. I never even saw the knife."

"She stabbed Samuel?" Abraham's barely contained rage seeped into his words.

"What? No." Tobias sniffed and wiped his nose on his sleeve. "He was looking at her, all dumbstruck and proud. Daniel stabbed me twice in the stomach, then pulled a gun."

"Daniel double crossed you guys?" Isaak's voice surprised Catarina. He had been so silent next to her that she had forgotten he was there. Tobias waved a hand at Catarina for her to take over.

"He was the reason we were all there." Her voice cracked. So many details she had forgotten about were making her emotions raw. "He was an international serial killer that went country to country, building small teams for robberies that funded one big one. Then at the big one, he would kill his team and kill any witnesses. Governments from all over the world had teamed up to catch him."

"Wait," Isaak interrupted, "that was on the news, wasn't it? He was the skinny white guy that looked like the bargain bin version of a mid-life-crisis." Tobias, Catarina, and Katie all chuckled lightly. "That means it was you guys at the Siyam Diamond Ball last year?!" Catarina openly gawked at Isaak, who looked offended at her surprise. "I was kicked out of the family, remember? I don't live under a rock." Isaak's eyes were darting back and forth as he put the pieces together. "That means you were the lady in the white dress! So, they kidnapped you and you just went along with everything?" Isaak stared at Catarina in confusion.

"I was being drugged." She said quietly. "It only stopped when I agreed to be a witness for incriminating Daniel. He tried to kill me, so they could at least have him on attempted murder if nothing else. I heard later that the plan for Tobias and Sam was a slap on the wrist with the charges for the robberies they were part of. Daniel was the one they were all worried about."

"So, what happened to Sam?" Abraham was getting impatient.

"Daniel stabbed me and got the gun." Tobias reiterated. "I don't know what his plan was to get out, but we were surrounded by police and federal agents. Somewhere in the time we spent in the cabin, he fell in love with Catarina. He demanded that she go with him when he realized he had been double crossed. It's like his brain cracked. He started screaming about all the ways he would kill her, about tearing her to pieces while she screamed and begged to die."

Tobias's eyes were glued to the floor as he relived those horrible few minutes. Catarina hadn't had to think about this same event in so long that she was trembling in her own miserable hell. Tobias continued with tears streaming down his face. "Sam thought he was a friend. They had bonded over so many things. He was so broken when he realized it was all a lie. He was trying to talk to Daniel when the shooting started. Daniel was going on and on about killing Catarina, and I was on the fucking floor trying to keep my guts from falling out. Daniel snapped and went to shoot her, knowing he was going to die. Roland tackled Catarina, but Jacob tried grabbing Sam when he jumped for the gun."

Abraham had reached over and put a hand on Tobias's shoulder while the man broke down. His whole life was spent protecting Sam, and in a matter of minutes his brother was ripped away. Catarina watched the exchange and struggled to keep her own emotions out of it. She had gone over that night in detail in therapy several times, but by the look of it, Tobias never had.

"He was trying to stop that man from dying, even if he wasn't really a friend." Isaak whispered his realization. Katie had tucked herself into a ball on the far side of the couch, watching as an outsider. Catarina felt a little lighter knowing that everyone saw that Katie was innocent. Katie gave her a nod of support.

"If he wasn't focused on her…" Tobias stood, towering over Catarina, blaming her for everything.

"Then he would've killed Sam first." Isaak got to his feet, standing eye to eye with Tobias, trying to diffuse him.

"He's right." Abraham's voice came from behind the two. Tobias turned in confusion. "Don't get me wrong, that bitch is a pain in the ass, and I would love to blame her. If that man wasn't focused on her, then he would've been focused on Sam."

Tension burned in the air. Tobias's eyes began to dart back and forth chaotically while he relived the moment over and over again in his head. What began as rage on his face, contorted into confusion, and finally rested on hopelessness. She could only imagine the images floating through the man's mind at the thought.

Sam would've been easy prey. Daniel would've gotten closer, more than he had already, slowly closing that gap, until Tobias was out of the picture completely. Sam would've died the horrible slow death that Daniel had screamed in such garish detail for Catarina. She watched similar thoughts race through Tobias when he finally focused on her.

"NO!" He stomped his foot and turned to the center of the room to pace while glaring at Catarina, who was still plastered into the seat of the couch. "No, no, no! It's your fault! Sam died because of you!" Even with him yelling, she could hear the doubt in his voice. "I would've gotten him out! If Daniel wasn't so focused on you, I would've seen the signs! Sam would've lived if you hadn't been there!" He was barely hanging onto reality now.

"Tobias, you need to breathe." Isaak said. Both he and Abraham were trying to provide some semblance of comfort.

"You know there's nothing you could've done!" Abraham's gruff voice was calming and even logical.

"You were in the way!" Tobias nearly screamed, jabbing his finger into her chest. It hurt, but Catarina remained completely still while he continued. "We were all so focused on you, and now Sam is dead!"

"Sam died at the hands of an evil man!" Abraham said stepping forward, ready to intervene. Tobias dropped to his knees in front of Catarina, grabbing the collar of the flannel she was wearing.

"Why did you have to be there?" Tobias was openly sobbing, anger seeping out of every cell. "Why the fuck didn't you just die when you hit your head at the bank?!" Catarina could feel herself shaking in sync with Tobias. She didn't open her mouth. Anything she would've said would've escalated this. "Why didn't Daniel just kill you and be done with it?!" He screamed, still holding tightly to the shirt, pressing his forehead against her collarbone. Catarina raised her head, blinking quickly to slow the tears she couldn't stop.

An alabaster hand rested on Tobias's shoulder, followed by a freckled one on the other. Catarina was doing her best to avoid looking at the men. She stole a glance at Katie who sat wide eyed in her little corner of the couch. Katie couldn't do anything to help right now, and Catarina knew it. Trying to offer some level of comfort, Catarina mouthed a silent, *It's ok.* Katie in turn mouthed back her own, *I'm sorry.*

Catarina's breath caught before tears blinded her view. Tobias pulled back, still hysterical, and started to shake her like a rag doll. Catarina grabbed his arms, tucked her head, and let him. He was still on his knees in front of her, but if he got to his feet, she would attack. This wasn't an act of vengeance, just the breaking of a damaged man. Catarina's back throbbed in pain each time it brushed the cushion behind her.

"He would be here if you had just died at the bank!" Tobias was nearly incoherent when he released her flannel and dropped into her lap sobbing. She desperately wished that he could see how much this wasn't her fault. This ripping sorrow was so much worse coming from the man she had had known. Abraham and Isaak were both crying quietly behind him, all grieving their loss.

"I'm sorry, I couldn't save him." Catarina whispered. She knew nothing she could say would change what happened. She didn't think anyone heard her until Tobias's hand shot up, wrapping around her throat. His hair had fallen in front of his face, but when he looked up at her, Catarina's heart sank.

"You don't get to be sorry." He ground out through clenched teeth. His other hand wrapped around the first, squeezing her throat even tighter. She was still breathing, but if this went any further, she would be in serious trouble. Catarina slowly brought her hands up to grab his wrists, if he was going to kill her then she would be ready.

"The only person at fault is Daniel." Catarina's voice broke under his pressure. "I tried to comfort him when he was dying, you watched me." Tobias cut her off when he damned near leapt to his feet, but Catarina matched his motion, stepping up onto the couch to look him in the eye and keep her airway open.

"I was protecting him, and you got in the way!" Tobias shook her, leaving her back screaming in pain. "Everything would've been fine if you weren't there!"

"You dragged me into this!" She was struggling to keep the tremor out of her voice while her knees shook. "I didn't have a choice! There so many times where you all could've stood back and let me go! You even asked me if I was using Sam! Do you remember that?" Catarina watched Tobias's face while he recalled the conversation. His rage was still boiling, but she could see him wavering with the memory. "You never talked about it, did you?"

The realization hit her like a brick. In every session with Tyrese, he always stressed the importance of talking through the events piece by piece so your brain could make sense of what happened. If she didn't, it was very likely that her own mind would take the events and turn them into a nightmare in her own head. What remained could be any mix of fact and fiction based on how in touch she was with reality.

"There's no point!" Tobias screeched, nearly colliding with her when his shins hit the couch. "Talking won't bring him back!"

In his blind rage, he didn't notice how Catarina had angled her body to the side. With his hands still wrapped around her neck and Tobias leaning forward, Catarina let go of his wrists. With quick and well-practiced form, Catarina reached between Tobias's arms to hook both her hands behind his neck. His eyes went wide a second too late. Catarina braced one foot on the back of the couch, using it as leverage to heave them both over the top and pulling Tobias beneath her to take the impact of the fall.

"It wasn't meant to bring him back." Catarina panted, her back spasming while her body tried to deal with her wounds ripping open again. Tobias's massive arms wrapped around her, locking her in place, but she wasn't trying to run. Looking down at him, she continued, only vaguely hearing the others springing into action. "It helps you remember the details, and make sense of what happened, so your mind doesn't create new horrors out of details that get lost in the big picture." Tobias stared up at her.

"Why didn't you just die?" Tobias sniffed. The impact seemed to have knocked some cognition back into him.

"Why is it my fault for wanting to live?" She whispered back.

His hands fell away, but several others hauled her back to her feet. Complying with muffled whimpers and groans, Catarina looked over her shoulder to see Katie still sitting patiently on the couch. Expecting her to bolt at the first opportunity, Catarina gave her friend a look that basically translated to '*What are you still doing her?*' Katie blinked back at her like she had no idea that she should've.

"So, she didn't kill Sam." Isaak said, bringing Catarina's attention back to their small group. Isaak was just shorter than Tobias, so when he looked at his cousin, Catarina watched the vein pulsing in his neck. Tobias was clenching and unclenching his fists.

"She can't bring him back." Abraham sounded confident, "but she can give us the next generation."

He was looking at Tobias, obviously waiting for approval. Isaak was staring at his father in horror, giving Catarina some relief that it was just as abhorrent to him. Tobias kept starting like he was going to ask, but couldn't get the words out, so Abraham continued.

"You weren't able to save your brother, but now you have the chance to raise many sons just like him. Teach him our ways and show him how to live a life that we will all be proud of."

"Yeah, that's not happening with me." Catarina spoke up. Abraham slapped her with so much force her knees buckled. There was a bit of shuffling while she got her feet under her again. Her body objected to just about everything with its own quiet groans.

"Discipline is for the husband or father only." Isaak said it like a reminder. Tobias was looking between the two men slowly shaking his head. Abraham was scowling at Isaak, blatantly ignoring Tobias's hesitation.

"You will marry her." Abraham said it like an order, turning his attention back to Tobias. "There's no way to bring Sam back, but this way we might be able to see pieces of him in your family."

"I'm not getting married or popping out little crotch goblins for you, Nuts." Catarina could see the rising tension in the family and figured it was a good time as any to push buttons.

Abraham swung at her again, but a hand shot out and grabbed his arm. Isaac had pulled her against himself when he stopped his father. Catarina did her best impression of a statue between them. Tobias finally snapped out of his bewilderment and stared at his cousin while the shadow of a look crossed his face. The four of them kept glancing at each of the others in the small group while Katie studied them from her spot on the couch.

"It won't do any good, marrying her." Tobias broke the silence. "I'm infertile." Abraham's neck nearly snapped when he ripped his head around to look at his nephew.

"I thought Sam was the infertile one." He objected.

"He lied for me." Tobias stepped back, leaning against the couch they had gone over only minutes before. "We found out when we went to that one doctor. Dad would've beat me to death for it, as the oldest, so Sam lied for us both." Tobias sighed and crossed his arms in front of his chest. "He didn't know about a lot of the shit that went down, but he saw the marks, and he tried to protect me."

"That's why you've spent your life protecting him." Isaak said quietly. Something in the way he said it had Catarina focused on the twitching muscles in his jaw. Despair radiated off Isaak like a nearly visible force. Blinking quickly, and sniffing, he straightened up. Abraham alternated his intense glare between his two relatives. No one wanted to be the first to speak, but when Abraham stared at Catarina, Isaak tightened his hold on her.

"Looks like you finally found a way to weasel your way back into the Gods good graces, boy." Abraham sneered at Isaak.

Catarina looked over at Katie, making sure she understood what the old man was implying. Katie, who had missed her earlier opportunity to escape, nodded once. Catarina flicked her eyes to the door, trying to convince her to run for help, but to her surprise, Katie shook her head slightly. God, she hoped the woman had a plan, other than being a witness at her reluctant wedding.

"You're the only one who has a problem with me." Isaak's voice was strong and sure. "What if we have a bunch of babies just like me? You going to throw them out too?"

"This curse is a reflection on me." Abraham stepped forward. "Do better, and you could save this family."

Catarina watched the old man put the last of his hope to continue their bloodline into the son he rejected. He didn't seem all that excited at the prospect, but the same bull-headed stubbornness that Tobias had shown on their last adventure, was prevalent on his face. Tobias, on the other hand, looked like he was going to have a stroke. The vein in his head was pulsing erratically.

"Again, I'm not agreeing to any of this!" Catarina's voice was incredulous at best. "I'm not even a virgin!" She knew she was grasping at straws now.

"And I was exiled for most of my life." Isaak smirked. "It doesn't make a difference now."

"You would go along with a forced marriage?" Catarina leaned back slightly to look up at the man, but her back spasmed in protest.

"I've done a lot worse in life than that." Isaak gave a sad smile before turning his attention back to his father. "We will need a rooster."

"I will grab one and the robes tonight." Abraham sighed. "We will need to get everything else ready."

Tobias still stood staring into the abyss while the others planned around him. Abraham made his way across the room to Katie. He pulled her to her feet before taking her upstairs. Katie didn't put up a fight, but Catarina saw her quick wink when no one was watching.

"Tobias." Isaak whispered, placing his hand on the stunned man's shoulder. That seemed to shock him out of his stupor. "I know it's not the justice you wanted, but I need you to tell me that you're ok with this."

The crushing weight of her predicament was settling around Catarina. When Tobias focused on her, she could see his internal battle. The seconds slowly ticked by and the churning in her gut was almost painful. Watching her fear, Tobias's conflicted look cleared. He didn't look relieved.

"Marry her." Tobias decided with a sigh. He almost looked defeated, until he spoke again. "Make her suffer." With that, he turned on his heels and stormed out of the house.

Catarina swayed on her feet. She could feel the blood dripping down her back while the room did a tilt-a-whirl around her. Isaak had been holding her arm, but readjusted to grab them both, keeping her on her feet. The smell of him invaded her senses, making her want to vomit. Every time her face brushed his shirt, she jerked away, making Isaak's grip tighter.

"Sit down so I can stop the bleeding." Isaak said, his voice was monotoned while he practically dragged her over to the table.

Plopping her down in the seat, he removed the flannel and untied her shirt. Catarina leaned forward, laying her face against the cool table while Isaak brought out the medical supplies... again. She probably could've run, but Katie was upstairs, and Catarina was just so tired. She hardly recognized the small movements it took to clean her back. It all burned and stung so much that her mind was processing it like one continuous electric current that zapped to life with every touch. There was no relief coming. If there was a bus driving by, she would've loved to jump in front of it, if only it would stop the pain. Her body flinched with a mind of its own when a particularly sensitive cut was brushed.

"The wedding will be quick. Keep quiet and behave yourself, and you might keep your ability to walk." Isaak said with a haughty tone.

"Why walk when you can run?" Catarina clapped back with a weak chuckle. "I run my mouth, my body, and my attitude all over the damned place. You should reconsider if you're not ready to marry all of me."

"Tobias is holding on by a thread," Isaak stopped working, and leaned closer. "You're getting dangerously close to being thrown out of a window."

"We're in a two-story house. I like my odds." Catarina smiled weakly before letting sleep take her.

# Chapter 16

Roland followed Brandt, Tyrese and Jacob down the hall to a room that had been converted into a traveling medical base. Director Johnston had hired a private team of medical professionals for whatever was needed. No expense was spared as equipment was spread all over the room.

Sarah sat on a chair beside a genuine hospital bed. She was holding the hand of her sister, who was the sunken in version of Sarah. Ava was still coming down from her last high, but they didn't have many options left. The heartbeat monitor beeped quicker when they had come into the room.

"I've got nothin' to say to you, feds." Ava's voice was quick and light. "You can't prove anything. I didn't have anything on me when I was arrested, and anything in my system, I was forced to take, and you can't prove otherwise."

"Ava..." Sarah interrupted, but Ava kept going.

"I'm not hurting anyone. I'm not getting government assistance, disturbing anyone's peace, and I'm actually putting money back into society since everyone's got to eat! I even pick up trash at the park when I stay there, so I'm helping better the city!" Roland watched her eyes darting around the room. If she was on the way down from a high, he was sure this conversation would trigger every bad memory and feeling she had growing up.

"As much as we appreciate all of that," Brandt held up a hand stopping her, "we aren't here for that. We need information on your family."

"What kind of information?" Ava whispered, looking over at Sarah for assurance.

"About the family." Sarah said with more confidence than Roland was expecting. The tears that immediately welled up in Ava's eyes doused Roland's intensity for answers.

"Ava." Brandt sat down in a chair near the bed. "Your drug use…. have you ever wanted to quit?"

"I've tried!" Ava snapped at him. "Everyone always treats you like shit, like I like to live like this! I was six months clean last time before it was too much! I just wanted to feel ok again. I hate feeling like a sideshow freak, like I can't even close my eyes at night, or even go out in daylight without waiting for someone to start beating me!"

She flipped the blankets off her legs, exposing layers of burn scars that ran up and down the freckled skin. The thing that sucked all the air out of the room, was her exposed foot, that was missing every one of her toes. Sarah quietly let go of her sister's hand. Lifting up her floor length skirt and removing her shoes, Sarah revealed her own matching scars and missing digits.

"I would never fault your life choices, especially after what the two of you have been through." Brandt kept his voice calm and soothing, easing some of the tension in the room. "We have been authorized to offer a paid contract for continuous information on your family. In return we will be holding them accountable for their crimes. Also, if you accept, and you are truthful about everything, we are offering immunity." He nodded at Ava who looked to her sister. They sat there having their own silent conversation.

Roland fought the urge to start tapping his foot. Jacob was still as a statue beside him, but Roland saw his jaw ticking. Tyrese took a chair from beside the far wall and placed it beside Brandt. His movements were slow and deliberate. Roland couldn't figure out why until he saw Ava and Sarah watching him warily. With all the teachings about a pure bloodline that they had discovered, it never occurred to him that the family could have racist ideologies. Tyrese leaned back in the chair, and the women relaxed.

"Ok," Sarah said, "but we do this together, and I get to stay with my sister."

"Deal." Tyrese said. He was speaking in his therapist voice, soft, calm, and assuring. Sarah and Ava still didn't relax though. "I have also arranged a spot for you at an exclusive rehabilitation facility. If you would like, your sister can stay with you, or we can have her located nearby while you recover. All of this would be covered by us if you accept." The sisters looked at each other in another silent debate, but it didn't last long.

"That would be nice, thank you." Ava nodded.

"Before we go any further, I have an idea of different things that your family might have taught, and I understand that you might have some of the same beliefs. I understand if you would want another psychiatrist working with you, but if you give me a chance, I think you might be pleasantly surprised at how open-minded I am." Tyrese said.

"It's not a belief that I hold anymore." Sarah explained. "We were always taught to be afraid of anyone with darker skin. That's why we couldn't understand why Isaak was 'cursed'. By the same logic, he should've been the purest soul of us all, but we were beaten when we asked questions."

"It's hard to shake something that was pounded into you for years, but I'm ok as long as Sarah is with me." Ava's eyes darted back and forth, never settling on Tyrese for more than a few seconds.

"Please let me know if we need to take a break." Tyrese gave them a friendly smile. "Now let's begin."

Roland and Jacob pulled up two folding chairs that had been left for this exact meeting. They gave Ava the same recap and information that had been provided to her sister. They had to double back a few times and simplify a few details to help Ava's racing mind. She was hooked up to a few different bags, but she didn't seem as out of it as before. Being addicted for as long as she was, Roland was sure Elliot had played around with a few drugs that would ease the detox process.

"We've been through all these locations marked in red. Yellow marks are where we haven't checked, and blue marks are any locations related to the family." Brandt pointed to the map that was laid across the foot of the bed.

"Did Isaak say anything about where they might be when you two met up?" Ava asked Sarah.

"No, he just said he was going to be getting back to get his revenge." Sarah sat back in her own chair, pressing her fingers into her forehead. "He sold his apartment and packed up his things. Something about making sure he had no distractions while he found his way back to the true teachings of the Gods."

"What about the family farm?" Ava asked. "The caves?"

It took less than five seconds for the confused look on Sara's face to disappear. And just like that, her eyes went wide, she sucked in a breath, and toppled forward off the end of the chair. Everyone jumped to catch her at the same time, but only Tyrese had the sense to dive forward, catching her face in his hands. Even with everyone else making a grab for her arms, her head still whipped forward. Tyrese literally stopped her from bouncing her head off the floor like a basketball. Ava tried to grab her sister but was so weak that all she managed to do was lean forward.

"Nice catch!" Brandt said before lifting her back into the chair.

"Why does this keep happening?" Roland grumbled and flinched when Tyrese elbowed him in the ribs.

"Best guess is an arrythmia or a tumor." Jacob said. He had been so quiet, Roland nearly forgot he was there. "Probably another hereditary issue." To his surprise, his friend never moved from his chair to check on her. In fact, Roland didn't remember Jacob reaching for her at all when she fell.

"Hypertrophic Cardiomyopathy." Sarah started listing off her symptoms. "Always lightheaded, habitually tired, and I have to be super careful when I exercise. Sometimes I get chest pains, but it's nothing like getting blood pressure spikes that make you pass out." Shrugging, Sarah changed the subject fast enough to make the tires squeal. "I'd forgotten about the caves."

"Tell us what you two remember." Jacob said, but his mind was somewhere else in his own personal hell.

"Why don't you take a walk?" Tyrese turned to him.

"No," Jacob sighed, shaking his head like he was trying to shake away the fog, "I need to know."

"You're in love with that girl, aren't you?" Ava asked, her eyes nearly sparkling.

"The agent that was taken with her is my girlfriend." Jacob cleared his throat and pointed to Roland. "Roland is in love with the civilian that was taken."

"Catarina is my girlfriend." Roland almost cursed at his own defensive tone.

"Didn't know you had clarified that, my bad." Jacob said the last bit with some mockery.

"You wanna look both ways before you get on my fuckin' nerves?" Roland glared at his friend.

"From the bottom of my heart, fuck you." Jacob matched his glare for a fraction of a second before they both stood down and returned to the conversation.

"I've got superglue if you two need Chapstick." Tyrese smirked. "You done, or should we wait?" He sure didn't, returning his attention to Ava, Tyrese continued. "Why is their love important?"

"As bad as it is, if they know that Catarina is in a relationship with you, there's a good chance that they'll keep her alive longer." Ava looked happier than Roland thought she should have. "The caves are here," she pointed to the map, "but I'm not sure they would be there, if they have Isaak with them. No one in our part of the family would've helped."

"What happens at the caves?" Brandt asked.

"Consequences." Sarah said quietly with tears filling her eyes. Ava reached over and took her sister's hand again in a show of support.

"Like what happened to you?" Brant pushed, but his tone was soft and welcoming, the way it always was when he was dealing with someone damaged.

"We were told who we were going to marry when we were twelve years old." Sarah said with a sigh. "I was supposed to marry Obediah, and Ava was promised to Zacheriah."

"We knew what kind of men they were." Ava jumped in. "They used to get together and kill animals in the woods. Not for food or anything, just for fun, in the most awful ways possible."

"So, when we were caught running away...." Sarah's voice trailed off.

"They were the ones who chose our punishment." Ava's voice was stronger than her sister's, but the pain was still there. "They said they would start at the toes so if we ran again, they would take the foot apart in pieces every time we tried."

"Once we were eighteen, every time we did something they thought was unacceptable, we were beaten and burned. We finally got out a year later." Sarah finished. "We spent that year in terror, trying to build up everyone's trust that we would be the perfect obedient spouses.

"What was the reason for waiting until you were eighteen, but cutting off your toes before?" Brandt asked, resting his elbows on his knees. "I'm just trying to understand the dynamic."

"We belonged to our father until we were eighteen, because of state laws, but once we turned eighteen, we belonged to our future spouses. They wait one year for the potential husband to take over responsibility for the bride, because the transition isn't always smooth. Then at the wedding, they are branded during the ceremony." Sarah explained.

"I would like to hear more about that later," Tyrese took back the conversation, "but for now can you tell me more about what happens in the caves?"

"Sometimes, people get chained to the wall and starved for days, depending on what they did. One of the wives was caught cheating, and her husband was forced to beat her to death before he skinned the other man alive." Ava looked to her sister who nodded at the memory. "One of the uncles was caught stealing from his sister's family, and they burned his hands with oil to 'purify the temptation within'. If he was a woman, they would've just taken one of his hands."

"So realistically, what are Catarina and Katie in for?" Tyrese asked.

"Katie wasn't involved at all, and the family believes that harming the innocent will bring consequences worse than death." Ava said with a soft smile. "She will most likely be let go since she is 'untrainable'. But Catarina is different."

"They could do anything." Sarah added. "Lock her in the caves, beat her, take limbs, or....." Sarah took a steadying breath. "What happened to Cecilia could happen to her."

"What did happen to her?" Brandt asked. Roland was doing his best not to fidget with the new information. Jacob on the other hand had his legs bouncing like he was trying to singlehandedly recharge the electricity in the building. "She just disappeared after she turned eighteen."

"She was given to the family of the child that died." Sarah shuddered. "They executed her."

"They took her to the caves and turned her into what regular people call a blood eagle, but they called her an angel. Something about watching over the other children for eternity to pay for letting the other child die." Ava said in a disconnected voice. "Only that was after they had cut out her tongue and made her eat it, then removed her hands. That's when we knew we had to leave, rather than risk dying like that. I've spent years trying to get that final image of her out of my head."

"Which is why you started taking drugs." Tyrese's voice was so understanding, but Roland was still reeling in his own head.

"It didn't help." Ava shrugged. "But no therapist wants to help a relapsed druggie."

"If you let me, I'm happy to help you both." Tyrese offered. "Take a few days to decide. Right now, we need to try to find where they would be at. Tobias knows Catarina is a handful, so we can assume that they are keeping Isaak involved."

They kept talking, but Roland was doing his best to keep it together. Now that they were sure Katie would be ok, he was consumed with what was in store for Catarina. He was sure there was a hurricane wreaking havoc on his brain from the inside of his head. His ears couldn't keep up with the current conversation over the roaring. Every single one of his old scars were tingling like he had ants crawling all over.

He only saw the blood eagle completed in movies. There was yet to be any concrete evidence by any historian that it was actually completed. Several religions throughout the years taught it in their history as a sure thing, but none had any proof it as far as he knew. The image of Catarina's body slumped over, with her entire back ripped open in the grotesque pose, sent Roland throwing himself at the nearest trashcan.

Still in the process of retching, a set of hands pulled his hair out of his face and secured it behind his head. Catching his breath, Roland scooped up the wastebasket, turning to sit where he fell. Jacob had popped-a-squat right next to him. The bastard seemed to find new life now that his other half was supposedly in the clear.

"If looks could kill, you'd still fail." Jacob smirked at him, but it didn't reach his eyes.

"If at first you don't succeed, it's only attempted murder." Roland spit into the trash, that was now propped in his lap.

"Or you're not nearly as good as you think you are, and it's time to get you checked into a psych ward." Jacob leaned back against the wall.

"All of the voices in my head think you're an asshole, and the last one wants to shoot you." Roland chuckled. "Feeling better knowing Katie should be in the clear?"

"It snapped me out of the mental spiral." Jacob nodded. "Looks like you plummeted all the way to the bottom though." After Roland nodded, he kept going. "Well tell me if you're still able to maintain your rubber mass and bounce off everyone's nerves to get our girls back."

"Yup." Roland set the trash bin down and climbed to his feet. Jacob clapped him on the back when he stood up.

"Maybe after we get her back," Tyrese had a smirk on his face even though Brandt looked unamused, "we all start weekly therapy sessions. On top of what all of you are doing individually.

I figure if no one is playing with a full deck, we ought to combine you all and get one out of this shitshow!"

"Anything is a shitshow with this idiot in the game." Elliot marched into the room followed by Director Johnston.

"Nice eye," Roland glowered at him, "did you not listen the first time your wife told you to clean the kitchen?"

"Did your application for the nut house get rejected again? Do the world a favor and donate your brain to science so you actually benefit humanity." Elliot sneered.

"You've got a big attitude for a dude built like a ticktack." Roland could feel the rage building.

"But your momma's breath smelled great this morning!" Elliot returned.

"At least my mom didn't scream 'burn it with fire' when I was born!" Spat Roland.

"I'm surprised Catarina's still alive after you two bumped uglies. Everyone around you dies, I didn't think she would be any different." The coward took a slight step to the side, putting Director Johnston between them, knowing he hit a nerve.

"And that's as cordial as it gets with these two." The Director jumped in before Roland could lose it, but he didn't miss the glint in his boss's eye. "I gave you two sixty seconds to get it out of your systems, so shut up and listen." He took a breath to start and stopped. Sniffing suspiciously, he started looking around himself. Eyes stopping on the wastebasket, he nodded once and continued. "I'll get someone to check the food. The last thing we need is mass food poisoning."

"No need." Brandt said. "Just new information not setting right, but we are all good now."

"Alright." Director Johnston switched his attention to the twins across the room. "Does Silver City mean anything to you two?" Ava and Sarah both thought and shook their heads.

"We traveled around for hours at a time to get from home to home." Sarah explained. "Women were never given the names or locations of any place unless their husband decided they were worthy of the knowledge."

"Knowledge is power." Director Johnston surmised.

"If we could see it, we might be able to help." Ava offered. We don't know the exact places, but we knew how long it would take to get from place to place. If we can pinpoint one on a map, we could find the others!"

"That's very intuitive, Miss." Director Johnston gave the girls a very unexpected and father-like smile. "Elliot, get set up in the large conference room. Brandt and Tyrese, please help the ladies get comfortably set up there as well so we can follow that lead. Jacob and Roland, come with me." He winked at Roland before discreetly tossing a pen. Roland caught it with ease.

"Let's move!" The Director said with a smirk.

Elliot made sure he was the first person behind The Director out the door. The smug asshole turned so quick, he didn't see the pen. As it happens, it wasn't a pen, but a micro tazer that Elliot designed. It seemed that The Director didn't like Elliot's comments either. As soon as they cleared the door into the hall, Roland zapped Elliot quick on the thigh. The man went stiff as a board, falling against the wall, and hands grasping at anything to hold onto. Everyone else walked casually around him. He made a choking sound for a solid five seconds before the moment passed and he limped along at the back of the group.

"Director, the Chernobyl survivor got his paws on a tazer. Permission to shove it up his ass?" Elliot complains in an almost whiney voice.

"Well with all of us moving from place to place, things are bound to get dropped, and he was just being a helping hand and picked it up!" The Director was facing away from them, but there was a smile in his voice. "Permission denied."

"I'll get you for that Hoeft." Elliot whispered quiet enough that he knew only Roland could hear. He was the one who designed the hearing implant in the first place.

They went up the hall to a room that had been closed off. There were still agents buzzing in and out like their asses were on fire, but there were several projectors aimed at the wall. Sheets from the hotel were being mounted to the wall, transforming it into a giant endless screen. Several lights flipped off and the display became even clearer.

Two projectors displayed maps of Rapid City and the surrounding states. One was a general bird's eye view, and the other had dots over known locations. The third projector was throwing up images of the locations at ground level, rotating through images on a five second interval.

Roland walked to the front of the room where a large table was set up with files and computers. Jacob was right on his heels, his eyes searching the map like something was going to jump out at them. He didn't look nearly as anxious as he had before. The disconnected look in his eye was gone.

"Alright everyone," Director Johnston's voice boomed across the room, sending everyone into an anxious silence, "Ava and Sarah are cooperating witnesses at the moment." He waved to the girls that were sitting in chairs, front and center. "We are going through the locations that they know of and branching out from there. There is a bird on route, with another source, if my information is correct. I will step out but continue while I'm gone just in case." With that he drew a circle in the air, signaling to the room to get going.

Sarah and Ava spoke up when they saw images of locations they recognized. That helped create a starting point for the map's teams and they began working their way outward. At one point they looked through Silver City like The Director asked about, but it didn't look familiar to them.

A call came in and Director Johnston left the room. Roland was nearly sweating with anticipation. The display on the wall read eight o'clock. He didn't want to spend another night without her. Three in a row had Roland's heart racing, thinking that the last time he saw her would be just that. The last time. Thats when the doors burst open.

A slim woman with an athletic build and a black bob stopped when she realized the room was full. Jacob was on his feet, sprinting at her before she could react. Katie leapt at him, her arms wide. The sound of laughter and tears echoed off the walls, but Roland's mind was racing. Catarina wasn't with her.

Roland looked at Director Johnston, nearly begging to know where she was. The man just held up a hand, encouraging him to wait as the seconds ticked by so slowly, he could feel time standing still.

"Roland!" Katie's soft voice broke the tension in the room. "Shes alive! She couldn't escape with me, but she's alive!"

"You left her?!" Roland roared. Everyone that could, took a small step backwards, except for those with the most familiar faces.

"She was safer there than in the woods risking infection!" Katie's voice was gentle but firm. "I know where she  is, but you have to get to her soon! They are going to force her to marry Isaak and have his babies."

# Chapter 17

It took several hours to for the men to realize Katie had escaped. She managed to get her hands on a pen that had been lodged in between the cushions of the couch. She had stuffed it into her bra, retrieving it with her mouth after her hands were tied.

She was nice enough to wait until after Catarina was there so she could try to take her too. It took some convincing to get Katie to leave, but when she pointed out just how bad her injuries were, Katie relented. She snuck out the window again, but this time, no one saw her.

Catarina woke up after dark to the yelling. It took a while to figure out what was happening, but after the last seventy-two hours, she was running on empty. She was so tired that she just tuned them out. Issak was the one who even bothered checking to see if she was alive.

He ignored her screams when they untied her from the bed and hauled her downstairs. Abraham basically dumped her on the floor. She tried to get up, but he put a heel on her side and kicked her over.

"Hey!" Isaak yelled. "If she is going to be my wife, then I will be the only one who lays hands on her." Isaak grabbed her biceps and dragged her to the wall where the shackles were. His movements looked harsh, but there was almost no pain with them when he locked the shackles closed. Catarina, for all her efforts, made her reactions to his show of force more severe than they were.

Tobias and Abraham ran all over the house, packing up items like their asses were on fire. It would've been funny if Tobias hadn't stopped every few minutes to glare at Catarina. It didn't seem like a conscious decision, but the rage was so apparent that she was sure his body was just taking over. That left Isaak stopping to put himself between them, staking his claim.

They were out of the house soon after, all loaded into an old dark green ford with an extended cab. The back of the cab lay down into a bed, and Catarina was doing her best not to roll around too much. Issak laid next to her, his legs curled up, with her own thrown over the top of his. It was a strangely intimate position, but he didn't seem bothered by the physical contact. Before they drove away, Abraham pulled a beanie over his red hair despite the heat. Tobias hid in the truck bed for a quick escape if necessary.

They drove with the lights off, for what seemed like hours. Catarina's hands were clammy, and Isaak kept feeling her face with his hot hands. The crease never left his brow. At one point she dozed off with her mind racing.

When they skidded to a stop, Catarina's bruised temple bounced off Isaak's shoulder. Abraham was out of the truck in seconds. Isaak sat up to watch what was going on outside. Catarina tried to discreetly undo the knots with her teeth, but Isaak reached back and put a hand over it, stopping her.

"He's not coming." Abraham growled when he climbed in. Starting the car, he peeled out before Isaak could ask questions. The motion threw him against Catarina, but he laid back down.

"Did we do this all for nothing then?" Isaak sounded almost resigned.

"No." Abraham's annoyed voice made Isaaks nose twitch like he was trying not to sneer. "He's not coming for the ceremony, but he will be there after. He can't watch, even when he knows what really happened."

"Funny, I was sure it would be you that would miss my wedding." Issak said blandly. Abraham reached back and punched him in the side. Isaak winced but only slightly.

They drove for what seemed like hours, but eventually pulled up to a small cabin in the middle of nowhere. It looked like a small hunting lodge. When they walked in, it was the definition of minimalistic, no fridge, no stove, and no microwave. The glare of the flashlights reflected off a small sink. It was attached to the wall with a hand pump on top. Unlit candles were strategically placed around the small interior.

"Be ready at sunrise." Abraham ordered before walking into one of two bedrooms and slamming the door.

"Let's get a few hours of sleep." Isaak said with a sigh.

He brought her into the other room that sported a full mattress. He took off the backpack he was carrying and had Catarina sit on the bed. In a few minutes, he had her tied up like a freaking pot roast, securing her feet to the frame for good measure. It was too warm for blankets, but he threw one over her anyways. Laying on top, he tossed an arm over her and was snoring in less than a few minutes.

Catarina knew that there would be better opportunities to escape if she could get a few hours of sleep. She knew nothing would stop the sunrise, so she closed her eyes in the black room and let sleep take her.

When the alarm went off, Catarina had forgotten where she was and jumped. That in turn set off Isaak who thought she was about to run. He clamped his arms down on her, straining all her injuries, leaving her silently screaming for mercy. It took a second for him to realize that she wasn't trying to run and let go.

"Let's get married, *Dear*." Isaak grumbled sarcastically and turned off the alarm on his watch.

"Wow, pet names already?" Catarina's filter didn't wake up with her this morning. "I thought you would've preferred pet or slave or something degrading like that."

"You're not special enough for that." Isaak cracked before rolling out of bed and striking a match. A small lantern cast light around the windowless room.

Catarina's body ached like she had been hit by a train. Watching Isaak tie his shoes, she looked around for anything she could use as a weapon. The backpack he brought in was sitting in the corner by the door. If she could get her hands on it, the possibilities would be endless.

"I have to use the bathroom." She groaned, purposely let her voice keep the groggy tone from her first comment of the day.

"I was wondering how long it would take you." Isaak chuckled. "It's been a while since you've been."

"It warms my heart to know you track my bowel movements." Catarina sighed. "I'm one sneeze away from a bad day, so I hope you remember how you did this."

To her surprise, Isaak had her untied in a matter of minutes with the rope neatly organized next to her. She briefly wondered what the hell he did in his extracurricular time, but decided she really didn't want that answer. She was just testing out her ability to move her back when an iron cuff clicked shut around her ankle.

"Don't say that I never got you anything." Isaak said as he picked up the chain and found the flashlight. Leading her out of the room and farther still, out of the house, they made their way through the trees. After a while, he pointed to a bucket next to the trees. It looked fairly new, but she wasn't thrilled.

"Two gifts in one day, you must really love me." Catarina snarked and walked towards it. When they got close, she kicked the bucket, just to be sure no animal came scurrying, or slithering out. Nothing happened though, and she gave a sigh of relief. "You love me enough to watch me take a shit in the woods?" In the moonlight, Isaak's chuckle was easy to see.

"I'm not going to maintain eye contact, but I won't be turning my back either." Isaak stepped back the length of the chain and tossed her a wad of toilet paper. When she caught it, he redirected his attention to another area while still keeping her in his peripherals.

She figured that was as good as she could hope for, so Catarina shook her head and took care of her business. Making sure he wasn't looking when she stood up, Catarina tried to keep a groan to herself. The sleep she got last night wasn't nearly sufficient, but it did take the edge off enough for her to plan her escape.

Isaak started to turn towards the cabin when Catarina tucked a shoulder and came into sack the quarterback. To her surprise, when she hit his side, he dropped the chain and wrapped an arm around her middle. Stepping back, he spun, and tossed Catarina into the nearest tree. The impact had stars bursting in her eyes. She hit the ground with a cry of pain. Isaak walked up, picking up the chain and holding out a hand help her up.

"Well played." He said with a full smile. That smile took her breath away, he looked like the ghost of Sam staring back at her.

"Can you blame me?" Catarina took his hand, climbing to her feet while coughing.

"I'd be offended if you didn't at least try."

They walked back to the house, Isaaks smile disappeared as soon as the cabin came into view. Abraham was in the yard out front, laying sticks in the grass forming a circle. A rooster slept in a wire cage beside him. He was working by the light of the moon, and out here in the middle of nowhere, it was as good as any fire would've been.

Two boxes sat on the tailgate of the truck. Isaak led her over to them and placed one in her hands. The boxes were polished wood, dark and beautifully carved. Isaak gave her chain to Abraham, who grabbed her bicep and essentially dragged her into the cabin. Once they were inside, Abraham walked her into the bedroom.

"Don't do anything stupid." He grumbled while pulling a gun from his waistband. Aiming it at her, he dropped the chain and tossed her the key. "Unlock it and open the box." Abraham watched while Catarina followed the instructions. Reaching inside, she pulled out a deep purple billowing robe that cascaded down to the floor. "Strip and put that on." He ordered.

"If you think I'm going to give you a free show, then I might have hit you too hard." Catarina nodded at the shiner that darkened Abraham's face.

"I don't have to kill you to make you pay for your smart mouth." He said, lowering the barrel to aim at her legs.

Catarina sighed and began removing her clothes. Trying to keep her dignity, she resisted groaning as the shirt scraped along her aching back. She grabbed the robe and pulled it away from the lighter dress fabric. It seemed to wrap around her somehow, but she wasn't quite sure.

"Everything off." Abraham's voice was clinical at best. "Wrap it around under your arms twice and tie it in a bow in front. The robe goes on top."

"Are you going to cut them off me if I don't?" Catarina dropped the gown back onto the bed."

"Yes. If you get cut in the process, then that's your problem." Abraham took a threatening step forward, but Catarina flipped a hand at him in dismissal.

Doing her best to hide what she could of her body, Catarina peeled off the rest of her clothing and wrapped the tent-like dress around herself. The robe was harder to put on, with her back torn, but she managed. Abraham led the way back outside, leaving her standing in the middle of the circle.

"If you run, I'll just start shooting." Abraham kindly informed her. She rolled her eyes at him, turning to assess her options. Looking around, she watched Isaak walking back through the woods towards them, his own purple cloak emphasizing his own lack of pigment. He had a lantern in one hand, but she was sure he didn't need it with how bright the moon was shining.

Stepping into the circle, Isaak gave the lantern to Abraham, who placed it on the tailgate and started fiddling with other things outside of her field of vision. The sky was just beginning to lighten in the east. Isaak took her shoulders and moved her to face the north while still in the circle. Before he let go, Catarina threw her arms between his, then wrapped them around locking his wrists against her ribs.

Taking a small jump, she planted her feet against his bare hips and yanked him towards her. Catarina's ass hit the ground with enough force to knock her teeth together. Pulling him towards her and kicking her feet up sent Isaak flipping in the air. He crashed into Abraham and the two of them collapsed in a pile on the ground.

Rolling to her side despite the pain, Catarina pulled her feet under her and took off. She could hear parts of the dress ripping under her feet, but she didn't care. She had almost made it to the first tree when something solid hit her in the back, hard enough to knock her to the ground. She screamed in pain, unable to move. In the middle of her scream, someone stuffed a rag into her mouth, securing it with duct tape.

"Another move like that and I will put you in a wheelchair permanently." Abraham threatened.

"Did you really have to throw the tire iron?" Issak asked while dusting off his robes.

"It was that or the ax." Abraham huffed. "You should be grateful I didn't start removing her leg."

Abraham yanked Catarina to her feet and marched her back to the circle. Isaak held her hands together while Abraham secured them with tape. She was trying to breathe calmly and not choke on the rag in her mouth, but tears still streamed down her face. She was sure her back was bleeding again. Isaak opened the front of her robe, pushing it back until it slid off the edge of her shoulders.

"Hold her." Isaak said quickly.

Abraham wrapped his arms around her, the immediate pain from her back had her screaming into the rag again. Blinking away the tears, she could just make out Isaak hurriedly closing the distance. She recognized what he was holding as soon as it seared the skin above her heart. Her legs lifted and shot out of their own accord, sending Isaak stumbling backwards and dropping the branding iron. Almost as an afterthought, she noticed the door on the oil lantern was open.

While still screaming, Catarina smashed her heel onto the top of Abrahams foot. His grip relaxed and she buckled her legs, falling through his arms to the grass. She grabbed the handle of the iron and swung it, hitting Abraham's knee over and over again. He dropped like a rock. The last thing Catarina saw was the heel of his other foot coming straight at her face.

Pain shooting up both of her legs was the first thing that caught her attention when she came out of the black haze that was so warm and comfortable. There was a sharp burning sensation near her heart, but when she tried to move her hands, they didn't do anything.

The throbbing in her legs stopped when what felt like a set of hands relaxed, moved to another section, and squeezed again. She inhaled sharply, her eyes flying open. Isaak's celeste blue eyes stared back at her. He almost looked surprised.

"If I'm being honest, I wasn't sure you were going to wake up this time around." Isaak said softly. His hands tightened to the point of pain, but when she flinched, he let go immediately. That's when she realized she was naked. Isaak lunged to cover her mouth when she opened it to scream.

"Quiet now." He whispered. "I may not give two fucks about you, but if you ruin my plans, then I'll make sure we die together." He let go and stepped back.

"So, we got married, and now it's time to claim your prize?" Catarina wanted to spit at him, but didn't hold out a lot of faith in her capabilities right now, especially with her legs tied to different corners of the bed.

"Normally that would be what's happening, but you're not my type." Isaak kneeled on the side of the bed, grabbing her forearms. He squeezed them hard enough to take her breath away.

"I don't look anything like your family." Catarina groaned when he let go. "But you weren't looking at Katie either."

Somehow it just occurred to her that he was only in his boxers. He sat down on the side of the bed, the light of the candles danced across his skin. Scars tracked all over his body. He never had an easy life, but now she could see the evidence of it with her own eyes. A bright new brand in the shape of a circle was burned into his chest where hers was.

"You probably would've enjoyed it more if Roland was here." Catarina whispered. "But Abraham probably would've parted you out himself."

"It took me years to figure it out." Isaak whispered back. "But being gay isn't something survivable with those monsters."

He stood and went back to work, grabbing her thighs in different spots. "Be grateful you bruise easily so we can both avoid something much worse."

"So, you're marking me up to make it look like we had sex?" Catarina didn't raise her voice at all. "What's the point?"

"If you're my wife then I'm in charge of you." Isaak said while throwing a sheet over most of her body. "If he strikes you unprovoked, then I have every right to kill him."

"And you need that excuse so you can get into your heaven without his death on your hands." Catarina tried to nod skeptically, but her body hurt too much.

"You're not listening." He climbed onto the bed, standing beside her. "They kicked me out, he killed my mother, and he beat me for years. Anyone can play a part and go along with whatever religious zealotry. It takes a special type of twisted to build someone's confidence enough to breach the inner circle, then tear it all down from the inside."

Before she could say anything else, Isaak started rocking the bed back and forth, knocking the headboard against the wall in a steady rhythm. The shaking jostled her body so much that she almost thanked him for the sheet. Every part of her felt like she had been hit by a truck, then lit on fire. She tried to keep it together, but even this distorted version of kindness was too much.

Squeezing her eyes shut, Catarina wept. It seemed to go on forever, and when he sped up, she wanted to scream. The only thing that kept her quiet was the possibility of Abraham walking in. Isaak stopped suddenly. Hopping off the bed, he walked to his backpack, where he removed a bottle of water. Wetting down a washcloth, he rubbed it all over his own body.

"You've got to smell like me." Isaak whispered before removing the sheet and smearing his dirty washcloth all over her. It did the trick though, she smelled foul. When she noticed the blood on the rag, she took another inventory of herself.

"Where is all that coming from?"

"Most of it's not yours." Isaak shrugged. "You aren't a virgin, so, they kill a rooster and splash the blood on the bride to," he did air quotes with his fingers, "restore the purity to the condemned." He clearly didn't believe it either.

"I mean this in the best way." Catarina sniffled, "That's completely insane. Right now, your plan is halfcocked and so filled with rage that you're either an evil genius or the definition of a major psychotic episode."

"But if we live, it'll be a hell of a story." Isaak smirked while he untied Catarina from the bed.

"I'll make sure to quote you in your eulogy." She cracked with a groan when her foot came loose.

Isaak continued to untie her, moving with smooth practiced technique. When he sat her up, Catarina had to bite her tongue to keep herself from screaming.

"What happened here, what is this?" Catarina blinked back tears when she noticed both her wrists were tightly bandaged. They stung like her back did when she moved her hands.

"Abraham was in the process of degloving your hands, as a punishment for your stunt in the marriage circle." Isaak said it so easily that Catarina wanted to throw up. "I thought talking him out of cutting them off would be good enough, but I guess I was wrong. He didn't get far in the process so you shouldn't have too much nerve damage after all this.

 Her clothes had been folded and set on top of his backpack and Isaak turned his back to retrieve them. She leaned forward to try and catch him off guard, only to retreat when the pain shot through her head.

"With the way your face looks, I wouldn't try anything for at least twenty-four hours." Isaak said. He tossed the clothed on the bed, but grabbed them piece by piece, and in a strange show of humanity, helped her put them on.

"I will hold off on the beauty contests for the next month." Catarina chuckled with a groan of pain. "But I have a bridge troll look-alike contest on Halloween I can't miss."

"Then use one of your personalities to act demure and stay out of my way, so I can finish this." Isaak stood back and acted like he was going to scratch his shoulder, but just remembered the matching burn.

"What about Tobias?" She asked while Isaak started to get dressed.

"He will do what he's told until he loses his mind." His voice was completely indifferent. Abraham is the reason I'm here, so stay out of my way, and stop trying to run, *wife*." He said it with possession, but not in the nice steamy way that men do in the books she had read. It was harsh and threatening in a way that kept her snarky retort to herself.

"Can you make sure I'll get out alive?" Catarina left the slightest hint of vulnerability evident in her voice. Isaak froze when pulling his dirty T-shirt back on and stared at her. "I figured we are clearly past the 'safe and unharmed' part of the request." She waved a hand at her own damaged face.

That managed to surprise a snort out of him. He didn't give her an answer but gave her a smirk before grabbing her bicep with the knife wound and led her to the door. Catarina was tense in anticipation, but when Isaak's hand squeezed slightly, she slouched, and turned her eyes to the ground, giving the 'demure' appearance he had asked for.

No one was in the main room, but when they went outside, the light nearly blinded them. Catarina could hear the voices before she saw anyone. Tobias was back and he didn't sound sane at all.

"I don't care what you decided!" His shriek vaguely reminded Catarina of Daniel. In his last moments, Daniel didn't even sound human. "I sat in a jail cell for the last year dreaming of ways to kill her! I'm not going to let that freak claim her as his wife when Sam's revenge is MY RESPONSIBILITY!"

Blinking against the light that was doing its best to blind her, Catarina shielded her eyes with her free hand. Isaak never stopped walking the both of them towards the truck where the men were arguing.

"It's too late for that!" Isaak yelled above the hysteria. He reached over and pulled the collar of her shirt down enough to expose the brand that now marred her skin. Tobias, who had been flailing his hands around in the air, froze. Still walking forward, Isaak let go of her shirt and moved the collar of his own, exposing a matching brand. "I've claimed her. She is my wife, and you won't touch her!"

"You've never belonged here! You don't have any standing in the family, no matter what you've done trying to come back!" Tobias was storming forward, ready for a fight.

Isaak shoved Catarina towards Abraham, who was sitting in a camping chair. His pants were cut from the ankle up to the knee and he wasn't getting up. The leg was wrapped with patches of blood that stained the bandage. His hands weren't injured though, and they shot out fast, latching down above her elbow. Wrapping her arms around her stomach in a display of reluctance, Catarina noticed a lifted truck that was painted camouflage.

"She's coming with me!" Tobias howled jabbing a back at the truck. "I won't let you take this from me!"

They lunged at each other and the fight began.

# Chapter 18

"This is almost over. We'll get her back." Jacob said for what seemed like the millionth time. They were riding up the mountain in vehicles the National Guard had given them, along with a few hundred in support.

"I know you're trying to help, but if you say it again, I'm going to shove my gun so far up your ass..."

"I got it, I got it." Jacob held his hand up in surrender. He was still feeling put out, because when he had Katie in his arms again, despite the dire situation, he popped the question. Katie, who had a more level-headed view of their current circumstances tried to postpone her answer. Jacob looked heartbroken until she kissed him and insisted 'good things come to those who wait'. Then she had to take a second to explain to him that when this was all over, and everyone was home safe, it might be a better time. Jacob had been stewing ever since.

Katie told them all the details of what happened in her escape and where she was picked up at. From there, they worked with Ava and Sarah to backtrack on the maps, using the images of locations, to go back to several houses until they found the one. Katie had run almost two miles through the mountains to get to

Silver City, where she stole a truck and drove to the next town about thirty miles from rapid city.

Director Johnston wanted to be sure it was actually her before he said anything to them, just in case. Tyrese was watching Roland over The Director's shoulder when he broke the news. If it hadn't been for his lanky friend, then Roland would've lost his mind right then and there. Tyrese would've benched him, and they would've had to haul him away in a strait jacket. Fun stuff.

Roland, Jacob, Director Johnston, Tyrese, Brandt, and Elliot all sat in the room while the medical team examined Katie. She recalled what happened while being inspected. Samples were taken and tests were being done, making sure nothing fell through the cracks when it came time to convict the family.

Katie gave a description of the house and route she took to narrow down the location. Sara and Ava stayed in the room with the rest of the team to continue narrowing down the location, updating The Director via tablet as they narrowed down the search.

Roland had to smile when she recounted Catarina's attack on Abraham, leaving him with a suspected fractured orbital bone. The relief that flooded over him, knowing she hadn't lost her spunk, was indescribable. The relief was quickly doused when Katie detailed their first escape, then the second. She was only able to fill in pieces from what she was told during her phases of unconsciousness. Roland's face drained when Katie told them about the flogging and Simon's death.

They would never know if it was the tumor that killed Simon, or one of the many injuries after the fights. The way Katie had described the so-called funeral had some of the doctors caring for her looking a shade of green.

Finally, they got the details on Tobias's mental break. Roland was doing all he could not to rush Katie through the story. He was aware that Tobias likely didn't have an accurate recollection of what happened, but this went far beyond what he was expecting.

When she explained the marriage proposition, Roland nearly threw his hands in the air and demanded that The Director let them go scorched earth to get Catarina back. The Director left the room for a few minutes before answering.

"Sarah and Ava have assured me that it would take at least ten hours go get the ceremonial robes that are used in their traditional weddings." Director Johnston was scrolling through the tablet in his hands when he re-entered the room. "Another important note is that they only do weddings with 'the rising of the sun', as they put it. So, we have at least until tomorrow at dawn to find her."

"If I can see a picture of the house we were kept in, that would speed this up." Katie winced when someone pressed too hard on a spot in her back.

"Be careful!" Jacob cautioned. He wasn't rude about it, but his nerves were clearly fried. The medical team gave him a sideways glance but not a lot else.

"I've got a few here." Director Johnston turned his tablet around and started scrolling through a few pictures. "These are a few that were within the distance you gave, even if they weren't on the sister's radar."

"Wait, go back." Katie held up a hand. "That's the one!" Roland wanted to pass out.

"Let's get a thermal reading on house forty-three please." Director Johnston was speaking into his phone on his way out of the room. Roland saw Jacob giving Katie a quick kiss before he followed the small group out. Roland was directly on his heels.

"Director, I can take the bird with a small team and be there in thirty minutes." Roland demanded. Passing through the doors of the conference room, Director Johnston nodded at Elliot.

"Director, the house is negative for thermal readings." An agent called out from the crowd. Roland's knees buckled, but he grabbed onto a table, avoiding a full collapse.

"Elliot" The Director called out. The sneaky little bastard raised that stupid single barrel gun and darted him again. Roland was able to grab a coffee mug out of the nearest agent's hand and chuck it before he hit the ground again.

That was last night. This morning Roland woke up with another round of vomiting and a headache that would knock out a mammoth. He went on a rampage for a while before Tyrese talked some sense into him, and they got ready to go.

Director Johnston was right to have him sedated. The bastard. What they found out, while Roland was dead to the world, was that the home had been vacated. No one had been in or out of the house for hours. Once they realized that Katie was gone, they abandoned the structure. Several birds were sent up to run surveillance on the surrounding areas, but there were no less than fourteen structures that could be used as cover.

Roland felt better, despite his still simmering anger. Now he bounced alongside his best friend in the back of a truck on yet another foot patrol. His hair was tied tight enough that it might be more of the cause of his headache than he wanted to admit. They were headed to a small hunting cabin off the beaten path on what used to be private property. Everyone was split into separate groups going to each location with a healthy amount of backup. After everything that had already happened, they were going in with the maximum amount of force.

Slowing to a stop just out of sight from the cabin, they all piled out of the vehicles. They made their way up to the house like a wall, blocking the road that led the way out. An old pickup sat in front of the cabin. With the sun high in the sky, he wondered if it would be an advantage or a vulnerability.

When they got closer, they spotted an old man sitting on a lawn chair. It was Abraham. Soldiers down the line brought their firearms to a low ready, causing a ripple effect. As they closed the distance, Roland could see what everyone was prepping for.

Isaak's form appeared as Roland rounded a tree. He was bleeding from several cuts, his nose, and his mouth. Someone had used this man like their own personal punching bag. His clothes were dirty and ripped. He had been in a nasty fight with someone.

"Looks like the cavalry's here!" Isaak's voice boomed in the silence. Abraham glared at him with his hands up in surrender. "Nice to see you two again. Jacob. Roland." Isaak acknowledged them with a quick look before returning his focus to the old man.

"You're going to burn in hell, boy." Abraham spat.

"I'm making sure that you burn right beside me, you old fuck." Isaak snorted. "Why do you think they got loose at the house when we first got there?" He giggled harder. Roland aimed his gun and everyone else followed suit.

"You let her go?" Abraham raged, but didn't move.

 Roland nodded to the soldiers on his right. Once he got a nod back, he circled his way around the truck. They were all trained on basic safety, he had to assume no one would shoot him in the ass when they were this close to the end. Abraham's leg looked badly damaged, propped up and wrapped in bloody bandages.

"Of course I did!" Isaak lowered his gun, but only slightly. "You beat the crap out of my mom and me for years! You helped turn Cecilia into a blood eagle! You've been the enforcer for years! Fingers, toes, and limbs all cut off like they were nothing! I've watched you beat men to death with your bare hands! Why do you think I put the idea in your head to marry Catarina? I knew you couldn't! If I did, at least I could protect her from you!"

"You married her for life, you ugly little bastard!" Abraham smiled thinking he had won.

"The wedding already happened?" Roland asked, not ready for the answer.

"You bet your ass it did! She'll never be yours!" Abraham shouted triumphantly. His smile only faded when Isaak lowered his gun completely, shaking his head with a sick twisted sneer.

"Delusional Monster." Isaak tossed the gun aside when he turned to face Roland. "She never said I do. She wasn't conscious to accept it, and it was never consummated." A soldier came up and began to cuff Issak, much more gently than Roland would've liked. The others spread out to search the area.

"LIAR!" Abraham screamed from his seat while he was cuffed. "I heard it!"

"Joke's on you." Isaak mocked. "I'll always be a better man than you. You heard a bed banging against a wall and drew your own conclusions. I'll see you in hell." Turning back to Roland and Jacob he continued. "I have a detailed history of every crime that Abraham and the family has committed from murder down to illegal child labor and tax evasion."

"Where is Catarina?" Jacob cut him off. "If we find her alive, you might be able to cut a deal."

"I don't want a deal." Isaak gave them a sad smile. "I'll give you everything and even testify, as long as we don't spend a day in the same prison."

"Where is she?" Roland wanted to shake him.

"I don't know where he took her." Isaak sighed. "I knew you guys were probably closing in and I tried to keep him here as long as I could, but we fought, and I woke up in the dirt."

"You'll never find them!" Abraham taunted. "The little shit failed."

Roland was about to storm over to the old man and demand answers, but Jacob beat him to it. Abraham was smiling until Jacob jammed his gun into the bloody bandages around his knee. It wasn't legal by any stretch of the imagination, but the way the other members of their group found the ground and the sky incredibly interesting, he didn't think it would be a problem. Once Abraham stopped screaming, Jacob asked again.

"Where. Did. They. Go?" Jacob put his foot on top of the man's knee that was propped up on a box. One wrong move would send it folding in the wrong direction. Abraham glared through his one good eye, the other was red with blood.

"He didn't say, and I hope you never find her. I don't care what Sam thought of her. She's a curse to this family." Abraham growled.

"Spread out!" Jacob yelled, stepping back from the man. "Look for any sign of where they could've gone!" Everyone scattered like roaches.

Roland ran towards the tree line behind the house. A few walking trails led into the woods, so he picked one at random. The others that had followed him that far each chose their own path. Roland didn't bother waiting for someone to pair up with him. He was confident that he could handle himself should it come to that.

The trail took him up over the top of the next hill, trees still blocking most of his view. He took off at a jog. There was no way that she was right there, only for him to miss her by minutes. There was the sound of another engine in the distance.

The trucks they had driven up in still roared behind him, but there was a different rumble somewhere up ahead. Picking up his pace, Roland stepped into the trees, making his way quickly through the foliage. In a small clearing up ahead, a camouflage painted, nineties Blazer sat waiting. Roland didn't see anyone near, so he crept up to the truck and opened the passenger door.

Laid across the seat in the back Catarina was tied up and unconscious. There was movement to his left. He barely had time to see Tobias's face before the man hit him in the head with a wooden bat and everything went black.

The floor bounced underneath him, making lightning flash behind his closed eyes. Roland was trying to get his bearings before opening his eyes again. His arms were tied behind him and looped around the one on his ankles. The carpet smelled of old dirt and cigar smoke.

"You know this isn't my fault!" Catarina's voice was full of sorrow. "Tobias, this won't bring him back!"

"SHUT UP!" Tobias's voice echoed off the walls of the truck. "Your fate has been decided! I've received guidance from my ancestors, and you won't change my destiny! Our fates are tied together because of your involvement with Sam's death."

The truck hit something that left Roland bouncing enough to groan out loud. Catarina groaned right along with him. Opening his eyes, Roland got a full view of the underside of the front seat. He was face down on the floor between the rows with no room to roll or adjust. He tried to lean the other direction, to look over his shoulder when they hit another rut, and he bounced to his side, with his legs awkwardly pinned against the seat.

Catarina had her hands bound behind her, but Tobias had the presence of mind to at least buckle her in in case he decided to drive them all into a ditch. Roland watched helplessly from the floor while she grimaced at every movement of the vehicle. His heart nearly broke when she looked down at him and he saw the bruises all over her face and neck. A bandage was wrapped around her bicep, but there was no blood, so that was at least something.

"Good to hear the sound of your voice, Tobias." Roland taunted. "You've still got one hell of a swing."

"I told you before, Scarface, I didn't figure I could make you look any worse." Tobias called back.

"Where are we going Tobias?" Roland wiggled as much as he could, trying to find a weakness in the bindings. "People everywhere are looking for you! Now that I'm gone too, they are going to be asking questions second."

"They can try, but they won't get here in time!" Tobias said proudly.

"Where is here?" Catarina was looking out the window.

"One of the caves that Sam and I used to sneak off too before we were thrown out." Tobias's voice was calmer than he had sounded so far. "I was going to take you back to the bank where it all started but it wasn't significant enough."

The vehicle skidded, and barely stopped before Tobias hopped out. There was a bunch of rattling around while he pulled something out of the back. Another door opened and Roland was dragged backwards. His knees hit the ground first since he was still hogtied.

"Agh!" Roland yowled through gritted teeth. "Not even a shred of decency after all our time together?" Tobias pulled him against what felt like a giant metal grate. With a heave, the wild game cart lifted him off the ground and started rolling Roland to the cave entrance.

"If that were true, I would've just dragged you by the feet and torn up the other half of your face." Tobias deposited him on the hard rock floor and walked back to the truck.

The walls glowed in the light from the setting sun, but in a small grouping near the center were several black plastic drums. He was only about ten feet away from the barrels, but he could smell the gasoline. Roland tried to reach his feet, and while struggling, managed to find the knot. Looking back at the Blazer, Roland watched as Tobias pulled Catarina out. She struggled a little, but her face was glossy with sweat. It wasn't that warm, so he had to assume that her injuries were holding her back.

Tobias had pulled her around to the back of the truck before he opened the tailgate. Roland couldn't hear what they were saying, but when Tobias pulled his gun from his waistband, and cut her bonds, he knew they had to figure it out quick. He was almost through the first set of knots when Catarina started to strip.

Tobias reached into the truck and pulled out a giant white ball of what looked like fabric. Catarina stood there in her underwear when he shoved the material at her. Roland pulled harder at the knots. Taking the fabric, Catarina unraveled what looked like a gown and started stepping into it. When she braced one hand on the truck, her back lit up in the light of the sunset.

Bright red gashes were splitting open when she moved, her back was nowhere near healed and began to drip red. The back of the dress laced up, and when Roland watched her reach back to try to tie it herself, Tobias turned her around. Tucking the gun into the back of his pants, he yanked and pulled the dress closed.

Roland's feet were free, but he held the position, until he could get at least one hand out. The whimpers that echoed up from Catarina had him pulling hard enough to make his wrists start to bleed. The dress was similar to the one Johnathan had made back at the gala. Catarina was swallowed up in the sheer mass of it while Tobias pulled her behind him. She tried yanking out of his hold, but when he clamped down on her wrist, Catarina screamed and dropped to her knees. That's when the ropes came loose.

Tobias had just turned, taking a fistful of Catarina's hair. Roland got his feet under himself and took off. They were about fifty feet away, and because of the noises that came from Catarina, the man didn't hear Roland until he was right on top of them.

Tobias got ahold of his gun, but didn't have a chance to raise it when Roland hit him. He must've had one hell of a grip on Catarina because they all went down in a pile of arms and limbs. The gun went flying on impact, but Roland didn't see where it landed. They were throwing punches and elbows, rolling in the dirt.

The obnoxious white dress was caught between them, dragging Catarina along with, but she wasn't making any noise or fighting back. Roland pulled back to see if she was ok. In hindsight it was a stupid mistake, but the consequences made stars burst in his eyes. Roland had ahold of Tobais's throat and tried to come down with elbows on the man's face, but he evaded like a pro, despite being in the bottom of the pile.

Tobias repeatedly punched him in the side in an effort to land a liver shot when he felt the dress start to pull away. Springing to his feet to give Catarina a chance, Roland began kicking Tobias as he writhed on the ground. Once she was free and everyone's view was unobstructed, Tobias locked his arms around Roland's leg and barrel rolled. The two of them scrapped in the dirt, gouging eyes, biting, and spitting. Each of them desperate to be the last one standing.

"HEY!" Catarina screamed. They both froze, blood was dripping down her left shoulder, but she had Tobias's old revolver in her hands aimed at the both of them. Swaying on her feet, Catarina's eyes were glassy. "Don't you move, or I'll shoot!" Her words slurred and she stumbled.

Tobias lunged into action, shoving Roland so hard to the side that he hit a rock. Roland didn't waste any time scrambling after the man. Several shots rang out and echoed off the cave walls. Tobias yelled in pain before ripping the gun away from Catarina and shoving her to the floor. He whipped around right before Roland tackled him and the gun went off.

# Chapter 19

Catarina heard the gunfire but couldn't orient herself quick enough. After they all went down in a pile, she managed to crack her head on a rock. The blood was slowly dripping down her left shoulder, soaking into the wedding gown and the giant poofy sleeves. She had tried to pull the trigger, but her hands were slick with her own blood, then the world spun around her. Climbing back to her feet, she saw the two men laying in a pile.

They were just inside the entrance of the cave, only yards away from the barrels. She stumbled again and ended up on her hands and knees. Doing her best not to vomit, Catarina watched as Tobias tossed Roland's limp body off himself. Roland wasn't moving.

"No." Catarina's voice was a whimper in her own ears. Tobias was laughing maniacally while he climbed to his feet. "No, no, no, no!" She couldn't even shake her head while the tears streamed down her face. Staring at the body on the floor, she could practically feel her own heart ripping apart inside her chest.

"I don't know why you're so surprised, Short-Stack." Tobias picked up the gun and sniffed. "I was chosen by The Gods to be a part of your demise. You won't get out of this one alive."

"My brain is telling me to keep quiet and try to figure a way out of this." Catarina slowly pulled one leg under herself and just barely made it to her feet.

"But you've always had a wild heart." Tobias mocked.

"And with all my heart, fuck you." Catarina's breath caught as the sentiment came out, riding on the pain that now coursed through her body. "Fuck you. Fuck your sick family. Fuck your psychotic funeral practices. Fuck your stupid-ass vendetta. Fuck you for not catching onto Daniel's antics sooner and getting your brother killed. And fuck your sorry-ass delusion thinking that I was the problem in the first place!" She nearly screamed the last part.

"Anything else?" Tobias sounded indifferent at best.

"Yeah, fuck your ugly shoes too, Johnathan would've been disappointed in you." She sneered right back at him and was shocked when he chuckled.

"Do you know why I made you wear that dress?" Tobias started walking in a wide circle around the drums. Catarina winced when she shook her head. "The last time I saw you, you were wearing that obnoxious white gown. Sam was dying while you whispered to him."

"I wasn't going to leave him there dying alone, scared, and confused." Catarina said. "No one deserves that."

"And you won't either." Tobias cleared the last barrel and walked up to her. "We will be rewriting history. You here, in the white dress and me dancing. We will walk into eternity together. Shame that your love couldn't join us." Tobias pointed the barrel of the gun at Roland.

"But if we never dance, then we never have to redo that god-awful night." Catarina looked down at Roland's body on the floor. "Because of you, I never got a chance to know him. I hope you choke on a dick on your way to hell you bastard."

"You should be ashamed of yourself. No one wants a bitch with a mouth on her like you." Tobias was rising to her combative tone.

"I should be." Catarina shrugged but her smile turned into a wince. "We both know I'm not, but I probably should be."

Tobias walked around Roland's body, giving it a wide berth. Catarina was barely able to stay standing, but she did try to keep the distance by matching Tobias's steps. She tried to hold the dress high enough that she wasn't tripping over it.

"Why the theatrics?" Catarina asked. "I thought you hated making things complicated." Catarina was trying to keep the barrels between them, but Tobias's steps were significantly wider than her own.

"In some sick way, they were for Sam." Tobias shrugged. There was a spot on his side that was leaking blood. If she could keep him talking, Tobias might pass out from the blood loss before he could kill her.

"How was any of this for Sam?" Catarina choked out. "He would be ashamed if he saw what you've done to yourself in his name!"

"You don't get to tell me what he would be feeling right now!" Tobias screamed, strode over and latched down onto her arm, digging the barrel of the gun under her chin. "We are going to dance, just like we did a year ago, and maybe I will be able to see Sam one last time before I blow us all to hell." Tobias pointed to the drums.

"Are those filled with gas?" Catarina almost couldn't get the question out. "There's no guarantee we'll die from the explosion!"

"It's a fate worse than death while you beg to die." Tobias tucked the gun into the back of his pants again and grabbed Catarina.

Tobias pulled her close. Catarina resisted until he pressed her back with purpose, the nerve endings screaming in pain at his touch. He led her slowly around the room, both of their injuries hindering their movements. A few times, her head started to spin, and Tobias stopped long enough for her to get her bearings before continuing.

Catarina could feel the walls closing in on her. She didn't even care that her face was wet with tears while she cried. She was sure her nose was running, but there was no fix for that either. There was another sniffle that mimicked hers. Catarina looked all the way up into Tobias's eyes. He didn't look away.

They shared a moment of misery in the silence, while they swayed in the mouth of a cave in the mountains that glowed in the light of the sunset. Tobias didn't blubber or cough, but his own grief broke some of the silence around them. At one point, Catarina's feet got tangled in the dress and she stumbled. Tobias caught her with a groan. His face was pale enough that she wondered if he would collapse while they danced.

"In another life, I might have loved you the way he did." Tobias whispered.

"You said you considered me a sister too, remember? Right after Sam decided that's what he thought of me." Catarina reminded him of their conversation in the cabin. Tobias looked down at her with the shadow of a smile.

"I remember," Tobias's hands were clammy, "but I wasn't talking about him."

Catarina stopped dancing and took a few steps back. Tobias gave a small shrug. In the sunset light, her head started spinning. The air was too thin, and she couldn't seem to catch her breath.

Tobias pulled the gun out of the back of his waistband again, aiming it at the ground.

"If this is some sick joke to fuck with my head, then congratulations, you win." Catarina put one hand on her stomach trying to quell the urge to vomit. Tobias strolled back to where Roland's body was sprawled on the rock. He circled the man she loved like a vulture, eyeing his next meal.

"It's not a joke." Tobias stood on the far side of the body. "I realized when I was rotting in that cell, that I wouldn't have been so distracted by you, and so hurt by your betrayal." Tobias sniffed, the tear that fell mixed with the sweat drenching his face.

"So, you never received 'guidance' from your ancestors." Catarina threw in air quotes to make it sting a bit more. "You're just a delusional idiot, that wants revenge for being human and growing feelings. Why didn't you just get a boner and deal with it the old-fashioned way? It would've saved us all a lot of time and effort over the last year!"

"You don't get to mock me." Tobias growled at her. "Spiritual guidance comes to those who are looking for answers. Not sirens that scream into the void."

"In case it escaped your notice, demons are spirits too! Why didn't you ask who the hell you and your neurotic family were praying to?" Catarina was raging now. "Did you even try to hear it when the devil on your shoulder was screaming for you to fucking stop, saying that you've gone too far? He was probably bashing you upside the head with a neon sign, you dense mother fucker! You hold onto your stupidity like a dog humping a stuffed animal, everyone tried to take it away, but you keep on humping!"

A barking laugh cracked through the silence, making them jump backwards. Roland, who was apparently very much alive, sat up and threw one mother of a punch directly into Tobias's crotch. The hulking man howled as he dropped to his knees. Roland locked both hands around the gun and tried to pull it out of Tobias's hands. By some miracle Tobias was still holding on.

Catarina scooped up the skirting of the gown and ran towards the two of them. Even though the blood had slowed to a trickle down her neck the cave still spun around her. The gun went off again before she could make it far, and she skidded to a stop. Catarina heard the ricochet of the bullet off the insides of the cave. Breath catching in her throat, she waited for the barrels of gas to explode, but they hadn't yet.

"RUN!" Roland screamed at her. Following his orders, Catarina ran past them, taking a second to stomp down on the bloody wound in Tobias's stomach. He screamed, and ripped the gun away from Roland, but it flew across the cave floor, going off again. Catarina instinctively ducked before Roland screamed again. "Get out of here, go!" She stumbled over the uneven floors when Roland cried out.

Whipping around, she saw Roland cupping his crotch in a ball on the floor while Tobias grabbed the gun. She had just started to run back at him, when the gun clicked. EMPTY. Catarina was frozen, watching Tobias and Roland make eye contact.

In the distance but coming up fast multiple engines grew louder with the passing seconds. The unmistakable sound of a helicopter closing in left Tobias's face falling in defeat before he looked at the gasoline barrels.

In a last-ditch effort, Tobias took off while Roland sprang to his feet and ran towards her. He leaned forward and threw her over his shoulder without breaking stride. Tobias pulled something small from his pocket and fumbled with it over the opening of one of the barrels. The roar of the cavalry grew louder as Roland raced towards the tree line. Once they cleared the mouth of the cave, he pulled her down, across his body, protecting her with his own.

She could still see over his shoulder as he ran, but Catarina watched the man from her nightmares openly sobbing while struggling to get a spark from the small lighter. Tobias paused, looking at her one last time with a sad smile before he struck the lighter, and the cave was engulfed in flames.

The force of the explosion practically lifted them off the ground and they landed hard, rolling over each other. Roland's body crushed the wind from her lungs several times before they stopped. Above the ringing in her ears, beyond the roar of the trucks that just pulled up, Catarina heard the crackle of the fire.

Roland let go, running his hands all over her, reassuring himself that she was alive. Catarina in turn, reached out, cradling his face in her hands. She knew he wasn't thinking when he scooped her up and squeezed her into his warm embrace. Crying out in pain, Catarina went limp against him. He hadn't seen her back, so it wasn't his fault, but this was killing her. She wanted him to hold her, she wanted to squeeze him tight and never let go. Now, because of her injuries, they could only sit in the grass while bodies circled the area, piecing together the tragedy until Catarina could move again.

Roland took her face gently in his hands and kissed her softly while their tears mixed. Pulling back, he tucked her against his chest and tried to hold her gently, being the comfort that she needed, knowing the nightmare was over. Roland's chest was shaking while he cried with her.

"There!" A familiar voice called out. Catarina leaned back and Roland only let go enough that she could see. Jacob and Katie came running up from the crowd. Director Johnston and several others were close on their heels. Jacob pretty much slid on his knees the last few yards before hitting them both hard.

"Careful you ass!" Roland growled at him, but it was halfhearted at best. Katie dropped to her knees next to them and joined in the group hug.

"Where is Tobias?" Jacob asked. Roland and Catarina looked back into the entrance of the cave that was engulfed in flames.

"It's really over then." Director Johnston said nearby, then in a louder declaration, he called out "We've got our people back." A roaring cheer went up in the sea of bodies.

"What the fuck are you wearing?" Katie laughed, happy tears falling down her own face. She grabbed a fistful of the obnoxious fabric. That got a laugh out of all of them.

"Another white gown and another time we almost died. "Catarina shook her head gently, the pain shooting down her neck. "At this point if I ever get married. I'm opting to wear gold. It's got to be less dangerous than this white bullshit." Jacob practically snapped to attention burning holes into Katie's face.

"NO! Don't you dare, this is not the time!" Katie snapped before Jacob could get a word out.

"But..." Jacob pointed to the both of them, leaving Catarina confused as hell.

"No." Katie dug her heels in. "Or that will be my answer." Jacob practically pouted before wrapping his arms around their little group. Catarina knew he was happy they were out of trouble, but she was going to be asking a ton of questions later.

After several hours, they were all packed onto the back of a military aircraft on their way back to a hospital in Rapid City. Director Johnston already had a team standing by ready to give them their full attention. Catarina was still in the obnoxious gown.

She was going to try and change back into her clothes, but Jacob insisted that the corset on the dress was keeping the wounds on her back closed. He also peaked under the wraps on her wrists where Abraham had tried to deglove her hands. Without a thorough inspection, he wouldn't know the extent of the nerve damage, which may have contributed to her not being able to shoot

Tobias sooner. He also put a temporary bandage where she split her head open. Then he reinspected the knife wound in her arm and the gash on the top of her head. Jacob didn't want to touch the brand mark on her chest, but he was sure Johnathan would have something to help with the scarring.

Roland kept physical contact with her every second since they got on the aircraft. Jacob gave him a once over as well. The new bulletproof T-shirt he was sporting was what had saved his life from the bullet. The only caveat was that it didn't stop the foot-pounds of impact. Jacob suspected that his sternum was badly bruised, if not minorly cracked because of it. He said something about the adrenaline masking the pain when Roland carried her, but she barely heard him.

Catarina was staring at two figures at the end of the plane. One was sitting, wrapped in chains with a spit bag over his head hiding most of his wounds, and a silver piece of tape keeping his mouth shut. The other, battered and bruised, sat in a simple pair of handcuffs and another around his ankles. A few agents sat between them, obviously acting as a buffer while Abraham glowered at his son.

Isaak looked much more relaxed, despite his two black eyes and extensive other injuries. He didn't stop staring at Catarina and it was making her skin crawl. When Roland saw the exchange, he silently switched seats with Catarina. When it was announced that they were going to begin their descent, Isaak stood up.

The agents around him all grabbed him at the same time, but he didn't make any effort to move besides that. Roland put an arm around Catarina in response. He spoke loudly despite the silence that echoed around them.

"I'm sorry for what happened." Isaak didn't break eye contact with her. "I'm not asking for your forgiveness, because we all know I don't deserve it. You're a badass. No one else could've gotten out of that." He slowly reached up and pulled his shirt collar down, exposing his burn. "This means fuck all without your consent and consummation. Cover it, cut it off, leave it, or do whatever. Live your life, you've sure as hell earned it."

# Epilog

Catarina threw the ball again. Buster and a few new additions went running after it in the giant yard. The ball disappeared into a pile of snow, but that didn't stop them. Snow went flying, one of the smaller dogs yipped, and Buster took off with it.

Her hands still got all tingly after a long day, but the doctor said that was pretty normal considering the depth of the cuts. She had nerve repair surgery, compliments of her employers. She did all her physical therapy and even picked up crocheting to help with the fine motor skills in her hands. The cold didn't bother her hands as much now.

It snowed really early this year, but she didn't mind. Thanksgiving was just around the corner, and it would be her second official holiday with Roland. Halloween was freezing, but they spent part of it in Virginia giving their testimonies and getting all the official paperwork done.

They recovered what was left of Tobias's body and the medical examiner said he died instantly. Abraham and Isaak had separate trials that wouldn't happen until sometime next year, but they were safely locked away for now. Roland was reassigned to help guard the safehouse with the occasional contract at his discretion.

"Hey, Firecracker." Roland's footsteps in the snow was the only reason she didn't jump. Wrapping his arms around her, he kissed the top of her head. He offered to get an apartment nearby, or even rent a house, but Catarina saw the slump in his shoulders when he offered. "I just got the confirmation for the new family needing the safehouse. They will be here tonight around six. A married couple and their daughter."

"OK, sounds good. It's almost three, so we will be cutting it close, unless you want to get the groceries, and I'll turn over the rooms."

"Sounds good to me." Roland gave her a small squeeze before whistling at the dogs. They all slid to a stop in front of them and Roland got the ball back before throwing it. "Are you ready for a new family so soon after everything? Director said we were the last option, but I can talk to him if you aren't ready."

"I'm ready. It will be nice to have our first official mission together." Catarina itched the rising scar over her heart where she had been branded, it had become a nervous habit. Over the last month. "All that time at the gun range has to pay off sometime."

"The butterfly design on all your equipment was an amazing idea. I'm just glad you are comfortable using them again. You know Pete and Annibelle would've been proud. I love you, Cat." Roland said. "We're in this together, and I'm right here every step of the way." He stood behind her, giving her a squeeze before stealing a few bags from her pocket.

"I love you too." She whispered, blinking back tears. After several bad relationships and being estranged from her family, when she heard those words, it nearly brought her to tears. He leaned down to kiss her before they both circled the yard, cleaning up after the dogs. They were both doing individual and couple's therapy every week, helping them get back into normal life.

"Do they have any dietary restrictions?" Catarina was making a shopping list in the kitchen after they came in and dried all the dogs. Roland walked into the office to grab the fax that came through with the information.

"Doesn't look like it. The daughter is our age though so no kids this time." Roland set the paper down on the counter beside Catarina. "I love kids, but if we have to go down to the bunker...." His voice trailed off.

"It will be good. And everything is insured, just in case." Catarina sighed. She knew she was ready, but that didn't stop the jitters.

"You know...." He stole the pen from her hand and set it on the counter. "They will be here for a bit, and I won't have you all to myself anymore." He turned her around and lifted her onto the counter.

"Sounds a bit crowded if you ask me." She smiled while he kissed a line up her neck, wrapping her in a hug before kissing her lips softly.

"So, we had better make the best of the time we've got now." Roland flicked his eyebrows at her with a wide smile before pulling back and throwing her over his shoulder. Catarina squealed when he ran the both of them up to their room, away from the numerous security cameras. They knew they didn't have a lot of time, so it was quick and full of laughter, but one of the ways that they found themselves growing closer as the days went by. Roland always took the time to kiss the scars that she was still so self-conscious about, and she made sure to always spend a few minutes after holding him close and savoring the moment.

Roland left soon after to the grocery store, mentioning in passing, that the agents assigned to stay with the family were two that were more than familiar with them. Agent Jacob Evans and Agent Katie Madison would be along for the ride this time. Catarina knew what room they would want to be in, so she got that one ready too. The familiarity of the routine helped ease some of the anxiety she had getting back into the swing of things.

Roland probably wouldn't be back before the family got there, so she made sure to let the dogs out and get them in the kennel room before the new family arrived. Several of the dogs were giant breeds, and she didn't want to scare them.

She had just closed the door when the alert that an authorized vehicle had just passed through the gate sounded. She gave a big sigh and pulled on an oversized sweater. She didn't want to freak the family out with all her newly acquired scars. The doorbell rang and she made her way down the stairs. Taking a breath, Catarina opened the door, ready for anything.... Almost anything.

"Mom? Dad?" Catarina's voice cracked.


To be continued.....

About the Author:

T. Reeves is a new author who self-published all her works. She also balances her writing life with being a mother, working a full-time job, designing nails, and maintaining a healthy relationship with her husband. She is the author of the recently published *WHAT DOESN'T KILL YOU* as her first work with plans to continue this series to its completion.